What if...
Everyone Knew Your Name?

a choose your destiny NOVEL

What if...
Everyone Knew Your Name?

LIZ RUCKDESCHEL AND SARA JAMES

DELACORTE PRESS

Published by Delacorte Press
an imprint of Random House Children's Books
a division of Random House, Inc.
New York

Delacorte Press and colophon are registered trademarks of
Random House, Inc.

www.randomhouse.com/teens

Educators and librarians, for a variety of teaching tools, visit us at
www.randomhouse.com/teachers

Library of Congress Cataloging-in-Publication Data
Ruckdeschel, Liz.
What if—everyone knew your name? : a choose your destiny
novel / by Liz Ruckdeschel and Sara James.
p. cm.
Summary: The reader's choices control the course of Haley's
sophomore year at a new high school as she navigates the social
scene, deciding whether she wants to become a queen bee, a
wannabee, a freak, or a geek.
ISBN: 0-385-73296-1 (trade pbk.) — ISBN: 0-385-90317-0
(Gibraltar lib. bdg.)
ISBN-13: 978-0-385-73296-3 (trade pbk.)—
ISBN-13: 978-0-385-90317-2 (Gibraltar lib. bdg.)
1. Plot-your-own stories. 2. Plot-your-own stories.
[1. Friendship—Fiction. 2. High schools—Fiction.
3. Schools—Fiction.] I. James, Sara. II. Title.
PZ7.R84Wha 2006
[Fic]—dc22 2005023570

Printed in the United States of America

10

First Edition

What if . . .
Everyone Knew Your Name?

Homebodies make for nobodies, unless you live where the boys are.

"Gross!" Haley moaned as Freckles, the Miller family's three-year-old dalmatian, woke her up with a sloppy wet kiss on her sunburned cheek. "Mom, I think the dog's been eating Mitchell's beef jerky again," Haley called out to the front seat, where Joan Miller was busy adjusting the radio dial.

Until recently, Haley hadn't thought of her mother as a classic rock enthusiast. But ever since the Millers had set out on their cross-country road trip, Joan had been scanning the airwaves, searching for Bob Seger, Crosby Stills & Nash and the Allman Brothers Band, occasionally even singing along to their peace-and-love-soaked lyrics.

Maybe it had something to do with the move east. The Millers had recently traded the Golden State of California for the Garden State of New Jersey. And they were all a little unsure of what awaited them in the suburbs just outside New York City.

"Mom, the jerky?" Haley said, wiping the dog's hickory-scented slobber onto the sleeve of her shirt.

Joan turned around and patted Haley's little brother, Mitchell, on the knee. "Honey, remember when we talked about feeding Freckles people food? It's not good for him."

But six-year-old Mitchell didn't respond. Instead, he kept staring catatonically out the back window of the station wagon, just as he'd done for much of the last two weeks, ever since the family had pulled out of their driveway in San Francisco. With good reason, Haley's parents were becoming concerned.

As was Haley. That is, when she wasn't obsessing over permanent scarring from her sunburn and the mosquito bites she'd picked up in Yellowstone, Glacier and the Badlands.

Two weeks of cold showers in national parks had whipped her long auburn hair into a tangled, dreadlocked mess. And after wearing the same four sets of clothes for fourteen days straight, she smelled worse than Freckles. "Are we there yet?" didn't even begin to describe the way Haley felt.

In fact, nothing seemed to matter to her anymore. Not leaving her friends behind in Marin County. Not the new school she would soon be attending—the first public school of her life. At this point, all Haley cared about was getting into a hot bath and a real bed as soon as she possibly could.

"Well, here we are," her dad, Perry Miller, finally said, turning into the driveway of a brand-new cedar-shaked colonial-style house with quaint white shutters and a wide front porch with a swing.

"This is it?" Haley asked. "Are you sure this is the right address?"

"Chez Miller," Perry said proudly, looking fondly at Joan.

Haley gasped. She looked back and forth between her parents' excited faces, the chemically treated lawn and green window boxes filled with bright red geraniums.

"But where are the solar panels?" Haley asked. "The 'Vote Green!' signs in the front yard? The blue recycle bins?"

"I thought you hated all our junk," Haley's father said with a frown. "You always seemed so embarrassed when your friends came to visit at the old house."

Old, of course, was the operative word in describing the Millers' former home in Marin County, California. Built in 1926, the ramshackle farmhouse had withstood countless earthquakes, though not without suffering some very visible wear and tear.

"What's wrong, Haley?" her mother asked. "Don't you like it?"

"I just didn't realize it would be so . . . perfect," Haley said, looking skeptically at the new house.

"Well, just wait until we move in," Joan said, reaching into the backseat to give her daughter's hand a squeeze.

"I have to say," Perry added, admiring the grass, "it is sort of nice having a lawn."

"Well, maybe we'll plant the vegetable garden out back," Joan said, leaning in to kiss her husband as he growled in approval.

Gross, Haley thought. There was nothing, absolutely nothing worse than seeing your parents make out. Except maybe seeing them make out while you were trapped in a car with them for two weeks straight. Haley was about to protest with her usual cry of "You're corrupting a minor!" when something caught her eye.

At the house next door, a group of boys were playing pickup ball. Haley stared—no, gaped was more like it. These weren't the crunchy No Cal guys she was used to, with pit-stained hemp T-shirts, playing footsie with Rasta-motif Hackysacks in the parks near the Haight. These were grade-A East Coast hotties, shirtless, suntanned and sweaty, their rippling muscles flexing and firing each time they connected with the ball or the court.

Haley couldn't decide which one she liked best.

There was the lanky blond with his arrogant, entitled charm. He passed the ball to an olive-skinned stunner who wore his dark hair a little long on the sides, sort of sexy shaggy, but way cute.

And then there was the brunet guarding both of them. With his tinted sunglasses, a tattoo across his washboard stomach and a chip on his shoulder the size of Haley's former home state, he looked like just the right kind of trouble. Haley was about to name their firstborn child when suddenly a fourth player emerged from the huddle.

As if in slow motion, the blue-eyed, coal-haired vision in soccer shorts and not much else dribbled to the top of the key. Haley climbed out of the car to get a better look as the boy pump-faked, crossed over his dribble, squared to the basket and leaped into the air. Just as he crested, he snapped his wrist, sending the ball on a perfectly arced trajectory that ended with a swoosh in the basket.

The blond grabbed the ball and threw it at the garage door.

"Damn it!" he yelled. The ball bounced against the house and rolled across the lawn, coming to rest at Haley's feet. She picked it up as her new crush jogged over to retrieve it.

Figures, she thought. *Of course I look like a bedraggled orphan on the day I meet my future husband.* She wanted to disappear.

"You must be our new neighbors," he said, still

catching his breath. He wiped his hand on his shorts and extended it toward her. "I'm Reese, Reese Highland. I live next door."

Haley blushed, sliding her hand into his and gazing intently into his baby blues, unable to speak.

"Your ball," Haley finally blurted out. "I mean, here." She shoved the ball toward him. "Sorry. We've been in the car for two weeks," she explained awkwardly.

"I get it," said Reese. "Road trip."

"Exactly."

"Yo, Highland, hurry up," the blond called out from next door, prompting Reese to throw the ball back to him.

"Don't mind him," Reese said, looking at Haley. "That's Spencer." They watched as he missed an easy layup. "As you can see, his manners aren't much better than his game." Haley smiled.

"And over there, that's Drew Napolitano," Reese added, pointing to the olive-skinned kid, who now had the ball. Drew dribbled to the basket and shanked off the rim. "Trust me. He's better on the football field than he is on the basketball courts."

"And who's that?" Haley asked, pointing to the bad boy of the group, who had just grabbed the ball from Drew. He took three giant steps, sailed toward the basket and landed a massive dunk.

"That, my friend, is the infamous Johnny Lane."

"I hope he's on your team," Haley said.

"Naturally," Reese replied, watching Haley admire Johnny's shot. "So what's your name?" he asked.

"Haley," she said.

"Highland, come on," Spencer yelled.

"Well, Red. That's my cue," Reese said, heading back across the yard to the court. "Guess I'll see you around."

"Definitely," she said, her face still flushed. She turned and walked quickly up the porch steps and into the house. *You've got to be kidding,* she thought. *Neighbors? Wait until Gretchen hears about this.*

Haley was just about to run upstairs and e-mail her oldest and best friend when she remembered that the computer, along with the rest of the family's belongings, hadn't arrived yet.

So much for that good night's sleep in a normal bed, she thought.

Facing the street in the new house were two big open rooms with polished hardwood floors, large bay windows, freshly painted white walls and lots of built-in bookshelves. Not that Haley really noticed, since she was still too busy thinking about another neighborhood amenity.

"Well, what do you think?" Joan asked enthusiastically as Haley entered the kitchen.

"He's adorable," Haley answered absently.

Joan was emptying the contents of the cooler into the fridge and threw a soda can at her daughter to get her attention. Haley caught it just in time.

"I meant what do you think of the house?" her mother asked.

Haley shrugged. "It's okay, I guess. I mean, if you like new and pristine and completely empty."

"It won't be empty for long," said Joan. "The movers are coming first thing tomorrow morning. Speaking of, you and Mitchell should really get some sleep."

"Mom, it's six o'clock," said Haley, peering through the kitchen window to get a glimpse of the basketball game that was still going on next door.

"Only six?" Joan said. "That's what traveling does to you. After living in three time zones for the last two weeks, I don't even know what day of the week it is."

"Yeah, and now we're in the JTZ. The Jersey Twilight Zone," Haley muttered.

"Oh, Haley, stop. It won't be that bad. And I see you've already made at least one new friend," she teased.

"Do you think he goes to the same school as me? Do you think he's in any of my classes? Do you think we'll have to study together after school?" Haley asked, her mind suddenly racing.

"Don't you think you're getting a little ahead of yourself? Come on, lovergirl. Let me show you to your new room," said Joan, taking her daughter by the hand and leading her up the stairs.

"Honey, where's the necessities bag?" Perry asked as Joan and Haley reached the top of the stairs. "My teeth are mossy and I'm dying for a shower."

"Be right there, babe," Joan said with a wink before turning to Haley. "Sweetie, you're at the end of the hall. Last door on the right." She hesitated before adding, "It's a little smaller than the other bedrooms, but we thought you'd want the one with the most privacy."

"Whose room is that?" Haley asked, pointing to an enormous open space with tons of natural light.

"That's Mitchell's. We thought it best to put him next to ours."

Perry came back into the hall wearing only a towel. "Honey, the necessities bag?" He snuck up behind his wife and began nuzzling her neck. Joan giggled as Perry goosed her and pulled her into the master suite.

Haley shuddered as the door closed behind them. Ever since they had decided to move east, her mom and dad had been acting like a couple of teenagers again, making out in public and sometimes even going to bed before sundown.

She almost preferred the way things used to be, when her dad was spending most nights on the couch and her parents barely spoke at the dinner table.

Haley still hadn't figured out exactly what had happened between them to repair their relationship.

One day, much to Haley's surprise, the Millers had just fallen back in love. And then just as quickly, they were all moving to New Jersey.

Parents, Haley had decided, were a lot like the weather—sometimes nice, sometimes cloudy, and always prone to sudden changes that were almost impossible to predict.

Haley entered Mitchell's room without knocking.

"Intruder . . . Intruder . . . Marcus will shoot," Mitchell said in his robot voice as he pointed a gun-shaped hand at Haley.

Marcus was Mitchell's imaginary friend, but really Mitchell was the one who was invisible. Back in San Francisco, none of the boys his age even knew he existed. In fact, Haley couldn't even remember a time when she'd seen him play with an actual living, breathing kid.

"Your room is enormous," Haley said in awe as she brushed her younger brother aside, walking over to the wall of windows.

Poking her head through a door, she said, "No way! You've got your own bathroom?"

"Intruder," Mitchell said once again.

"Okay, chill out, buddy. I'm leaving," Haley said, patting him on the head on her way out the door.

Seeing that her parents' door was still closed, Haley walked down the long hallway, past a sky blue communal bathroom with a pedestal sink, and another small room that was empty. *Dad's office,* she deduced.

Haley's father had recently been offered an adjunct professor's slot at the Columbia University film school, and though he planned to keep office hours on campus and lecture at least three days a week, he would also be working from home, finishing up his latest documentary, on the growth cycle of deciduous trees.

Reaching the last door at the end of the hall, Haley closed her eyes, took a deep breath, turned the knob and stepped inside. Much to her dismay, when she opened her eyes and looked at the space, she found that the room was barely large enough for her to turn around, even before she brought in her bed, a dresser and various personal effects.

This can't be right, she thought. And yet there in the corner was her luggage, neatly stacked, confirming that this was indeed her new room.

Haley wasn't exactly thrilled. She considered going to her parents and making a case for why she should have Mitchell's room instead. But then she remembered how difficult it was to convince her parents of anything once they had made up their minds.

While unrolling her sleeping bag, she kicked up a huge cloud of dust that had been collected at all the national parks the Millers had visited in the last two weeks. In the midst of a coughing and sneezing fit, she leaned her head out of the only window in the room to get some fresh air. Instead, she stared across the yard in disbelief.

From her second story window, she had the perfect view of the basketball hoop next door, and beyond it, what looked to be a boy's bedroom, with posters hanging on the walls. *So maybe this isn't the worst room in the house after all,* she thought, suddenly liking the looks of her new room, her new neighborhood and maybe even her new life.

In the days that followed, the movers came and the Millers unpacked. Haley seemed to be settling in swimmingly until the morning of her first day of school.

Convinced that everyone's first impression of her would determine what her life would be like for the remainder of her high school career, Haley spent hours running between her closet and her mother's full-length mirror, trying to find something suitable to wear.

Every article of clothing she owned was systematically rejected as too something. "Too West Coast." "Too last year." "Too unflattering." "Too Montessori."

"Haley, breakfast!" Joan called from the kitchen, before Haley was fully dressed.

With not another second to spare, Haley grabbed a pair of khaki pants and a pink sweater, in fact the first outfit she had tried on nearly two hours earlier.

"You don't want to be late," Joan said from the bottom of the stairs.

"I'm coming!" Haley replied, grabbing the blue book bag off her chair. She was still putting her hair up in a ponytail when she arrived in the kitchen, walking right into the shot her father had set up with his movie camera.

"So Haley, thoughts? Impressions?" he called out from behind the equipment. "It's your first day as a sophomore at Hillsdale High. What are you looking forward to this year?"

That was the thing about growing up with a documentary filmmaker for a father. You lived your life in front of a vintage Super 8 camera. Every awkward stage, every embarrassing moment, the bad haircuts, the braces, it was all captured on film.

"I'm looking forward to being one year closer to getting out of this house," Haley said, faking a smile before swallowing her vitamins in a single gulp of freshly squeezed orange juice.

"Haley, breakfast," her mom pressed.

"Sorry, Mom, gotta run," Haley said, dashing out the door as Freckles snatched her buttered bagel off the table.

Outside, Haley checked herself out in her mirrored pencil case. *Not bad,* she thought. Her sunburn, thankfully, had faded to a tan, and miraculously, there wasn't a sign of a breakout in sight.

As Haley walked down the driveway toward the street, Perry loaded Mitchell into the station wagon.

"You sure you don't need a ride, sweetie?" he called out to Haley as Mitchell stared at her blankly from the backseat.

"No, I'm fine, Dad. Really," she said. The last thing she needed was to be dropped off at school by her dad on her very first day. Besides, she had just spotted Reese standing at the end of the driveway, and she wasn't about to pass up the opportunity to share a seat with him on the bus.

"Really. Go ahead," she said, waving.

"Okay. Suit yourself," her father said. He honked the horn and waved to Reese as he pulled out onto the street.

Haley took her time walking to the curb, forcing herself not to look in Reese's direction. *Don't seem eager,* she thought. She was just about to casually glance up, feign surprise and say hello when a white convertible full of girls peeled around the corner and screeched to a halt in front of Reese's house.

"Morning, handsome. Need a lift?" a pretty brunette with perfect skin and intense green eyes asked from the passenger seat.

"Hey, Coco," Reese said in a familiar tone. "Ali, don't you ever get sick of carting your little sister's friends around?"

"As if I have a choice," Ali said. "Why do you think my parents gave me the new car?"

Meanwhile, a perky blond in the backseat was dismissively eyeing Haley's khaki pants and pink sweater. "Who's your friend?" she asked Reese. "Or is this another one of your charity cases?"

"Whitney, you know you really shouldn't frown so much," Reese said. "You'll get wrinkles."

"Shut up!" Whitney cried, reaching for her compact. "That's it, I'm asking my father for Botox this Christmas."

"Whitney, you're Jewish," the driver said coolly from behind a pair of silver shades.

"Actually, Ali, the Kleins celebrate everything these days," Coco said with a snide glance.

"My soon-to-be-stepmonster is Catholic," Whitney said, staring at her reflection. "Am I really getting laugh lines?"

"Maybe if you didn't spend forty-five minutes a week in your tanning bed, you'd have less to worry about," Coco replied. "So are you coming or not?" she asked Reese.

"Guess I'll see you later, Haley," Reese said, smiling and winking at her as he jumped into the backseat next to Whitney.

"Haley. That's so cute," said Whitney, exaggerating her words. "Like the star."

"You mean comet, stupid," Alison said, her foot already on the gas. As the convertible disappeared around the bend, Haley was left standing dumbstruck on the sidewalk, plagued by the nagging suspicion that Reese Highland was way more than just friends with one of the girls in the car.

• • •

Boy, does Haley ever have a lot to learn. She's about to be thrown to the wolves of the New Jersey public school system. And if she's not careful, they're going to tear her apart.

It was sort of cute, though, wasn't it? Haley thinking someone like Reese Highland would have to ride the bus to school? And speaking of Reese, will he come to think of Haley as more than just the girl next door this year? Or will he fall under the spell of the wicked Coco De Clerq?

Haley is about to face the toughest choices of her young life. And guess what, she's all yours. What if Haley becomes the most popular girl in school? What if she falls flat on her face? Or . . . what if no one notices her at all? Who will Haley Miller become in your hands?

It's time for you to make the first move. To have Haley call her dad's cell phone and beg him to come pick her up, turn to page 27. To make her brave the bus alone, turn to page 17.

It's a brand-new year at Hillsdale High, and for Haley Miller, it's a brand-new life. Her grades, her friends, her love life, her future—it's all up to you. So get ready to change the fate of the girl with the most potential at Hillsdale High.

In Hillsdale, those who ride the bus usually get busted.

Haley was still choking on the convertible's exhaust fumes when a dingy yellow bus rounded the corner and stopped in front of her driveway. A pair of graffitied doors with cracked glass opened. Bracing herself, Haley stepped inside.

"This isn't the bus for Hillsdale, is it?" she gasped, looking around at the sea of misfits.

"No, it's the bus to Disneyland, kid," the driver said. "Take a seat," he ordered.

Haley wobbled down the aisle as the Millers' quaint new house became a speck in the distance.

She scanned the rows, looking for a seat, while goons with facial hair and girls pierced six ways to Sunday glared back at her.

Haley had heard that her bus route began in the Floods, an undesirable section of Hillsdale where rainstorms turned backyards into lakes and streets into rapid-flowing rivers. *How bad could it be?* she had thought when her mother warned her. *Pretty bad,* she now realized.

Halfway down the aisle, a boy's leg was outstretched, blocking her path.

"What have we got here?" he said.

The boy was wearing a black tank top and had a wad of chewing tobacco stuffed in his lip. One look at him and Haley knew that his bell had already reached its curve and that it was all downhill from here. "Aren't guys like you supposed to *drop out* of high school?" she asked.

"But then we wouldn't have met," the boy said with a smirk.

"Leave her alone, Garrett, you freak." Johnny Lane delivered the ultimatum without looking up from the Paul Westerberg biography that lay open in his lap. Haley recognized the good-looking brooder as one of the boys who had played basketball at Reese Highland's house the week before and wondered why he, of all people, was riding the bus.

"Easy, tough guy." Garrett laughed. "Guess I'll check you later," he said to Haley, finally letting her pass. He stared at her as he put his headphones on and resumed singing aloud to an obnoxious tirade of rap lyrics.

"Hey, thanks," Haley said to Johnny, but he either didn't hear her or didn't care, because he continued to read his book.

Haley kept walking and finally found a seat in the back next to a boy with pale skin and crooked teeth that were covered in braces. It was, Haley thought, like looking at a set of train tracks snaking through a jagged mountain range.

Across the aisle, Haley noticed an Asian girl hiding beneath an oversized gray sweatshirt, doodling in a large black book with frayed edges. The artist seemed oblivious to her surroundings and clearly unaware of Haley, who was now craning her neck to get a better look at the sketchpad.

With Haley in midlean, the bus lurched to a stop, slamming her into the seat back in front of her. Startled, the Asian girl turned and made eye contact with her. She then closed her sketchbook and tucked it into her backpack.

Great, thought Haley, *just my luck.* She hated getting caught snooping.

As the doors of the bus screeched open, a burly girl in white spandex came lumbering down the aisle. Everything about her was huge: her arms, her legs, her lips, her boobs. She had black hair that was matted and greasy and stuck to her wide, dimpled forehead. Her enormous feet were wrapped in a pair of sandals that tied at her ankles and crisscrossed up her tree-trunk calves.

Hasn't anyone ever explained to her the slimming properties of black? Or a good pair of jeans? Haley wondered as the girl marched toward the back of the bus. She seemed to divine Haley's insults as she shoved past, gave Haley a mean look and grabbed the boy with braces, plopping down on his lap. Much to Haley's dismay, the girl then nearly swallowed him whole with her kiss.

"Gross!" Haley shrieked, and hastily scrambled out of the seat. "Since when is it mating season in New Jersey?"

"If you're Darla, it's always mating season," said the Asian girl. "Why do you think they call her the Jaws of Death?"

"Shouldn't we help him?" Haley asked, looking at the flailing boy attempting to come up for air.

"What, you mean save a fourteen-year-old boy from getting to first"—the Asian girl squinted at the couple—"no, make that second base? I don't see Russ complaining, do you?" The Asian girl motioned toward the boy, who had been momentarily released from Darla's grasp. He had a dopey smile on his face and a glazed look in his eyes.

"Hey, do you mind if I sit here?" Haley asked the Asian girl. "In case they reengage?"

"That depends. Are you going to look through my bag next?" the girl replied. Haley's lightly freckled face turned a deep shade of red. "You shouldn't spy on people," she added. "You might uncover something you didn't want to know."

"Sorry. What can I say? I'm a curious person," Haley offered.

"I haven't seen you around here before," said the girl.

"My family just moved here from California. This is officially my first public school."

"Seriously?" the girl asked, her interest suddenly piqued.

"Yeah. I grew up outside San Francisco. My parents sent me to special magnet schools from the time I could walk. You know, politically correct teachers, everybody sensitive to each other's feelings, nothing you did was ever completely right or wrong."

"Well. That explains the sweater," the girl said, motioning toward Haley's pink top.

"Hey, easy. I've worn uniforms my whole life."

"I'd wear a uniform too if that's what was hanging in my closet. I'm Irene, by the way. Irene Chen."

"Haley Miller. Do you think just the T-shirt would be better?" Haley asked, lifting up the pink sweater to reveal a vintage-looking green baby T with a Yellowstone logo on the front.

"Absolutely." Irene nodded encouragingly as Haley

pulled off the sweater and shoved it into her back-pack. "You know, that's actually a cool shirt," she noted.

"Thanks," said Haley. "My parents bought it for my little brother on our cross-country trip this summer. Mine was too big so I swiped his."

"Now, let's see, what else? Take your hair out of that ponytail." Haley obliged. "Hmmm. You don't by chance wear glasses, do you?"

"Sometimes for class. But they're so nerdy," Haley said.

"Let me see," said Irene. Haley reached into her bag and pulled out a pair of old square frames. She hesitated and then slid them onto her face.

"They were my mom's," she explained. "She had my prescription put in."

"I love them!" Irene said. "It's so hard to find good glasses nowadays. See, now you've got a look." Irene held up a pocket mirror for Haley to see herself. Haley had to admit that with her hair down, in the tight T-shirt, wearing the modish glasses, she looked interesting, like some of the college kids she'd seen milling around outside her father's office at Berkeley.

The bus pulled up to its drop-off point, and Haley got her first look at Hillsdale High. It looked . . . blurry. She took off the glasses, which were really only supposed to be for reading. A modern, institutional-looking building formed a quad around a patch of green grass. Haley noticed a girl holding up a sign with Haley's name on it. Irene spotted her too and said, "Ugh, do you know that girl?"

"Never seen her before in my life," said Haley.

"That's Annie Armstrong. The welcoming committee. Figures. She says yes to anything that'll improve her transcript, including adopting new students and showing them around campus." The bus doors opened. Irene pulled her hood up over her head, handed Haley a comic book and said, "Come on."

With their heads ducked, Haley holding the comic book in front of her face, the girls got off the bus and hurried past Annie, who called out, "Hi, Irene!" As she caught up to them, breathlessly matching their pace, she said, "You're Haley, right? I know because I logged on to your old school's Web site and found a yearbook photo of you. I'm Annie, Annie Armstrong. I've been assigned to be your guide this week at Hillsdale High."

Haley looked at Irene, who was making faces behind Annie's back, and said, "Gee, thanks, Annie. That's really nice of you, but I think I can probably find my way around Hillsdale on my own. It doesn't seem too difficult to navigate."

"B-but—" Annie stammered.

"How 'bout I call you if I have any trouble?" said Haley, backing away with Irene in tow. "Okay? Really, thanks again. Sooo nice meeting you." Haley waved, turned around and pushed through the double doors of the school.

"But wait," Annie called after them, "don't you need my cell phone number?" Haley and Irene were already halfway down the hall, enveloped by the throngs of students reconnecting with each other after three months apart.

Everywhere, kids were slamming lockers, slapping high fives and snapping bra straps. Irene seemed to glide through the crowd unfazed. As they walked past the first open classroom door, Haley looked inside at a handsome teacher in a beige corduroy blazer, taking a sip of coffee at his desk. "That's Travis Tygert," Irene said. "He teaches honors history. Oh, and he's also the girls' soccer coach. Some people think he's cute."

"Wait a second." Haley stopped and reached into her backpack. "The name Tygert sounds familiar." She pulled out her class schedule and sure enough . . . "Oh, that's why. I have him for third period."

"You're taking honors history?" Irene asked, as if she objected to the idea.

"Guess so," said Haley.

"Let me see that," Irene said, and grabbed the paper from her hand. "All honors, except Spanish? Have fun," she said sarcastically, and gave the schedule back to Haley.

"You don't think I should take Tygert?" Haley asked.

"Take art with me that period instead," Irene

suggested. "You could certainly stand to lose one honors credit."

"I don't know . . ." Haley hesitated. "If I switch out of that class, it might throw off my whole schedule."

"Well, just come today and see what you think. You can always tell Tygert you got confused and went to the wrong class. He'll let you in tomorrow."

Just then, Johnny Lane walked by and grabbed Irene's arm. "Hey, see you in art class later, right?" he asked.

"That guy takes art?" Haley said after Johnny walked away.

"Yep. And so could you. Now, are you switching or not?" Irene demanded.

Haley bit her lip. The halls were clearing out as students filed into their classes. She knew she had to make a decision.

"I'll just see you in third period," Irene said matter-of-factly, leaving Haley standing in the hall. As the bell rang, Haley headed toward her first class, still wondering what she should do.

● ● ●

Our little Haley sure does look green riding the bus with the derelicts. But then again, maybe Haley Miller has more in common with this band of outsiders than we think.

Her new friend Irene seems to be *different*, to put

25

it kindly. Will Haley be able to bring out the best in Irene? Or should she wait to see who else she meets at her new high school before she forges her first alliance?

Should Haley follow her free-spirited curiosity and pick up a paintbrush? If she does, will she know where to, well, draw the line?

If Haley chooses history instead, who will she hang out with? And what if she doesn't meet anyone she clicks with like Irene?

It's only the first day of school and already two paths are diverging in a yellow hallway. The rest is up to you. Make Haley take the one less traveled by turning to page 38. Or have her preserve her perfect transcript on page 46.

Even the simplest choices will affect Haley's social and academic standing. But no matter what she does next, you can be certain that Haley's whole world is about to change. . . .

SPANISH CLASS

Everything makes sense when you're speaking the international language of P-O-P-U-L-A-R.

It was passing period on Monday morning, the first day of school, and the halls were congested with students slamming lockers, slapping high fives and snapping bra straps.

Haley followed Annie Armstrong, clutching her books and fending off a pair of rowdy linebackers playing a game of touch freshman. Basically this game involved one of the boys tossing a football at an unsuspecting freshman girl while the other made like he was going in for a catch but instead reached for the girl's breasts.

"I like to think of Hillsdale High as a sort of training ground for real life," Annie said to Haley while ducking out of the path of the ball. "Sure there are obstacles to overcome, but whatever your major field of interest, you can explore it here."

Annie had volunteered to be a part of the welcome program that helped new students acclimate to Hillsdale High. Haley had been assigned to Annie because they had similar class schedules—all honors except for Spanish, which was a third language for both of them. Annie, Haley discovered, had also studied French in junior high.

"Impressive, isn't it?" Annie said with pride, as Haley noticed a long glass case filled with trophies and rows of photographs. "For a public school, we do more than all right. In fact, we have everything," she added, beaming. "A debate team, a fencing squad, archery, Spanish club, soccer, basketball, cheerleading, lacrosse. We have skiing—downhill, cross-country and water. Band. There's golf, dramaturgy, Francophiles, Model UN, student council, badminton, tennis. We have Young Scientists and math Olympics, home economics and Econ Ten. Horseback riding, chess, Young Philanthropists and ballet."

Haley's head was spinning. She began to worry that she didn't have enough extracurricular activities on her résumé. In just a few years, she would be competing for college placement with girls like

Annie, who could probably build the world in five days, as opposed to seven.

"And last, but certainly not least," Annie sighed, "we have . . ." She paused and looked around to make sure no one else was listening, then in a reverent whisper said, "SIGMA."

"What's Sigma?" Haley asked, without bothering to keep her voice down. Several girls craned their necks to get a look at her.

Annie laughed nervously, shrugged and announced, "She's new here," before grabbing Haley by the arm and pulling her around the corner. "Boy, do you have a lot to learn," she said, shaking her head disapprovingly and bumping into a girl fiddling with the combination on her locker.

The Asian girl she'd hit was wearing an oversized gray parka with a fur-lined hood that nearly covered her dark almond-shaped eyes. Her plaid schoolgirl skirt was paired with men's oxford shoes and striped socks, and she wore a pair of tortoiseshell barrettes to pin her straight black hair behind her ears.

"Oh, hi, Irene," Annie said. Haley could tell by Annie's tone that she felt superior to the girl.

"You should watch where you're going," Irene said without looking up. She continued fidgeting with the lock until Annie and Haley had passed.

"Irene Chen, serious outsider," Annie said matter-of-factly. "I mean, I like her, of course, but then I'm probably the only friend she has in the world, poor thing. She should be glad I even bother to talk to her. Without me, she'd be a complete social outcast."

Somehow Haley found this hard to believe. Back in San Francisco, Irene, with her vintage clothes and cool, detached demeanor, would probably have fit right in with her friends.

"Have you been to the Golden Dynasty yet?" Annie added. "No, of course not. Well, the Chen family owns it. They own the whole chain. They're about to open their fifth franchise in Bergen County this year."

As Haley and Annie reached the door of their Spanish classroom, Annie's expression suddenly changed.

"What's her story?" Haley asked, pointing to the pretty brunette she had seen that morning picking Reese up for school.

"That is Coco De Clerq," Annie said solemnly. "God's gift to the sophomore class." Coco was flanked by two gorgeous blonde wingbabes. One of them Haley recognized as Whitney, the blonde from the backseat of the white convertible. The other was taller and seemed slightly bored.

Of the three, Coco was clearly the least beautiful, but then, that was like saying a lily wasn't as pretty as a peony or a rose. What did she care that she was two inches shorter than one blonde and two cup sizes smaller than the other? She was still clearly the alpha female of the group.

"That's Whitney Klein, and over there, that's Sasha Lewis," said Annie, pointing to the girl on Coco's left. "They've been friends since we were all in preschool together."

Haley watched as Whitney, who had just dropped her pen on the floor next to her desk, leaned down to pick it up. Whitney, in her low-cut top and curve-hugging miniskirt, smiled at the boy seated next to her, and just like that, the kid was reduced to a puddle of boy flesh, all oozing hormones, with acne and bad teeth.

"Whitney has a terrible reputation," Annie said. "But she's best friends with Coco, so she can act as slutty as she wants to and still be one of the most popular girls in school."

Annie seemed to know an awful lot about these people, Haley observed. Maybe too much.

"Anyone who's friends with Coco is automatically granted social immunity," said Annie. "It's kind of sad, really, since there's no way Whitney could ever land a real boyfriend, considering. They all just use her up and move on."

Haley watched as Whitney leaned back in her chair, unwrapped a lollipop and proceeded to suck the color off her candy. *How could anyone possibly use a girl like that?* Haley wondered. In her opinion, girls like Whitney ate boys for lunch. Right after they finished their lollipops.

"Someone should really take her aside and give her a few pointers," Annie said smugly.

"And what about her?" Haley asked, pointing to Sasha, who was dressed in a military jacket, faded blue jeans and broken-in leather boots. Her MP3 player was blaring glam rock through the headphones as she stared dreamily out the window, watching the clouds float by.

"That's Sasha," said Annie. "She's a total mystery. In French club last year, one of our advisors nicknamed her the Enigma. No one can figure her out."

The bell rang and Annie and Haley entered the classroom to take their seats.

"Hello, Ms. Frick. Don't you look nice today," Annie said, her voice lilting.

"*Hola, Anita. Cómo estás?*" the Spanish teacher asked. "And who do we have here?" she added, looking at Haley.

"I'm Haley Miller," Haley said. "I just moved to Hillsdale." She felt the need to establish that she and Annie were far from being great friends.

"Well, all of my students have Spanish names, Haley. For you, I think Mariposa Blanca. Why don't you sit right there, Mariposa," Ms. Frick said to Haley, and pointed to the seat behind Coco De Clerq.

"Sure," Haley said, plopping down in the desk. Annie, eyeing Haley jealously, trudged to the other side of the room and took the last empty desk, next to a boy who seemed to have so much pent-up energy he sizzled like an old appliance.

"Hola, chicos y chicas!" Ms. Frick said with flair as she clicked up to the chalkboard in her strappy high heels. *"Yo me llamo Isabella."*

On the green chalkboard, she wrote in a flowery script three irregular verb conjugations, starting with *ir, to go.* She turned to face the class and looked right at Haley.

"Mariposa, why don't you tell us about your summer?" she said.

"Okay," Haley said, and then began speaking in near-perfect Spanish, divulging that she had just moved to New Jersey from California. She went on to tell the class about the drive across country with her family; about her father, who was a documentary filmmaker, and his new job at the Columbia Film School; about her strange younger brother and their dog, Freckles.

"Señorita, excelente!" Ms. Frick said when she had finished.

Haley blushed as the door to the classroom opened. Standing there dressed in khakis and an open-necked white linen shirt was a reason to learn Spanish if ever there was one. He had dark tanned skin, broad shoulders, smoldering eyes and wavy black hair that was still damp from a recent shower. The boy smiled at Ms. Frick, who directed him to sit in an unoccupied folding chair next to Annie Armstrong's desk. Annie looked over at Haley and gloated.

"Everyone, this is Sebastian Bodega, our new foreign exchange student from Spain," Ms. Frick said breathlessly. "He is on the swim team and will be living with the Shopes for the rest of the year. Now, to begin the lesson, let's try using the verbs I've written on the board."

Sebastian raised his hand. "Sebastian," Ms. Frick said, more than happy to call on him to speak. "Why don't you share something about your summer vacation?"

Sebastian's voice was deep and sultry, while his Spanish was, of course, impeccable. After all, it was his native tongue—his tongue being a piece of the Bodega anatomy every girl in the classroom clearly wanted to explore.

Too bad none of them, aside from Haley, Annie and Ms. Frick, could understand a word the boy was saying. Nevertheless, his *r*s kept rolling off his bow-shaped lips. He talked about his mother and growing up on the outskirts of Seville. He talked about learning to swim in the Mediterranean.

As if challenged to a duel by Sebastian's speech, Ms. Frick suddenly showcased her own language skills. She shamelessly ignored the rest of the class and launched into a private conversation with Sebastian, speaking so rapidly that even Haley had trouble deciphering what she was saying.

"I bet you our little Enrique here keeps Isabella occupied all year," Coco said to Sasha, who just shrugged.

Haley sat quietly, straining to hear what Sebastian was saying to Ms. Frick about bullfights. That was next to impossible with Coco blathering on about summering on her family's yacht, the *Lazy Daze,* in some town in the Hamptons called Quogue. Apparently, Coco's father, Maury—Maurice De Clerq—owned a couple of furniture stores on Route 17 and had found stratospheric success with a gel-filled recliner he had developed, patented and licensed to a national furniture chain.

"It was total boys of summer," said Coco. "I mean Malcolm was cute, but he worked on our boat. If my mother found out, I could say goodbye to ever getting a car next year."

"You never know, maybe your mom likes Malkie," said Whitney.

"I told you not to call him that," Coco snapped.

Whitney was now filing her nails. "I love summer. It's the perfect time to try new things. You can get away with anything."

"What happens in Quogue stays in Quogue," Coco vowed. Haley was intrigued.

"*Por favor,* class. Everybody quiet down," Ms. Frick said. "I have an assignment for you. This year, class, we're going to try something very exciting. We're going to have group projects that will last for the whole semester."

Annie gasped. "Does that mean our whole grade basically hinges on one project?"

"Everyone get into groups of four and I will tell you all about it," said Ms. Frick.

Whitney looked at Sasha, Sasha looked at Coco and Coco sighed, turning around in her desk chair to face Haley.

"So. Mariposa. Your Spanish seems decent. How would you like to be in our group?" Coco asked.

Out of the corner of her eye, Haley could see Annie signaling for her attention. Clearly, Annie wanted Haley to join her group with the spastic boy and the luscious Sebastian Bodega.

"Remember, students, this will be your group for the next four months. You will be graded heavily on the project," Ms. Frick advised.

"Whatever. She's such a pushover when it comes to grades." Whitney yawned.

"How do you know?" asked Haley.

Coco chimed in, "My sister's had her for the last two years. Besides, it's not even honors. How hard can it be?"

Haley looked at the three gorgeous girls in front of her, and then at Annie, who was smiling at her desperately from the back row. Suddenly, she knew exactly what to do.

● ● ●

Well, Haley certainly seems to be hitting it off with the right sort of people at Hillsdale. But are the Coco puffs really interested in her? Or are they just after her perfect conjugation? And if she picks them, will hanging out with the populettes be all it's cracked up to be?

And what of Annie? It's sort of sweet the way she's so obsessed with Coco. Then again, it's sort of pathetic. Maybe if Annie had real friends who accepted her as she is, she wouldn't feel the need to try so hard all the time.

And let's not forget that bodacious Sebastian Bodega. Talk about hotttnnesss, this guy is approaching the equator. What will happen if Haley gets to know this Spanish import better?

If you think Haley should see how the other half lives and give Spanish lessons to the popular girls, turn to page 62. If you think she should go for the sure A and stick by Annie, who's so far stuck by her, skip ahead to page 56.

It's only the first day of school and already things are heating up at Hillsdale, so just imagine what the rest of the semester will bring.

Even artists
sometimes paint
themselves into
a corner.

"**A**rt is mystery," said Rick Von as he turned on the overhead projector and a blurred image appeared on the wall behind him.

"Yeah. What the heck is it?" a tall, skinny African American boy with round glasses sitting next to Haley muttered. Haley looked at him and shrugged.

"Impressionism," Mr. Von said, looking at Haley. "That's where our journey begins today."

"Ain't nothing impressive about that one, Mr. Von," a chunky kid with a blond mullet called out from the back of the room.

"Thank you, Shaun," the teacher said, and then cleared his throat. Mr. Von's voice was raspy and rarely rose above a whisper.

"Sometimes, class, the further we get from our subjects, the better we can understand them." He seemed to almost tiptoe around the room as he said this, walking on the balls of his feet and slightly favoring his right leg, occasionally stopping to adjust his glasses or rub his stubbly beard.

"I'm Dale," the boy next to her whispered.

"Haley," she introduced herself.

"I heard he fought in Vietnam," Dale whispered, motioning toward Mr. Von. "It totally wigged him out."

"He's too young," Irene said. "I heard he worked in a salmon cannery in Alaska. That's how he got the limp."

"That was after Nam," Dale said. "He spent most of the eighties in a psychiatric ward. They did experiments on him and stuff. Now every time he goes near Newark, he thinks he's back in Saigon."

Johnny Lane leaned forward casually from the row behind them. "No, man," he said. "He just got some bad acid in Hawaii. Went up in the hills outside Waimea and lived off goats and oranges for six months. That's his deal, man. Acid Rick."

"No, I heard they call him Rick Von Wrinkle," Dale said, nodding toward Mr. Von's rumpled flannel shirt. "He can sleep for, like, three days straight."

"I don't know, man," Johnny said. "You think about eating goats and oranges for six months. Think about what it would do to you."

"Right," Irene said, nodding as if she understood. Johnny went back to tapping out a drum solo with his number two pencils, and Irene's eyes lingered just a moment too long.

"First we look wide, class," said Mr. Von. "We try to remove ourselves from the work." Mr. Von shifted the slide and began focusing the projector. "Then we begin to narrow the lens." Slowly, an image took shape on the wall.

"This is easily the most bizarre art class I've ever been in," said Haley. "And I'm from California."

Irene leaned toward her and said, "I know he might seem unconventional." Haley raised an eyebrow. "Okay, so he's totally weird. But I'm telling you, if you stick with this class, Mr. Von will change your life. Or at least that's what some senior told me."

Pointing to the slide, Mr. Von continued, "Only when you begin to understand the context of a piece can you begin to delve deeper, to find out the particulars, the brushstrokes, the artist's choice of subjects . . . *La Petite Rêve.*"

"*Little Girl Dreaming,*" Haley blurted out the translated title, then slapped a hand over her mouth. "Sorry."

"No. That's right," Mr. Von said. "Does anyone know who the master was?" he asked.

"Paul Gauguin," Haley fired back.

"Class, what would you say if I told you the girl lying here is Gauguin's daughter?" Mr. Von paused. "How does that information change your impression of the painting? Dale?"

Dale thought for a moment. "You can tell from the way he's looking at her that he's feeling protective. What's her name?"

"Aline," said Mr. Von.

"Aline is, like, the ultimate painting for him. I think that's why you can only see her from behind. Because he knew his brush couldn't do justice to her face."

"Thank you, Dale."

"Nice," Haley said.

"Does anyone else have anything to add?" Mr. Von asked. Shaun stared gape-mouthed at the ceiling, watching a fly circling above him. Johnny Lane continued to tap out a drum solo with two pencils. And Irene had already begun to draw in her sacred black notebook.

"Well, then," Mr. Von said, "your assignment for today is the same assignment you will have every day in this class. I just ask that you produce. Even if you're not interested in the lecture, pick up a pencil and doodle. Remember, we don't judge material here based on the size of the picture or the time it took to make it. I am only interested in the act of expression. So. Express yourselves. There are supplies in the cabinet. You have the rest of the hour." And with that, Mr. Von took a seat at his desk at the back of the room.

It was a loose, freewheeling approach to teaching that reminded Haley of her teachers on the West Coast. Maybe, she thought, public school in New Jersey wasn't so different from a Montessori education. At that moment, Shaun walked by and belched loudly, blowing his warm cereal breath into Haley's face.

"Like that, don't you?" Shaun asked, his thin lips curling into a deviant smile. "Mmmm, mmmm, good."

"You know, Shaun," Irene snapped, "I can't really decide if those sugar flakes are more flattering on your hips or your breath. What do you think, Haley? Hips or breath? Breath or hips? I don't know. It's a toss-up."

"You're forgetting option C," Haley said.

"What's that?" Irene asked.

Haley stood up and faced Shaun, brushing a collection of yellow crumbs from his faded flannel sleeve. "The sugar flakes on his shirt."

"Hey, gitcha lily-white paws off my lunch, bee-yotch," said Shaun, shoving Haley aside and intentionally knocking the papers off her desk. He walked to the front of the room and threw open the double doors of the art supply cabinet. "Ah, dude, yes. Paint thinner."

Haley bent down to collect her scattered belongings from the floor. "Well, that was annoying."

"He's like an evolutionary experiment gone horribly wrong," said Irene.

"I'll say," Haley replied.

"You don't know the half of it," Dale whispered. "He can read backwards."

"What do you mean?" Haley asked.

"I mean if you say something to him, he can recite it back to you, only backwards."

"Sdrawkcab ylno uoy ot kcab ti eticer nac eh mih ot gnihtemos yas uoy fi neam I," said Shaun, moonwalking backward down the aisle and carrying the jug of paint thinner back to his desk. "Sugar flake that, yo. Snap, crackle, pop."

Haley stared at Shaun, dumbfounded.

"I know," said Irene. "And what's worse, he can actually draw."

"It looks like a spider," Haley sighed, looking down at the sketch she had made of her left hand.

"Or an octopus," said Irene. She turned the page upside down. "Or maybe a rooster?"

Haley's brow furrowed. "I'm terrible at this."

"It just takes time," Irene reassured her. "You'll get better."

"Maybe with hundreds of hours of practice. What are you doing later?"

"I have to work."

"Where?" Haley asked.

"At my parents' restaurant. The Golden Dynasty."

"Best Chinese food in town," said Dale.

"Let me see yours," Haley demanded, pointing to Irene's drawing.

"No. It—it's not finished yet," Irene stammered, covering it up with her hands.

"Come on. I want to see," Haley said, prying Irene's hands off the page. She didn't notice that Irene looked upset.

"Lay off," Irene said seriously.

Haley couldn't understand why Irene was putting up such a fight until she looked down at the page. There, staring back at her, was a perfect likeness of . . . Johnny Lane.

"Why do you have to be like that?" Irene grabbed the sketchbook as the bell rang. Without bothering to say goodbye, she shoved her books into her bag and hastily exited the room, leaving Haley standing there all alone.

● ● ●

Boy, the drama. Sometimes girls can be so touchy, especially these sensitive artist types. From the way Irene was acting, you'd think her sketchbook was a window into her soul or something. And guess what? You'd be right.

Now that Haley's landed at Hillsdale, she needs all

the friends she can get. The wrong move here could potentially cross Irene off that list. Then again, if Irene's going to be so secretive all the time, does Haley really need her in her life?

If you think Irene is overreacting, send Haley home at the end of the day on page 82. If you want Haley to apologize to her new friend and try and work things out, go to page 77.

It's not even second period yet and already alliances are shifting at Hillsdale High. Will Haley and Irene's friendship break up before they've even gone out? Will Johnny remain the ultimate mystery in Mr. Von's art class? And will the strange phenomenon that is Shaun ever learn to interact with his classmates?

For now, Haley is your piece of clay. Sculpt her as you will. Just remember, a masterpiece always captures the essence of its subject. Otherwise, there's no point in getting your hands dirty.

Everybody has a past, but
few will make history.

Ohmigosh, here he comes," a girl in a yellow sweater gasped while fanning her face with fluttering hands. She seemed to be trying—unsuccessfully, Haley noted—to stop a rosy blush from rising to her cheeks. Catching Haley's eye, she added, "My older sister had him twice, and I've seen pictures. He's gorgeous."

"Who?" Haley asked at precisely the moment Travis Tygert breezed in from the hall carrying a worn leather briefcase. His skin was a deep shade of golden brown, and there was a light dusting of freckles on his forearms and the bridge of his nose.

A pair of intelligent hazel eyes peered out from his angular face. His sandy brown hair was a bit long on top and still had the mussed air of a recent college grad. In fact, he looked barely out of high school himself.

Mr. Tygert deposited his things near his desk and turned to face his students as a chorus of sighs echoed around the room. For the first time, Haley noticed that most of her classmates were lacking Y chromosomes.

"Good morning. I'm Mr. Tygert, and I'll be your honors history teacher this year." Another collective sigh. Haley rolled her eyes as Yellow Sweater cleared her throat.

"Um . . . Mr. Tygert?" Yellow Sweater said meekly. "I'm April. Tracy Doyle's sister?"

Mr. Tygert concentrated on the girl's round face for a moment and then smiled. "Hi, April." The way he said it only intensified the girl's blush. "I see your sister wasn't able to dissuade you from taking my class?"

"Oh no, Mr. Tygert," April said reverently. "If anything, she talked me into taking this class."

"Oh, really?" the teacher asked, bemused. "Don't tell me. Tracy liked civics so much, she purposely took it twice?" April nodded, and Mr. Tygert laughed.

"Well, I trust you'll only be studying the U.S. government with us for one year, April?" She nodded again and smiled while several of the other girls eyed her jealously.

Haley had never witnessed anything like this. True, Mr. Tygert had charisma. But the effect he had on his third-period history class bordered on ridiculous.

Even the studious Annie Armstrong was acting as if she were staring at a teen idol poster ripped from the pages of a magazine and taped to the wall above her bed.

What's come over them? Haley wondered. Mr. Tygert was hardly some biscuit with six-pack abs and a seventh-grade IQ. According to his Hillsdale High bio, which Haley had downloaded from the Internet and saved on her desktop as soon as she'd gotten her course schedule in the mail, Mr. Tygert was an Ivy League grad, the recipient of a MacArthur "genius" grant, a triathlete and a card-carrying member of the ACLU. He certainly wasn't someone to be ogled like a common calendar boy.

"War," said Mr. Tygert, striding around the classroom, turning the shiny gold wedding band on his left ring finger with his thumb. "Who here has ever played a game of war?" He leaned against the edge of his desk and looked out at the class as a number of hands tentatively went into the air. "Come on, don't be shy," he said, raising his own hand, then

taking aim as if he were holding a rifle. "I've played."
The room fell silent as everyone waited to see what
Mr. Tygert would do next.

As Haley raised her own hand, she cast a glance
over her shoulder and suddenly noticed Reese Highland sitting in the corner. Somehow, she had failed
to see him when she walked into the room, and yet
there he was, not three rows behind her.

Oh my god, Reese is in this class? Haley thought,
trying to suppress the silly grin that was creeping
across her face. Too late. Reese had spotted her. He
smiled back and lifted two fingers off his desk as if to
wave, but Haley quickly turned her head.

Mr. Tygert lifted his cup of coffee and took a sip.
"Why do you think we play at war?" He sur-
veyed the room, waiting for someone to answer.

After a long silence, Reese asked, "Isn't that a bit
like asking why girls play with dolls?"

"What do you say to that, April?" Mr. Tygert
asked.

"Well," April began hesitantly, "I think we play
with dolls to practice. So that we'll know what to do
when we become mothers." She batted her eyelashes
profusely, which had exactly zero effect on Mr. Tygert.

"What I'm hearing from you, Reese, is that you
think we're trained to fight?"

"Yeah, sure," Reese said confidently. "Just look at
sports teams, man. I mean Coach. I mean sir—"

Mr. Tygert interrupted. "You don't have to call

me 'sir' in here, Reese. And neither does anyone else in the class. 'Coach' works. Or 'Mr. Tygert.' But 'Travis' would be better." He looked at the seating chart again. "Now. Haley?"

"Yes, Travis?" she replied without missing a beat. A few of the girls sitting near her snickered at the sound of the teacher's first name.

He smiled at Haley. "Tell me about a time in your life when you or someone you know was taught to act a certain way but deliberately chose to behave differently."

"Well." She thought for a moment. "Take this morning. I'm supposed to let our dog, Freckles, out for a walk first thing every morning. But today was different."

"Why?" Mr. Tygert asked.

"Because I saw the paperboy coming. He can barely even reach the pedals on his bike. And he's afraid of dogs. Not the best career choice, right?" The class laughed. "So I kept Freckles inside an extra fifteen minutes, until he was gone."

"Thank you, Haley. You see that what we're trying to get at here, class, is the difference between being capable of a certain response and that course of action's becoming inevitable because of our training. Now, if you'll all open your textbooks to page . . ." Mr. Tygert's voice seemed to trail off as Haley, lost in her thoughts, became increasingly convinced that she had found the coolest teacher on the planet. Here was someone you actually wanted to be influenced by. Someone who was . . . checking her out?

Haley was shocked. Mr. Tygert had just given her the once-over as he handed out the first homework assignment, photocopied excerpts of Thomas Hobbes's *Leviathan* and John Locke's *Tabula Rasa* and an essay on the American vs. the French revolution. Before Haley could even fully register what had just happened, the bell rang.

"See you tomorrow," Mr. Tygert said as the students got up from their desks and shuffled into the hall. As Haley stood up to leave, he called out, "Oh, Haley, can I have a word with you?" She slowly walked toward him, wondering what he could possibly want. "Tell me something," he said. "Have you ever played . . . soccer?"

"Um . . . excuse me?" Haley asked.

"You know, Haley. That sport where the players kick around a little round ball and try to score by kicking it into a rather large net?"

"No. Sure, I mean, I've p-played, but I've never *played* played," Haley stammered.

"But you do know the basic rules?" Mr. Tygert asked.

"I guess so." Haley awkwardly shifted her weight from one foot to the other and looked down at Mr. Tygert's shoes.

"Your homeroom teacher tells me you've just moved to the area?" he asked.

"From California."

"Joining a team can be a great way to meet people. We have an excellent group of girls. The varsity team made all-state last year. And one of our best forwards graduated, unfortunately, so there's room on the team."

"Thanks, Mr. Tygert. I mean Travis. Or Coach. I mean, I'll think about it," Haley said, noticing again the wedding band on his left hand. She grabbed her books and bolted out of the classroom.

"Hey, slow down," Reese said, grabbing her arm. "What's the rush?"

"Oh, just trying to make it to my next class," she said.

"Was Coach Tygert trying to recruit you?"

"Yeah, little does he know how bad I am."

Reese playfully punched Haley's arm. "Nah, you have the legs for it," he said. "Maybe I'll even give you some pointers after school. I'm on the guys' team."

"He's not just on the team. Reese is the captain," Coco De Clerq said. She and Whitney Klein and a tall, beautiful blonde Haley hadn't met yet had appeared out of nowhere. "You're so modest, Reese," she added, flirtatiously clutching his arm.

"Hey, Coco," Reese said in a slightly bored voice. "Hey, Whit, Sasha."

"So, Reese, now that you're taking honors classes

this year," Whitney said in a pouty voice, "does that mean you have to hang out with the honors geeks?"

"Reese can hang out with whoever he likes," Coco said, looking at Haley. "Even mousy little brainiacs from his history class." She turned to Reese. "So, Highland, my sister tells me the seniors are ordering pizza and skipping second period. She said we could join them in the courtyard if we wanted. Wanna come?"

"Wow, pizza," Reese said, holding his sculpted abs. "Can Haley come too?"

"I don't know if that's such a good idea," said Coco. "I don't know how many they ordered. And my sister specifically mentioned you by name."

Haley got the hint. "Go ahead," she said, trying to be a good sport. "I've got English class right now anyway."

"That sucks," said Reese. "I have a free period. And I'm starving."

"Well, there's no way I'm dissecting anything in second period on an empty stomach," Whitney said.

"We're skipping bio, you nitwit," Coco said as Whitney followed her down the hall.

Sasha looked at Haley and smiled. "It's nothing personal. It's just how they are," she explained. "Once you get to know them, you'll see that they're . . . well, that they're exactly the way they seem." Reese laughed.

"What is my deal?" he added, holding his growling stomach. "I think I could eat a whole pizza by myself. That's what happens when you play soccer, Haley. Just ask Sasha. She's on the team."

Sasha nodded. "Yeah, try having a healthy appetite around those two," she said, pointing at Coco and Whitney. "No eat and repeat."

Haley had no idea what she meant but nodded in agreement.

"Haley's thinking of trying out," said Reese.

"Really? You totally should," Sasha said as Reese suddenly grabbed her arm and dragged her down the hall.

"Maybe," Haley said.

"Well, I hope I see you at practice!" Sasha screamed as Reese scooped her up in his arms and carried her into the courtyard.

● ● ●

Now, here's a girl Haley could be friends with. Sasha seems like the most promising candidate who's come along so far. Finally, someone who proves that being pretty and popular doesn't equate to being obnoxious.

So why is she friends with Coco and Whitney? Is it just out of habit? Or is she more of a Coquette than Haley would like to believe?

And what about Reese? Turns out, Haley's hottie next-door neighbor is in at least one of Haley's classes. But is she naive to think of him as anything more than a surrogate big brother? Isn't Reese already cuckoo for the Coco puffs? And what will Haley have to do to change his mind?

At least Haley has found a class she likes. History may repeat itself, but when Travis Tygert's teaching, no one seems to mind.

To have Haley spend more time with Coach Tygert and Sasha, turn to page 87. Or if you think Haley should be skeptical of the overly familiar teacher and the prettiest girl in the popular crowd, send her back home to spend some time nesting in her new bedroom and turn to page 82.

Keep in mind that for every one of Haley's actions, there is an equal and opposite reaction. She's about to find out where that peer pressure will come from next.

Never judge a bookworm
by her cover.

"So, are you in or out?" Coco demanded, her silky brown hair and gleaming white teeth taunting Haley with their perfection. In a bathrobe and no makeup, Coco would be a walking shampoo commercial, Haley realized.

She looked at the alternative. Annie waved and held up her arms as if to say, *Well, what are you waiting for?* Meanwhile, Sebastian was showing Ms. Frick some of his salsa moves, as the third member of their group sat flipping through the Spanish-English dictionary, already preparing note cards for the first exam.

Haley couldn't remember when she'd seen such a motley crew. The spaz sitting next to Annie, in particular, looked as if he might spontaneously combust if a girl even tried to talk to him. And yet somehow Haley knew that was where she belonged.

"Actually, Coco, I'm out," she said.

Coco frowned. "What do you mean?"

"I already have a group. But thanks for the offer."

"You can't seriously mean *them*?" Coco said, pointing across the room.

Haley shrugged. They all turned to look as the boy sitting next to Annie slipped his left index finger up his right nostril.

"Gross!" Whitney squealed. "Do you think he touches the doorknob with that hand?"

"Whitney, this is Dave Metzger we're talking about." Coco smirked. "That hand sees much worse than the inside of his nose."

Whitney shivered. "Haley, hon," she began, taking Haley's hand, "really and truly. You should trust us. These people are like social piranhas—"

"Pariahs, idiot," Coco interrupted.

But Haley stood her ground. "I've made my decision," she said. The temperature in the room seemed to plummet as the corners of Coco's mouth curled into a vicious smile, and now it was Haley's turn to shiver.

Coco glared at her. "Suit yourself," she said without flinching. "But good luck fitting in at Hillsdale hanging out with those geeks."

Haley gathered up her books as Coco and Whitney turned their backs on her for good.

"Okay, everybody, get together in your groups, please," instructed Ms. Frick. The teacher smoothed a few stray hairs on her head and clapped her hands together twice. "Chop-chop."

Haley pulled up a desk and parked herself between Sebastian and Annie.

"Sebastian was just telling me about his house in Seville," boasted Annie.

"Hi, I'm Haley Miller," Haley said, extending her hand toward Sebastian.

"Haley just moved here from California," said Annie, eager to trade on the one commodity she always seemed to have in abundance: information.

"It is my pleasure to make your acquaintance, Miss Miller," Sebastian said in a thick accent, kissing Haley on each cheek.

Suddenly, Haley noticed something else about the exchange student that was foreign to her—a tuft of brown chest hair peeking out of his white linen shirt.

"And this is Dave," Annie said as Dave smiled awkwardly and flipped to the *B*s in his dictionary, lowering his nose back into the book.

"Okay, class, now each group is going to be

58

assigned a city in Spain," Ms. Frick said. "You're going to research everything you can about your city. At the end of the semester we're going to have a fiesta in which you'll share with the rest of the class what you've learned about the culture and its history— you will cook the local cuisine, dance the native dances and wear the traditional costumes.

"Annie, Sebastian, Haley and David, your city will be Seville." Sebastian smiled.

"Like that's fair!" Coco protested from across the room. "It's Sebastian's hometown. They won't have to do any research."

"Settle down, Cocita. Your group will research the most important city in all of Spain. *La capital*. Madrid."

"Where's Madrid?" Whitney asked, frowning at the map.

"Gracias, Señora," Coco said, satisfied to have been given an assignment with such distinction.

"Look at her gloating," Annie whispered to Haley. "You know Coco thinks she got the best city just because it's the capital. Wait until she realizes it's ten times the work."

"And they only have three people," Haley added.

As Ms. Frick doled out the rest of the assignments, Haley's group began to talk among themselves. "So Sebastian," said Annie. "Tell us about Seville. How should we begin?"

"Well, Annie. Seville is a place of great hospitality,"

said Sebastian. "So, for our first study session on my city, allow me to cook for you some of my favorite dishes, tomorrow evening."

"Sounds great," Annie said.

"I don't know," said Haley skeptically. "Shouldn't we start putting together our report first?"

"Haley, this is the best form of research I can offer. Trust me," he said, caressing her arm.

Dave, meanwhile, blew his nose into an obviously used tissue. "I have food allergies," he said. "My mother usually likes me to eat at home. But I'll ask."

● ● ●

Well, the good news is Dave Metzger is a workaholic and Sebastian knows everything there is to know about Spain firsthand, so Haley's guaranteed an easy A on the report. The bad news is this motley crew may be too much for even the patient, levelheaded Haley to handle.

Was Coco right to warn Haley about associating with the freaks and geeks? Has Haley just assured her own social suicide by picking a group that includes, in no particular order, a pickup artist, a nosepicker and a girl whose desperation is so palpable, her every expression screams, "Pick me!"

If Haley goes to dinner at Sebastian's house, will she be subjected to more of his unwelcome advances? Or can she trust him to keep the heat on the stove? And if she opts out of the dinner, how will it affect her grade?

To have Sebastian prepare an authentic Spanish dinner for Haley and the rest of the group, turn to page 92. If you want Haley to skip the dinner, send her back home after school by turning to page 82.

A little wardrobe update might do Haley some good. Then again, a girl's got to eat.

Happy meals are few and far between when you live in a McMansion.

"So, are you in or out?" Coco demanded.

Annie Armstrong was now waving at Haley frantically from across the room, in her preppy headband and long pleated skirt that seemed like an outfit a grandmother would pick out. In fact, so hopelessly clueless was Annie that Haley almost felt sorry for her. Almost.

"I'm in," Haley said to Coco, turning her back on Annie for good. Even if Coco and her crew were stuck on themselves, studying with the popular girls seemed far more appealing than suffering through four months of Annie's suffocating attentions.

"Wonderful," said Coco, clasping her hands together and winking at Whitney. "As our official group leader, my first order of business is to nominate Haley for secretary." Haley sat up in her chair. *Uh-oh,* she thought.

"That means Haley will be taking notes in class and cc'ing us all over e-mail at the end of each day," Coco explained. Her voice was chipper and confident, but above all insistent. This was a person it would be difficult to say no to, Haley realized.

Coco fished around in her leather bag for her favorite black fountain pen and carefully wrote something out on a piece of monogrammed stationery. Her flawless script reminded Haley of the looping calligraphy used on formal invitations, and Haley suddenly wondered if maybe perfect wasn't just as annoying as needy, after all.

Haley read the note Coco handed her. "Add to your address list . . ." She looked at their screen names, hotcocodeclerq, sashastoletheworld and lilmisswitnee.

"Shouldn't we get Mariposa, I mean Haley's e-mail address?" Whitney asked. "I mean, in case there are any questions about the homework." She looked at Haley and explained, "I always have questions."

"Yeah, and they usually start with 'What's the answer to . . . ?' " Coco added.

Whitney looked hurt.

"You know I'm dyslexic. I can't help how my brain works."

"Now, that's assuming you have one, Whitney." Coco looked at Haley. "Well?" she said.

"Um." Haley hesitated.

"Don't tell me you don't have an e-mail address?" Coco scoffed.

"No, of course I do," Haley began, "it's just . . . I use my family's account."

Whitney snickered. "So does that mean your mom reads your e-mails? That's so beyond invasion of privacy."

"Cool it, Whitney," said Coco, sticking up for Haley. "Come on, you can tell us," she said, leaning ever so slightly forward in her desk. Haley noticed there was nothing Coco enjoyed more than drawing information out of people.

Whitney frowned. "Yeah, you can tell us," she said, echoing Coco's sincerity.

Haley looked down at her own shabby retro sneakers and ill-fitting khakis, lowering her voice as well as her gaze.

"I didn't pick it," she sighed, finally giving in. "But it's fancyfreckles." Whitney erupted in a spasm of giggles. Haley was mortified.

"That's so cute," Whitney said, clearly mocking

Haley by patting her on the arm. "Do you really think your freckles are fancy?"

"It's my dog's name," Haley said, trying to explain. "Freckles. He's a dalmatian."

Coco smiled sadistically. "Fancyfreckles? That really is hideous. I refuse to e-mail anyone called fancy anything."

"I—I don't even remember how my mom came up with it," Haley stammered. "It's just one of those stupid family things."

"Ugh, I know just what you mean," said Whitney. "My future stepmonster totally embarrasses me in public all the time. Like the other day, she told me my dad has jock itch in front of all these people at the club."

"Whitney," Coco snapped. "Too much information. Remember that little talk we had last week?" She turned to Haley. "Listen," she said, "why don't you just give us your cell phone number? So that we don't have to e-mail your dog."

"Fine, whatever," Haley said. Coco and Whitney took out their cell phones to program in Haley's number. Coco's was sleek and small and silver, while Whitney's was bubblegum pink and covered in rhinestones. Sasha, who was still busy listening to her MP3 player, didn't move.

"You know, I'm really losing patience with this whole punk glam phase, Sasha," Coco complained. When Sasha didn't respond, she rolled her eyes and turned back to Haley. "Ever since she discovered MC5 and the Velvet Underground, she's been impossible to live with."

"Five-ten," Haley began.

Whitney stopped, her face twisted in confusion. "Five-ten? What kind of area code is that?"

"The Bay Area," Haley explained. Coco raised an eyebrow.

"What bay?" Whitney demanded.

"San Francisco," said Coco.

Haley nodded. "I just moved here from California."

"You're Reese Highland's neighbor, aren't you?" Coco asked. "Your family bought that little bungalow next door to his. Isn't your mom building, like, a giant garbage heap in the backyard or something?"

"It's a compost heap," Haley said. "My mom likes to garden. She grows all our own vegetables."

"How . . . earthy," said Coco. "I didn't know people did that anymore."

Having seen the three girls chummily exchanging digits from across the room, Annie was now staring daggers at Haley.

"Uh-oh, girls, psycho alert," Coco said, motioning toward Annie. "You don't know her, do you?" she asked Haley.

"No," Haley said. "I mean I just met her this morning. She was assigned to show me around campus."

"Oh, sweetie. You don't need her," Coco said. Whitney frowned. "We'll show you everything you need to know. Won't we, Whit." Coco kicked her friend's desk, causing Whitney to yelp.

"Oww!" she cried. "What'd you do that for? You totally bruised my shin."

"Show some hospitality. You're being rude." As Coco unleashed one of her trademark smiles, Haley felt herself being drawn into the girl's hypnotic, if slightly terrifying, gaze. "Besides, you don't need Annie Armstrong getting one of her freaky little girl crushes on you," Coco added. "Scary."

"Yeah," Whitney added, shivering. "Psycho scary."

With that, Ms. Frick sashayed back to the front of the room. "Okay, class! *¡Silencio!*" The students continued to talk until Ms. Frick clapped her hands. "Now. Each group is going to be assigned a city in Spain. You will have to research everything about your city and at the end of the term we will have a fiesta in which you will share with the rest of the class what you've learned, cooking the local cuisine, dancing the native dances and wearing traditional garb from the city you have been assigned."

Coco rolled her eyes. "How do you say 'nightmare' in Spanish?" she whispered to Haley.

"Sebastian, since you are from Sevilla, that will be the city for your group." Annie smirked and gave a gloating glance toward Haley.

"Oh, like that's fair," Coco protested. "Their group won't even have to do any research."

"And Cocita, your group will have a most important city, *la capital*," the teacher said. "Madrid."

Appeased to have landed what seemed like the most coveted piece of real estate in all of Spain, Coco said *"Gracias"* and relaxed once again.

"Madrid," Whitney said, puzzled. "Is that where madras comes from?" Whitney debated the merits of plaid cotton and was still talking about piqué when the bell rang twenty minutes later. Kids began grabbing books and backpacks.

Haley, hoping to avoid an all-out interrogation by Annie, didn't even bother saying goodbye to Coco and the other girls. Instead, she left the class and ducked into the nearest restroom, hiding in a stall near the window. Sure enough, ninety seconds later she heard Annie's voice imploring, "Haley, are you in here? Haley?" Finally, after several passes through the room, Annie gave up and left.

As Haley emerged, checking in both directions to make sure Annie wasn't waiting to ambush her, her phone vibrated. She fished the black standard-issue cell phone out of her backpack and read the text message on her way to her next class. "So now do you know why we call Whitney the foxymoron? Study group at my house on Tuesday . . . 120 Kings Court, 6:00 pm. Don't be late. C."

● ● ●

"It's a palace," Haley said, gawking at the sprawling stucco facade of the De Clerq residence as her mother pulled up the driveway.

"Don't be intimidated, honey," Joan said. "They're people, just like us."

"Yeah, only with gobs of money. And servants."

"Well, they've certainly got a gardener. Look at those shrubs," Joan said, pointing to a pair of bushes shaped like lions. She parked the station wagon and started to get out.

"What are you doing!" Haley asked, mortified.

"Haley, I want to at least meet this girl's parents."

"Negative. No way," Haley said defiantly.

"Don't be so self-conscious," her mother said. "You need to loosen up." Haley frowned. There was nothing, absolutely nothing she hated more than having her mother tell her she was uptight. It was like being told you were uncool by a math geek.

"I'll be fine," Haley said, exasperated. "I've got my cell phone. I'll call you if I need to be picked up." With that, she jumped out of the car before her mother could even lean in for a kiss goodbye.

Joan rolled down the window and yelled after her, "Remember what I said! Just like us!" Haley cringed, waving goodbye so her mom would just leave already. When she was sure her mother had finally pulled out of the driveway, Haley walked up to the rosewood double doors and rang the bell. Chimes echoed inside, and a short Latina housekeeper opened the door.

"Good evening, *señorita,*" said the housekeeper. "You must be A-ley. Ms. Coco, she ask me to have you to wait in the kitchen." Haley followed the housekeeper through the foyer and down a long hall.

The kitchen was clearly a focal point of the De Clerq estate, even though it looked as if no one ever used it. The bleached oak cabinetry, marble floors, countertops and stainless steel appliances were spotless, without a single nick or sign of wear.

"I go and find Ms. Coco," said the housekeeper as Haley took a seat at the bar. Across the kitchen, the pantry door was ajar, and Haley noticed several rows of shelves that resembled the aisles of a gourmet grocery store. Everything was arranged in multiples, labels facing out. Obviously, there was more than one controlling, Type A person in this house.

An intercom crackled and came to life. "Haley. Haaaleeey," Coco teased. "What are you doing in my kitchen?"

"Um," Haley began, pressing a button that said Talk, "you invited me?"

"We're on the second floor. Take the staircase just past the living room. Third door on your right. And bring up some diet sodas, would you? They're in the fridge."

Carrying a cold six-pack, Haley entered what she thought was the living room. Enormous paneled bookshelves lined the walls around a huge stone fireplace. But what cowed Haley the most were the animals.

There was a black bear stuffed and standing in the corner. An eland was frozen in an alert position, looking up, near the window, while an emu was perched near the stairs. Haley could only imagine what her animal-loving mother would do if she saw this room. Haley felt as if she were being watched from every direction.

She quickly exited the room and walked up the marble staircase, following the general direction of blaring Top 40 to Coco's door. She knocked, but there was no answer. She knocked harder. Still no answer.

"Coco, it's me, Haley," she called out. Suddenly, the door swung open, and there stood Whitney in a pink velour sweat suit with perfectly ironed honey blond hair and massive diamond studs twinkling from her earlobes.

Coco was staring at her laptop intently as she sprawled on the L-shaped couch in front of a giant flat-screen TV that was flashing music videos and blaring surround sound. Obviously, she was far too busy to acknowledge Haley's arrival.

"Coco just figured out Spencer Eton's e-mail password," Whitney explained, and hurried back to the couch. Haley sat down near them on the edge of Coco's four-poster mahogany bed. It was topped with gauzy mosquito netting, a cloudlike down comforter and piles of white pillows. A ceiling fan with bamboo blades spun lazily above the bed.

Over in an alcove near the window, Sasha was curled up half asleep, her earphones securely in place, her nose in a book.

"Get this—Spencer made all the freshmen on the football team go swimming wearing bras, panties and football helmets at the country club."

"So that's why he wanted my underwear," Whitney said. "That's so mean."

"And creepy," muttered Sasha.

"Jackpot," Coco said victoriously.

"April Doyle? That's who he's been seeing?" Whitney exclaimed. "Ohmigosh, ew. She sent him pictures of herself."

"That slut," Coco said in disgust, closing her laptop. "I always knew she was handing out more than water bottles to the football team. It's common knowledge she's the cheerleader who always ends up in the boys' locker room. Ugh, I have to eat something now or I'm going to be sick." Coco pressed the intercom button.

"Consuela?"

"Yes, Ms. Coco?" the housekeeper answered.

"Is our Chinese food here yet?"

"Coming right up, Ms. Coco."

"I love me some Golden Dynasty," said Whitney.

"It's empty calories," Sasha complained. "Real Chinese people don't even eat that garbage."

"Doesn't your sister get served there with her fake ID?" Whitney asked Coco, purposely ignoring Sasha.

"All the seniors do. They get a corner table and drink mai tais on Saturday nights."

"Her boyfriend is so cute." Whitney sighed.

"You would like him," Coco noted. "He's prematurely gray."

"What are the boys like in California?" Whitney asked Haley. They all turned to look at her.

"I don't know. Laid-back?" Haley said. "They all surf or skate and don't really pay much attention to girls."

"Well, maybe they just weren't paying attention to you," Coco suggested.

Consuela entered the room carrying a silver tray full of Chinese food and put it down on a table in front of the couch. First, Coco and Whitney dished up full plates. Haley waited until they had served themselves before grabbing an egg roll and some rice and veggies.

"Baby corn is so cute," said Whitney, lining the ears up on her plate. "Someday I want to have a dinner party and just serve baby vegetables, with little corns and little carrots and baby spinach and those little broccoli rapes."

"How old are you?" Coco asked, clearly annoyed. "It's broccoli rabe. *R-a-b-e*. It sounds like Rob."

"Baby carrots are fine, but those little corns are so rubbery," Haley added.

"Wait, why are you here again?" Coco asked, dismissively eyeing Haley. Coco shoved her plate away after two bites. "Oh right, Spanish class. Well, at least we got the best city," she added, reaching for one of the diet sodas Haley had brought upstairs.

"Actually, Madrid has a lot of information to cover," said Haley.

"Oh, have you already started the project?" Whitney asked. "That was nice of you. See, Coco, I told you we picked the right partner."

"I just did some preliminary searches on the Web," Haley explained.

"Me too." Whitney giggled. "I did a search for hot Spanish men, and Sebastian Bodega popped up."

Coco reached for the fortune cookies and handed one out to each of the girls.

"Uh-oh," Whitney said with trepidation.

"What?" Haley asked.

"Well, everyone knows the best part of Golden Dynasty is the fortunes."

"Why?" Haley asked.

"Because they always come true." Whitney watched as Coco cracked open her cookie.

"Okay, me first," said Coco. " 'In a perfect world, you would not chase or be chased but find peace in the life that is right before your eyes.' Cryptic."

Whitney cracked her fortune open and read aloud, " 'Your rival is cunning and will not stop until she has all that you possess. You have been warned.' Oh no. The stepmonster strikes again."

Next, Haley read hers. " 'The doors to new worlds

are constantly opening for you, but just as quickly others are closing. All that you desire is within reach. You must have the wisdom to not turn it away.' "

"Uh-oh, Haley, what do you desire?" Coco asked. "Or should I say who? Sebastian? Spencer? Reese?" Haley blushed.

"Leave her alone, Coco," Sasha said. Coco, rising to the challenge, picked up a fortune cookie and tossed it to Sasha.

"Now read yours," she said.

"I don't believe in that stuff." Sasha stared at the cookie.

"Come on." Coco prodded her. "You know how it works. You're next."

"Come on, Sash," Whitney added. "It's fun."

"Fine." Sasha cracked open her cookie. " 'There is a deceiver who shares half your heart. In his hands, your future will be plundered.' Yeah, real fun, Whitney." Sasha put her headphones back on and slumped farther down in her chair.

"Well, well, well," Coco said as Haley opened up her Spanish book. "Looks like someone's in for a rough semester."

● ● ●

Well, that's certainly not the fortune anyone would expect for the lovely Sasha Lewis. Just last spring, Sasha was the golden girl of Hillsdale High's freshman class. Captain of the JV soccer team. Best friend of Coco

De Clerq. Whip smart, athletic and beautiful beyond belief.

Lately, though, Sasha has been acting sort of strange, cultivating that obsession with her MP3 player and barely even speaking to her supposedly best friends. Will Haley be able to break through and finally figure out what's going on with Sasha? Or will Sasha stonewall her, too?

And what about Coco? At the De Clerq estate, happiness is apparently a ten-car garage. But are material possessions really all that Coco wants? Or is she simply looking for someone to stand up to her? Is a challenge all she needs to soften her mean-spirited edge? Or will this leader of the spoiled brat pack never change?

For someone who could have her pick of boyfriends, Whitney seems to spend an awful lot of time with the girls. Was Annie right about her? Is she really just a slut in sheep's clothing? Or is Whitney a good girl at heart who's just a bit mixed up, thanks to her evil stepmonster-to-be?

Haley's fate is up to you. To draw her further into Coco's inner sanctum, turn to page 107. If you think Haley is out of her league, send her to page 82.

Remember, while you can't always judge the person, you can tell a lot by the company she keeps. So as long as Haley associates with the populettes, she'll be treated like one too.

**Even a bitter fortune
is softened by the
sweetness of the cookie.**

As Haley biked up the hill to the Golden Dynasty restaurant, she paused to admire the sunset over Hillsdale Heights, one of the nicest neighborhoods in Bergen County. It also happened to be the bread and butter of the Golden Dynasty's thriving delivery business.

Visible from most points in town, the Golden Dynasty's hunter green and gold pagoda was practically a local landmark. Haley locked up her bike as the sun disappeared behind the trees. Entering the Chens' restaurant through the heavy carved wooden doors, she walked down the long hall toward the main dining room.

Irene was standing behind a marble counter. When she saw Haley coming toward her, she frowned.

"What are you doing here?" Irene asked as she opened the fish food dispenser and started feeding the koi in the restaurant's indoor pond.

"My parents wanted Chinese takeout for dinner and I overheard someone at school say the Golden Dynasty is the best in town. My dad phoned in an order."

The koi fish stuck their lips out of the water to catch the food.

"How are you?" Haley asked.

"I'm at work on a school night." Irene glanced back at her. "How do you think I am?"

Haley shifted her weight from one foot to the other. "Listen. I wanted to apologize for what happened earlier. I shouldn't have looked at your drawing."

"Whatever. Your order should be ready in a few minutes," Irene said, wiping off a stack of laminated menus that were covered in dried soy and duck sauce.

Haley took a moment to admire the elaborate paintings of waterfalls and cranes and pink cherry blossoms on the walls. "Cool murals," she said.

"What are you talking about? They're awful," Irene said.

Haley looked around the restaurant and suddenly had a revelation. "You painted them, didn't you?"

"What if I did? It's just a bunch of stupid cherry blossoms."

"Oh, get over yourself."

"What?" Irene gasped.

"You heard me," Haley said. "Don't waste your talent being shy. That picture of Johnny Lane belongs in a gallery, not hidden in your sketchbook."

"Whatever," Irene said, unsuccessfully suppressing a smile. "You think so?"

"I know so." Haley smiled too.

Just then, Coco De Clerq, Sasha Lewis and Whitney Klein breezed into the restaurant. Haley tried not to but couldn't help gawking. Coco had on a green silk tank top and a tiny suede miniskirt paired with knee-high boots. Whitney was in a tight pink sweater and even tighter black leather pants and had tons of makeup caked on her heart-shaped face. Sasha, meanwhile, was in a loose, multicolored sweater dress layered over jeans.

"Our usual table," Coco snapped. Irene frowned at them but grabbed three menus. Haley stepped out of the way of the gorgeous trio.

"Aren't you in my Spanish class?" Coco demanded, looking at Haley.

"I—I think so. Yes," Haley stammered.

Coco looked her up and down. "Love the cardigan,

hate the shoes," she said, staring at Haley's mismatched low-top sneakers. "You should burn them. Now."

"Right this way," Irene said, leading Coco, Whitney and Sasha across the room to a reserved table next to the indoor fishpond.

A waitress wearing a turquoise cummerbund arrived at the hostess stand carrying two plastic bags full of takeout food.

"Miller?" she asked.

"Yeah, that's me," Haley said, suddenly wondering how she was going to get all that food home on her bike. She picked up the bags, waved goodbye to Irene and headed back out into the night, the image of Coco and her posse still etched in her brain.

● ● ●

So, Haley has fulfilled her good-person obligation by apologizing to Irene for prying. But now that they're on speaking terms again, will Haley continue to cultivate the friendship? Or is it time for her to move on and get to know other people? As there are other fish in the indoor Koi pond, there are other girls to befriend at Hillsdale High. Isn't that the best part about being new—exploring all your options before pinning yourself down to one group?

Now that Coco and her Coquettes seem to be taking an interest in Haley, will Haley develop a mutual interest in them?

To keep the talented Irene in the picture, turn to page 115. To widen Haley's circle and possibly edge her toward the popular crowd, turn to page 163.

Remember, you're in charge of telling Haley's fortune. And all you have to do is turn the page.

CHOOSE THE SHOES

Fashion may be forgettable, but first impressions last forever.

Haley was finally settling into life in New Jersey. Now and then when she went to sleep at night or woke up in the morning, she actually felt at home in her new room, although this was a development she wasn't ready to share with her parents just yet. They were still in their we-just-moved-our-family-to-another-coast-and-are-still-feeling-guilty mode, and Haley wanted to milk it for all it was worth.

Academically, going to a public high school and taking honors classes wasn't turning out to be that big an adjustment. The most surprising challenge so far, Haley was discovering, was the no-dress-code lifestyle. Who knew the simple task of picking out an outfit for school in the morning would turn out to be such an endless struggle? All those times she'd cursed the perennial white shirt and gray pleated skirt of her California school as suffocating her individuality, she could not have imagined ever arriving at a moment of appreciation for the uniforms.

Not only did Haley suddenly feel pressure to be in style, but wearing new, expensive clothing seemed to be the norm at Hillsdale. Some of the girls even prided themselves on never wearing the same outfit twice—all year long. Who could compete with that? For weeks, Haley had resigned herself to a public-school dress code of her own making: T-shirt. Jeans.

She had taken to getting dressed from the clean laundry pile, finding it too upsetting to even look at what was behind closet doors number one and two. Her outdated wardrobe still consisted of the childish dresses and matching sweater sets she'd owned since the sixth grade. There was even a felt vest that her grandmother had made for her. It had an owl on it. With googly eyes.

Those eyes alone were reason enough not to look in her closet.

Which was why Haley felt in desperate need of help this particular Thursday afternoon, frustrated after yet another day of wearing her boring "uniform" to school. At the very least, she wished for her parents' guilty generosity to sponsor, say, a spontaneous trip to the mall. Until that miracle arrived, Haley was forced to endure another day in the same old, same old.

As Haley was realizing, though, there was one significant loophole in the code of acceptable high school attire at Hillsdale. And that loophole was shoes. She had narrowed down the shoe possibilities in her closet to four acceptable pairs.

For the first option, there were her broken-in, mismatched low-top sneakers. One was moss green, the other black, a trade that had been masterminded by Gretchen, Haley's best friend in California. The sneakers were now starting to fade a bit, and Haley had drawn all over the sides and soles, one of which was peeling off. But she didn't mind. *All the artsy kids wear low-tops,* she noted to herself.

Next, there were the pale blue suede ballet flats Haley's mother had talked her into when they had arrived in New Jersey several weeks back. At first, Haley thought they were too girly for her taste. But once she put them on with jeans, even she had to admit they were comfortable, and flattering. *Didn't I see Annie Armstrong with the same pair on last week, in kelly green?* Haley wondered.

The third pair of shoes Haley had deemed within the realm of okay was a pair of black leather pumps she had worn to a piano recital the previous year.

They were a little on the fancy side, sure, but Haley could live with that. "High heels are the only way to go," she'd overheard Coco De Clerq say in the girls' bathroom.

Finally, there was the riskiest option, the one souvenir from the Miller family's recent cross-country road trip that Haley was actually happy to own—a pair of tan leather cowboy boots. *I could totally see Sasha Lewis in these,* she thought.

Even though she was basically wearing the same outfit day after day, the shoes could totally alter her look. In the ballet flats, with her hair pulled back in a ponytail, Haley looked like a fresh-faced good girl. In the cowboy boots, with her long auburn hair in loose waves, she was bohemian and sexy.

Not only did each pair of shoes affect the way Haley looked, but they also seemed to change the way she walked and talked. Haley didn't mean to strut, but it was hard not to in high heels. And somehow when she put on those old sneakers, her normally straight posture turned into a slouch.

The only problem was deciding which shoes to wear each day to school. So far, Haley was barely beyond eeny, meeny, miney, mo. . . .

● ● ●

Haley so needs your help.

It's probably safe to say that every girl at one point or another in her life has known the shoe dilemma. But

for Haley, this decision is not quite as simple as picking the most comfortable or flattering pair.

Haley is at a new school. Just as she's trying to size up all the unfamiliar faces and figure out where she fits best, they're assessing her and deciding whether or not to let her in—into their homes, into their parties, into their study groups and into their lives.

Right now, what might seem like the subtlest of changes in Haley's appearance will have a big impact on her life during the school year. Who she'll be friends with, what kind of grades she'll get, what sort of boys she'll date, will all be determined by choices you make now. So choose the shoes.

If you pick the ballet flats, turn to page 137. If you think Haley should wear her sneakers, go to page 115. Go to page 129 if you want Haley to wear cowboy boots. And if she's in pumps, send her to page 163.

Haley's steps from here on out will be determined by the shoes you put her in. So don't be surprised if this one little fashion choice completely, irrevocably alters her life.

SOCCER PRACTICE

Sometimes,
a girl just feels like
kicking something. Hard.

Travis Tygert, the handsome history teacher and soccer coach, was already on the field when Haley arrived for tryouts. Dressed in his snug white T-shirt and blue gym shorts, Coach Tygert was addressing the returning team members and new recruits.

Sasha Lewis, whom Haley knew to be one of Coco De Clerq's best friends, stood to Coach Tygert's right. On his left was a cluster of athletic-looking girls in ponytails and shin guards.

"Glad you could make it," he greeted Haley as she

joined the group. Haley smiled and looked around the circle of new faces.

Great, she thought. *Not only have they all played before, but they all seem to know each other.*

After they had finished their warm-up lap and stretches, Coach Tygert said, "I want to see your mile times. When I blow this whistle, sprint four laps around the field."

Haley hit her stride in the second lap. On the third, Sasha took the lead. As they sailed across the finish line, Sasha first with Haley a close second, the stopwatch read just over six and a half minutes.

"Not bad, not bad," Coach Tygert called out. "Let's partner up for some passing drills," he added, hardly giving them time to catch their breath.

"Hey, speed racer, you want to be partners?" Sasha asked Haley.

"Sure," Haley said. They kicked the ball back and forth casually. Sasha was clearly better at dribbling, so she kept the passes easy to let Haley get the hang of handling the ball.

"Sorry if Coco and Whitney were sort of rude to you the other day. They're very territorial," Sasha said, wiping the sweat from her brow.

"What do you mean?" Haley asked.

"Well, you're new. You're different. That threatens them."

"I don't see why," Haley said, shooting the ball

back to her. "I mean, look at me. It's not as if they have anything to worry about."

"You don't get it, do you?" Sasha asked. "There's an advantage to being the new girl."

"What's that?"

Sasha stopped the ball with her foot. "As far as anyone at Hillsdale is concerned, you're still perfect. You haven't done anything to change their minds yet." And with that, she kicked the ball past Haley and into the net.

After practice, Coach Tygert caught up with Haley and Sasha. He was wearing his aviator sunglasses and his warm-up jacket with his name embroidered in gold on the breast pocket. Haley suddenly wondered if her hair looked as matted and greasy as it felt.

"Sasha, I see you picked up a few tricks at camp this summer," Coach Tygert said. He was carrying a mesh bag full of soccer balls.

"You like the footwork, huh? I thought you might." Sasha took a big gulp from her water bottle.

"Watch out, Ridgewood," Mr. Tygert said, beaming. "Haley, I'm glad you came out. There aren't many open spaces on the team this year, but you keep up the level of play you showed out there today, and one of them is yours."

"Thanks, Coach," Haley said.

"See you girls tomorrow," Coach Tygert said, heading toward the parking lot and his black SUV. "Annabelle's cooking, and if I'm not home by six, she starts to worry."

"Who's Annabelle?" Haley asked Sasha once he was out of earshot.

"His wife," Sasha said. Haley took a deep breath and sighed. "I know, *married*, right?" Sasha added sympathetically.

As they made their way to the locker room, Haley noticed a hooded figure on a bicycle in the main quad. She didn't think anything of it until she and Sasha turned the corner.

Haley could hardly believe it. The back wall of the gym had been vandalized and was now covered with an elaborate mural, bearing all sorts of symbols and figures. The wind shifted and Haley caught a whiff of fresh paint.

"Wow," Sasha said. "Principal Crum is going to have a fit about this."

"Shouldn't we tell someone?" Haley asked.

"Nah," said Sasha. "They'll find out soon enough. Haven't you ever heard the phrase 'shoot the messenger'?" She suddenly put her hands on her stomach. "Besides, I'm ravenous. I totally forgot about the best part of soccer season."

"What's that?" said Haley.

"The postpractice pig-out." Sasha blew through the locker room doors as Haley trailed close behind.

What better way to celebrate a good, hard practice than with burgers, french fries and milk shakes? Now that Haley and Sasha are hitting it off, will they start spending time together off the field as well?

And what's up with that graffiti on the side of the school? Are the usual suspects from the Floods to blame? Or is the tag the work of some harmless merry prankster? And will Principal Crum uncover the boy—or girl—who's responsible?

To have Haley go hear what the principal of the school has to say about the graffiti, flip to page 119. If you think Haley and Sasha should leave the crime scene ASAP, send them to page 129 to refuel.

Soccer balls may be black and white, but not much else is at Hillsdale. Luckily for Haley, she has you to keep her head on straight and looking toward the goal.

Even smart people
look stupid when they have
too much to drink.

"**A**re you sure we can't help you with anything?" Haley asked Sebastian. She and Annie were sitting at the bar in the Shopes' kitchen, watching as he juggled a dozen different tapas dishes.

"I can set the table," Annie offered.

"Please. You are my guests," he replied, stirring the large pan of paella with a wooden spoon as the doorbell rang. "There is one task for you, however, Haley," he said. "To answer the door."

Haley got up to greet the final guest and found Dave Metzger standing on the stoop, his damp hair still wet from a bath and slicked over to one side. In his hands, he carried a book bag and what looked to be a bouquet of wildflowers, shrink-wrapped in plastic.

"Hey, Dave," Haley said.

"Good evening, Haley. Don't you look nice." Actually, Dave could barely look at Haley for more than a nanosecond before his gaze darted away. Over Dave's shoulder, Haley saw Mrs. Metzger's minivan still parked in front of the house.

"Is that your mom?" she asked.

"No. Where? Oh, sure. That's her." He waved as Mrs. Metzger rolled down her window and called out, "David, who's your friend? Is this the Haley I've been hearing so much about?"

"Yes, Mom," he said. Haley was startled that the woman already knew her name.

"Haley, I just spoke with your mother," Mrs. Metzger continued. "She's asked me to bring you and Annie home after supper."

"Um, okay," Haley said hesitantly, surprised that her mom would just turn her over to a complete stranger.

"I'll be back to pick you kids up in forty-five minutes. And remember, David, be careful with that lavender. You give it right to Mrs. Shope."

"Sure, Mom," Dave answered as Mrs. Metzger rolled up her window.

"Um, why was your mom talking to my mom?"

Haley asked as they watched Mrs. Metzger pull out of the drive.

"Oh, that. It's nothing. She just likes to check in with the other parents sometimes." Under his breath, he added, "Always."

Haley noticed that there seemed to be red welts rising on Dave's neck.

"Do I smell shrimp?" he asked nervously.

"Yep. Prawns in butter. Yum." Haley offered him a welcoming smile. "Can I take those for you?"

"Oh, right." He handed her the lavender wrapped in plastic. "I'm allergic."

Haley was about to ask him why he'd brought flowers if he was allergic, when Dave blurted out, "I went ahead and printed out some information on Seville for everyone." Reaching into his book bag, he pulled out a thick binder and handed it to Haley.

"Wow, impressive," Haley said, a bit taken aback at Dave's detailed and cross-referenced notes. "There's even an index."

"That way the footnotes won't get lost."

"I see," Haley said, slightly disappointed. "Between you and Sebastian, Annie and I won't have to do any of the work."

"David!" Sebastian said when they arrived in the kitchen. He temporarily left the paella and lunged toward Dave.

"Um, hi," Dave said, jumping out of Sebastian's way. If Dave got jittery just standing next to a girl, there was no way he could handle a European man kiss.

"But this is how we greet our friends in my country," said Sebastian, scooping Dave up in an embrace and lifting him several inches off the ground.

"Wow, okay," Dave said, dangling in the air. "Are we friends?"

"Of course!" said Sebastian, planting a kiss on each of Dave's cheeks. "My new American boyfriend."

"Watch the trousers," Dave said as Sebastian set him back down on the floor.

"I hope you brought hunger with you tonight," said Sebastian. "We have many foods and only four mouths."

"Where are the Shopes?" Dave asked.

"My host family has the parents' night at elementary school," said Sebastian, pulling a bottle of red wine out of the liquor cabinet. "So we are alone."

"All right," Annie said, eyeballing the bottle. "Now we're talking."

"Are we drinking?" Dave asked.

"This is a Spanish wine Mrs. Shope bought for us for the occasion," Sebastian said with pride. "It is not quite as good as the Bodega wines. But it is close."

"Your family has a vineyard?" Annie asked, clearly impressed.

"Yes, but only a small one. We don't make wine to sell. We make table wine to drink at home with our guests."

"Wow . . . That's . . . ," said Dave, laughing nervously. "You know it's a law here. You can't drink until you're twenty-one." He instinctively looked over his shoulder.

"In Spain, wine is to have with the meal, for pleasure, for taste. Not to get drunk," Sebastian said as he opened the bottle and smelled the bouquet. He poured a small amount into each of the four glasses. *"Salud!"* he said, lifting his glass. "To your health!"

Dave looked anxiously at his glass. "To your health, that's funny. Because I'm actually not feeling very well." He loosened his bow tie and sipped a glass of ice water.

"Bottoms up," Annie said, gulping down her wine.

Haley stared at her glass. *Well, we are supposed to learn about the culture,* she thought. Then she imagined what her parents would say if they found out she'd had wine with dinner.

● ● ●

To have Haley drink, continue reading below.

If you think she should sit this one out, turn to page 104.

● ● ●

"Um, is this tap water or bottled?" Dave asked Sebastian as Haley took a sip of her wine and set the glass back on the bar.

"Bottled," Sebastian said.

"Distilled, spring or mineral?" said Dave, growing increasingly concerned.

"I don't remember," Sebastian said.

"Is there a problem?" Haley asked.

"Only if it's mineral," Dave mumbled.

"Can I have some more?" Annie asked, helping herself to the bottle of wine.

"We eat in the kitchen tonight," Sebastian announced, setting out four celadon green plates.

"Sebastian," Haley said, "should this milk be just sitting out like this?" She picked up a jug of warm milk that had been left on the counter and sniffed it.

"Of course. In Seville, we always have on the table a jug of wine, a bowl of butter and milk."

"You mean you don't refrigerate anything?" asked Dave.

"Why should we refrigerate? It is fresh from cow that week."

"That week?" Dave exclaimed.

"Well, don't mind if I do," Annie said, once again refilling her glass.

"Now," Sebastian said, laying out the elaborate spread on the bar in the kitchen. "For you, my American friends, tapas!"

Among the piles of prawns, lamb and veal, there were chickpeas and spinach; grilled octopus with paprika; dried cod and potatoes; sole with pine nuts and red currants; fried cheese; the paella, which had been topped with mussels, squid, a white fish, scallops and flat-leaf parsley; and an eggplant dish, accompanied by diced cucumbers and a light, creamy yogurt sauce.

"What's wrong?" Haley asked Dave.

"I'm allergic to seafood," said Dave. "And pine nuts. And dairy."

"Try some potatoes," Sebastian offered. "And perhaps, a little wine. It will help with the digestion."

"But I'm allergic to tannins," said Dave.

"David, it is as if life is denying you all of its pleasures. Do not tell me you are allergic to women, too?" Sebastian asked, giving Dave's arm a good slap.

Haley tasted a little of everything on her plate. It was . . . different. "The paella's great," she said. Truthfully, the seafood-and-rice dish had so much saffron in it, she couldn't tell the fish from the scallops.

"This wine is strong," Annie suddenly blurted out. Haley glanced over at her friend and realized that Annie's lips and tongue were now stained the color of an overripe plum.

"How much have you had to drink?" Haley asked, watching Annie sway in her seat.

"Why? I'm not drunk," Annie slurred, and then hiccuped.

At that precise moment, a car horn honked in front of the house. Dave darted to the window. "It's my mom," he said. "She's early." He added quietly, "She must have done that thing where she just circles the block."

"Great," said Haley, explaining to Sebastian, "she's giving Annie and me a ride home."

"Leave this to me," said Sebastian, wrapping Annie's arm around his neck and helping her to her feet. He walked her slowly to the minivan as Dave ran ahead to distract his mom.

"Haley," said Sebastian, "we did not have as much of a chance to talk tonight as I had hoped. I hope you will come to my swim meet this weekend?"

"We'll see," Haley said. "Thanks for dinner, Sebastian." She jumped into the front seat as Sebastian loaded Annie into the backseat with Dave.

"Hi, Mrs. Metzger," Haley said, buckling her seat belt. "Thanks for offering us a ride." Mrs. Metzger looked at her suspiciously, so Haley added, "I thought I'd sit up here with you to show you how to get to my house."

"What about Annie?" Mrs. Metzger asked.

"She's staying with me tonight," Haley said.

"On a school night?"

"Yeah. Our moms work together. They have some big case they're prepping, so my dad's taking Annie and me to school in the morning."

"Your mother didn't mention any of this to me on the phone earlier."

Haley shrugged. "Last-minute change of plans. She called me on my cell phone during dinner."

Annie groaned from the backseat.

"What's going on back there?" Mrs. Metzger asked.

"Oh, it's probably just something she ate," said Haley. "That Spanish stuff Sebastian cooked was really spicy." Haley held her stomach. A look of terror spread across Mrs. Metzger's face.

"David, did you eat anything?" she asked, looking over her shoulder into the backseat.

"Don't worry, Mom." Dave laughed. "Just those crackers you packed for me. And some water."

"Bottled or tap?" Mrs. Metzger demanded.

"Bottled," said Dave.

"Was it mineral?" she asked.

"No. God, no," he reassured her. She turned back around and started the car, pulling out of the driveway and onto the street. "At least I don't think it was," Dave added under his breath.

During the long drive to Haley's house, Dave did his best to keep Annie sitting up straight.

"Everything okay back there?" Mrs. Metzger asked from time to time.

"Ah, young love," Haley said, motioning to the backseat. Mrs. Metzger frowned.

"What did you girls have to drink with dinner?" she suddenly asked Haley.

"Well," Haley began, wondering which would be worse, lying to a parent or ratting out her friend. "Sebastian served us an authentic Spanish fruit drink." Changing the subject, she added, "Do you know they leave their milk and butter just sitting out on the table at room temperature in Spain? Isn't that crazy?"

Mrs. Metzger was horrified. "David," she gasped, "promise me you will never go to Spain."

"Um, okay."

Haley rolled down her window and let the crisp autumn air deliver a sobering chill to the backseat. By the time they pulled onto her street, Annie seemed to be feeling a little better.

"Make a left at the next drive," Haley said to Mrs. Metzger. "And here we are—home, sweet home." They pulled up to the Millers' house, and for the first time since her family had moved to New Jersey, Haley felt happy to be home.

"Thanks again," she said to Mrs. Metzger, buying Dave a few extra minutes to help Annie out of the backseat.

"Bye," Dave said softly to Annie. "Hope you feel better."

"Thanks," a still wobbly Annie whispered in his ear, planting a kiss on his left cheek. Dave turned crimson and smiled, holding his face with his hand as if to seal in the kiss, as Haley and Annie made their way up the sidewalk. The girls stood on the doorstep waving goodbye until the Metzger minivan had pulled away.

"We'll have your mom pick you up in a few hours. You should be fine by then."

"Whatever you say," Annie said, preparing a big fake smile for Haley's mom as her new best friend opened the front door.

"Girls, you're home early. What a nice surprise!"

"Change in plans," Haley said casually, already leading the charge to the TV room. "We're going to watch a movie, okay?"

"Hi, Mrs. Miller," Annie said politely, doing her best to act normal.

"Nice to see you, Annie," she called out as Haley and Annie disappeared into the den.

● ● ●

Well, that was certainly a close call with Dave's mom and Haley's. In fact, Haley surprised even herself by how well she handled the situation.

Annie, as usual, was too eager for her own good. Fortunately, Haley was there to bail her out. But what about next time? Is Annie really the kind of friend Haley wants to have around?

It's clear Sebastian is attractive. It's also clear he's attracted to Haley. But are his suave European ways too fast for her? Or will Haley's sweet California charm slow him down to just the right pace?

To have Haley hang out with Annie and see more of Sebastian's bodacious bod, turn to page 137. To put a little distance between Haley and her oddball study group, send her to page 119.

It's another day, another drama at Hillsdale High. But if you think Annie's little experiment with binge drinking was high stakes, just wait.

DON'T DRINK AT DINNER

There's something to be said for holding on to your inhibitions.

The minute Haley decided not to taste her wine, she noticed how much Annie was gulping down.

"Don't you think you'd better slow down?" Haley said as Annie polished off her first glass.

"Who are you, my mother?" Annie asked, reaching for the bottle. "I just want to see what it's like."

Haley finally had to recork the bottle and give it to Sebastian to put away in the Shopes' liquor cabinet.

"I think you'd better hide this," Haley said. "Unless you want a drunk classmate passing out on your kitchen floor."

"You crazy American girls," Sebastian said, shaking his head. "Sometimes I think I never leave this country. Sometimes, I think I never come back."

When Mrs. Metzger honked the horn to pick them all up, Sebastian walked Haley to the door. "You must come to my swim meet this weekend," he said, placing his hand on the small of her back. Haley felt a tingle race up her spine.

"We'll see," she responded. "Thanks for dinner."

"Some night that was. You're no fun," Annie said to Haley on their way out the door. But Haley didn't care. The only thing she cared about was making sure there were no drunk girls riding home in Mrs. Metzger's minivan. Haley had the impression that that wouldn't go over very well with Dave's mom. And, of course, she was right.

Annie boldly climbed into the front seat to sit next to Mrs. Metzger, who immediately smelled the alcohol on her breath. When Mrs. Metzger pulled up to the Armstrongs' house, she marched inside and told Annie's mom that her daughter had been drinking. Annie was grounded for the rest of the month.

● ● ●

The word *moderation* **is just not in Annie Armstrong's vocabulary. As usual, she had to take it to an extreme, and look what happened. Busted. It really seemed to annoy Haley the way Annie got sloppy at study group for no apparent reason. What was the point?**

And to think that when they first met, Haley thought Annie was a goody-goody. Maybe Annie isn't the girl Haley thought she was. So what's Haley going to do about it? Forgive her or forget her?

And what about Sebastian? He just invited Haley to his swim meet. To have Haley forgive Annie and go check out Sebastian in his Speedo, turn to page 137. To have Haley put a little distance between herself and her oddball study group, send her to page 119 to find out the latest in school affairs.

It's another week of experimentation at Hillsdale High. Just remember, if you mix the wrong cocktail of personalities, a party will either fizzle or explode.

When you make a change, your life can get better, or it can get much, much worse.

"Okay, that's officially disgusting," Coco said, turning away from the plasma television screen on the wall in her bedroom as an aging rock star gyrated with a maroon guitar between his legs. "It's one thing for these old geezers to rock the classics, but dry-humping an electric guitar? That's a young man's game."

Over on the sofa, Sasha stared reverently at the TV, her normally hard-to-read face registering only one thing: complete hero worship.

"I don't know," Whitney said, tilting her head

sideways and watching the spandex-clad dinosaur lick the neck of his guitar. "I think he's sort of cute."

"Come on, Whitney," said Coco. "If you're attracted to fifty-year-olds now, who are you going to date when you're thirty?"

Whitney frowned. She held up three fingers as if to count, then paused. "Won't I be married by then?"

"Yeah, and widowed," Coco surmised. She glanced out the window. "Ohmigosh, you guys, the gardener is totally swimming in our pool again." She opened the window to get a better look, and Whitney jumped up to join her.

"Wow. Good abs," Whitney said, ogling Jorge, the De Clerqs' elderly yard man.

"I suppose you like that forest of gray hair on his chest?" Coco asked. "Out of the pool, Jorge!" she yelled through the window, then slammed it shut.

"What about you, Haley?" Coco said, sitting down next to her on the bed and wrapping a finger around a lock of Haley's hair. "You're awfully quiet."

"Am I?" Haley asked nervously.

"I have an idea!" Coco exclaimed.

"Does it have anything to do with your gardener?" Whitney asked. "If so, I'm in."

"I think we should give Haley a makeover," said Coco.

A look of grave uncertainty crossed Haley's face. "I don't know. . . ."

"Awesome!" Whitney squealed. "That's even better!"

"Trust me, Haley," Sasha warned. "It's a horrible idea. Coco's victims tend to come out looking like sluts or poodles. And sometimes both."

"Relax, it'll be fun," Coco said, dragging Haley by the arm and adding, "Sasha, you know, we can't all look perfect in everything we put on. And some of us need more help than others."

"I get to do her makeup!" Whitney shoved a chair behind Haley and grabbed Coco's toolbox-sized makeup case filled with professional brushes and a rainbow of eye shadows, eyeliners, lipliners, blushes and foundations. It was like a department store makeup counter, only portable, Haley noted.

Flicking on the mirrored vanity lights at Coco's dressing table, Whitney began brushing Haley's long red hair. "Hey, great highlights," she said. "They're so natural. Where do you get them done?"

"I don't. It's from the sun."

Coco laughed. "I use that line all the time." She threw open the double doors of her enormous walk-in closet, and Haley's jaw dropped. It was bigger than Haley's bedroom and was near to bursting with clothes, most of them still bearing tags from the stores. After rummaging through the racks, Coco tossed a slinky green silk tank top and a suede miniskirt at Haley. "Here. Try these on. They should fit. What shoe size are you?"

"Um, an eight," said Haley.

"Your feet are almost as big as Coco's," Whitney said as Coco shot her an evil look.

"Here," Coco said, handing Haley a pair of knee-high brown boots. "These should fit." Haley looked down at the supple calfskin and realized that the boots probably cost more than her entire wardrobe.

"Thanks," Haley said casually as Whitney came at her eye with a charcoal pencil.

"Ohmigosh! You look seriously hot!" Whitney shrieked as Haley emerged from the bathroom wearing the skimpy tank top, short skirt and boots. At first, Haley felt self-conscious, but when she caught a glimpse of herself in the full-length mirror, she was stunned and spun around several times to get a better look.

"Goodbye, Haley. Hello, Hot Mama!" Whitney said, grabbing the miniature silver digital camera off Coco's nightstand. Coco looked annoyed as Whitney snapped about a dozen photos of Haley in various poses.

"Do you diet?" Coco suddenly asked.

"No, I just eat healthy," Haley said, shrugging. "Everything's organic in our house."

"How many times a week do you work out? Do you eat bread?" Coco asked. She was circling Haley like a hawk.

"Of course. I love bread. And I don't work out unless I'm playing a sport."

Sasha looked up and asked, "Do you play soccer, by chance? Tryouts are this week, and we need a forward."

"Ugh, I hate people like you," Whitney said to Haley playfully. "If I eat one chocolate chip cookie it goes straight to my hips."

"Shut up, Whitney. It goes straight to your boobs and you know it," said Coco.

"I wish I had curves like that," Haley said, looking at Whitney's C cups.

"Oh, like you're flat as a board. You're almost as big as she is." Coco's voice was shrill and surprisingly high-pitched.

Haley blushed and crossed her arms over her chest. Eyeing Coco's thin frame, she smiled weakly. "You're lucky, Coco. You have the perfect body type for fashionable clothes."

Coco stuck her chin up and preened for a moment. "Ugh, but I have to lose five pounds this semester. Haley, promise me you won't let me eat any more Golden Dynasty for at least three weeks?"

They all looked at the willowy Sasha, who was still curled up on the sofa, picking at the Chinese food leftovers. "What?" she asked, her mouth full of lo mein. To try to talk to Sasha about body types was pointless. She was in another league.

"Well, I think you look great," Whitney said to Haley.

"I liked you better before," Sasha said.

"Whatever, Sash. You're such a downer," Coco complained, but Haley couldn't help feeling that maybe Sasha was right. The makeup, especially, was a little overdone. Suddenly, all she wanted was to go home and take a hot bath.

"In that outfit, you could have any guy you wanted," said Whitney.

"That's a good point," Coco added. "Haley, you must have a crush on *someone* after your first week of school. What do you think of the boys at Hillsdale?" she asked pointedly.

"I haven't really had time to, you know, scope things out."

"Just tell us who you think is cute," Coco pressed. "And we'll see what we can do."

"Yeah, are you a bodacious Bodega fan or are you sweet on Spencer Eton?" Whitney teased.

"I'm not. I mean neither. I don't even know them."

"Come on, you must have seen somebody you've liked by now, Haley. Who is he? Or is it a she?" Coco smiled sadistically.

"I . . . I mean . . ."

"Tell us."

"Well, I guess my neighbor's sort of cute." Haley instantly regretted saying it.

Coco's eyes narrowed. "You mean Reese Highland."

"Well, good luck there," Whitney scoffed. "Coco's been trying to land him all year." As soon as the words had tumbled out, Whitney clapped a hand over her mouth.

"Whitney, that's preposterous," Coco said.

"You're the one who said you wanted a boyfriend this year," Whitney said. "You know, double the parties, double the cool friends, double the trouble, double the fun."

"That doesn't mean I like Reese. Reese and I are just friends. If Haley likes him, by all means, she should go after him. In fact, I'll even help you get to know him better if you like."

"Really?" Haley asked. "You'd do that for me?"

"Sure," said Coco. "What are friends for?"

While Haley wanted to believe her, she couldn't help noticing that Coco's voice didn't seem all that sincere.

● ● ●

Well, that didn't take long. A few hours with Coco, and Haley's already become another Cocobot.

But is her sexy makeover an improvement or a disaster? Should Haley go back to being her plain old lovable self? Or should she claim her hottie status in the Hillsdale sophomore class?

If Haley does morph into another Coquette, will

Hillsdale's newest sweetheart sour overnight? Or will she thrive on the attention that comes with her new look?

And what about Reese? What will he think of the new Haley? Will he be seduced by the makeup and new clothes? Or will the racy changes turn him off?

What comes next is your call. If you want Haley to keep the makeover, go to page 163. If you'd rather have the wholesome Haley back, send her to take that hot bath on page 147.

Remember, appearances are only deceiving when they don't match what's inside. Haley's in your hands now, and she's trusting you to make the right choice.

IRENE'S ACTING FUNNY

New friendships take
a little while to work out
the quirks.

On the day of a mandatory schoolwide assembly, as the art teacher Mr. Von was checking off names, Haley looked over at Irene's empty desk and quickly came up with a story to tell Mr. Von to keep her new friend from getting in trouble.

When he called Irene's name, Haley explained that Irene wasn't feeling well and offered to go find her in the girls' bathroom and then meet up with the other students in the gym. Irene, of course, wasn't in the bathroom when Haley went to look for her. In fact, she wasn't anywhere on school property, as far as Haley could tell. After searching the halls near Irene's locker and circling the parking lot, Haley was about to give up. She had even braved the stairwell by the teachers' lounge, where some of the kids from the Floods went to get high. Irene wasn't there, either.

Haley was just about to head to the assembly alone when a figure in a hooded sweatshirt slipped through a back door into the yard behind the school. Haley knew instantly it was Irene. She followed her outside and around the corner of the building and found her standing there with Shaun. Neither one of them said anything.

"What are you two doing out here? Mr. Von is pissed," Haley said, looking around to make sure there weren't any teachers outside to catch them cutting assembly.

"Pissed isn't in Acid Rick's emotional vocabulary," Irene said, staring at the back wall of the gym. "Annoyed, maybe. But not pissed. Anyway, shouldn't we ask you the same question? Are you checking up on me again?"

"I covered for you," Haley said.

"Did I ask you to?" Irene asked. She pointed to the bottom right-hand corner of the wall and said to Shaun, "There, that's the signature."

Shaun looked at her and smiled. "That's the hand cock, all right," he said, flipping his wrist as if he were shooting a basket. "Lady knows her business."

"It's a craft not many people can appreciate," said Irene.

Haley finally turned her attention to the wall. She was astounded by what she saw. Patterns spilled into vivid shapes. Gothic figures rose up and towered above them. This wasn't your everyday graffiti. This was high art. And there, in the center of the chaos, lit with vibrant color, was a pair of almond-shaped eyes with the words *The Hedon* lurking beneath them.

"Wow" was all Haley managed.

"Wo-ho-how," Shaun mimicked.

"So you're impressed?" Irene asked.

"Well, one thing's for sure," Haley said. "Now we know why Principal Crum called the assembly. Who do you think did it?"

A funny look passed between Irene and Shaun before Irene said, "I thought you of all people would at least have a guess, Haley."

Haley couldn't understand why Irene was acting so strange. She was about to go back inside when Shaun put on his shades and belted out in a swooping falsetto, "Hale bop, she bop a wee bop. Hi bop, hey bop a way bop." He bobbed his neck like a chicken as he sang, while simultaneously grabbing Haley in a headlock.

"Shaun, have you been bingeing on eighties music again?" Irene demanded.

"Girls, they wanna, wanna have fun, girls," Shaun sang in a deep baritone, continuing his Cyndi Lauper medley. "Wanna have . . . They just wanna, they just wanna." He slipped back into his falsetto, pulling both girls into a three-way group hug. "Ahhh, now kiss and make up," he said, pushing the two of them together. "Oh, yeah. That's hot."

Still wary of Irene, and not even sure why she was saying it, Haley mouthed, "Sorry." Irene just shrugged and said, "Whatever, dude." And then the three of them headed inside to catch the tail end of the assembly.

● ● ●

Shaun and Irene are certainly acting rebellious. But is it with or without a cause?

Haley can't help wondering what's up with all their sneaking around. Will she be able to get to the bottom of it? Do Shaun and Irene have something to do with the vandalism? Or are they, like most artists, simply misunderstood?

If you think Haley should be suspicious of Irene's behavior, turn to page 178. If you think she should trust her friend, send her to page 171.

Artists make molds and break molds, but they don't try to fit into them. In order to keep hanging out with this crowd, Haley's going to have to forget about rules for a bit.

PRINCIPAL CRUM'S LITANY

Nothing about the word
"lecture" is appealing.

The entire student body was assembled in the gym so that Principal Roland Crum could talk about the recent rash of vandalism at Hillsdale High.

Instead of sitting with their scheduled classes as they were asked to do, kids naturally began gravitating toward their cliques. The pretty cheerleaders sat together. So did the awkward math geeks. Up at the top in the nosebleed sections were the social misfits, the goths, the punks, the wastoids, the warlords. Down in front, the popular crowd clustered together, regardless of grade. And sitting smack in the center of it all was Haley Miller, watching Coco De Clerq and her friends play Spot the Padded Bra.

"Vicky's got a secret," Whitney said about a girl named Victoria walking by in a tight blue sweater with high and oddly shaped boobs.

"Yeah, that she's sporting A cups under that C-cup bra," Coco said, just loudly enough for the girl to hear. Victoria crossed her arms over her pointy boobs and hurried to her seat. "Wait until some guy gets his hands on that fake-out," Coco added while weaving braids into Whitney's heavily highlighted hair.

"Coco, did you notice that as soon as you started braiding my hair, everyone else in our row started braiding too?" Whitney said.

"Honey, haven't you learned? They're like sheep. They do whatever I do." Sasha rolled her eyes.

"What's taking so long?" Whitney complained, staring at the empty podium.

"Honestly, Whitney. Would you rather be in class?" Sasha asked.

"Hold still," Coco barked, but Whitney kept squirming.

"Maybe she forgot to take her A.D.D. medication," Sasha said.

"My mother doesn't think it's good for me to take that stuff anymore."

"But didn't your dad tell you you had to take it if you wanted to live with him?" Coco asked.

Whitney frowned. "When your parents get divorced, how do you know who to listen to?"

"That's easy," said Coco. "You listen to the one who gives you the biggest allowance."

"Hey, did you guys see the graffiti yet?" Sasha asked. "I wonder who Crum is going to pin it on."

"I'm sure it'll turn out to be some jerk from the Floods. He'll get expelled and start pumping gas a year early," Coco said snidely. "Big deal."

"That's harsh, Coco. Even for you," Sasha said.

Sasha turned her attention to Reese Highland, Spencer Eton and Johnny Lane, who were sitting in the row behind them. Haley noticed the way Johnny was staring at Sasha and wondered if they were dating. *If they aren't, they will be soon,* she thought.

"What's your deal, Sash?" Whitney asked, examining her fingers for hangnails. "You've been, like, totally checking out the danger zone lately."

"What?" Sasha asked defensively.

"She's right," Coco added. "You have seemed curious about the dark side. I don't suppose that graffiti wall out back was painted for you?"

"As if." Sasha took out her MP3 player and put in her headphones as Whitney and Coco began whispering to each other.

Poor Dave Metzger, who was seated directly to Haley's right, seemed to be in the midst of another one of his allergy attacks. Dave was prone to attacks of all kinds, particularly in crowds. Also when he was alone. In small spaces. And enormous rooms with vaulted ceilings. During the winter, when heavy clothes made him itch. Also during the high pollen months in the spring, summer and fall.

In fact, there didn't seem to be a time of year or a situation that didn't induce some sort of attack in Dave. As his mother often remarked, sometimes in handwritten notes that were pinned to Dave's button-down shirts, he had a very fragile constitution.

Haley watched as Dave's eyes darted around the gym anxiously. His forehead was now covered with beads of sweat, and he was furiously scratching a red patch of hives on his forearm that looked worse than the poison ivy Haley had suffered during her family's cross-country road trip.

"Don't scratch. It'll only make it worse," Haley offered sympathetically. She fished through her book bag and found the tube of antihistamine cream her mother had given her on the first day of school, when her poison ivy had still been bothering her. "Here," she said, handing him the tube.

"What is it?" he asked with some trepidation.

"Antihistamine cream. It should stop the itching," Haley explained.

"Oh, I can't use that," Dave said, shrinking away from the tube.

"Why not?" Annie asked. Annie Armstrong was

seated behind Dave. She never missed an opportunity to butt in.

"I'm allergic," he said.

"You're allergic. To antihistamine?" Annie was incredulous. Dave nodded.

"But antihistamine is what people take when they have allergic reactions," Haley said. "How can you be allergic to an allergy cream?"

"I'm allergic to everything," said Dave.

"You can't be allergic to everything," Haley said reassuringly, patting his arm.

"Yes I can. I'm allergic to nuts, flour, milk, cheese, soy products, pollen, dust, antibiotics, alcoholic beverages, wool, silk, acrylic fibers and nylon. I'm allergic to shellfish, fish that eat shellfish, fish that eat other fish, and all forms of fowl. That means chicken, duck, turkey, eggs, goose, and definitely foie gras." Haley shivered. "I'm allergic to beans—lima, black, pinto and kidney. I'm allergic to tomatoes and any root vegetable in the nightshade family. I'm allergic to spelt, pasta and bread. . . ."

"Okay, okay, I get it, Dave. You are allergic to everything. So why aren't you in some sort of plastic bubble or something?" Haley asked.

Dave looked her in the eye. "I'm allergic to plastic."

Annie said, "Wow, you must know your doctor really well."

"He's my godfather," said Dave.

"Well, my mother said"—Annie looked at Haley— "that your mother said that you'd be into coming to the mall with me this weekend to look for Halloween costumes?"

"Let me get back to you on that," Haley said. "Hey, look. You stopped scratching." Sure enough, Dave was sitting perfectly still and the swelling was beginning to go down on the red lumps on his arm. He smiled just as Principal Crum stepped up to the podium and blew into the microphone. A blast of feedback rippled through the large black speakers that were mounted on the walls with thick metal chains.

"This morning, students, I sent out a memo to all parents and teachers, notifying them that we are now on turquoise alert."

"Whoopee," someone said sarcastically. Haley turned around and locked eyes with Irene Chen, who was sitting in the row behind Annie. "The last time Hillsdale was on turquoise alert," Irene said, "there was a milk shortage in the cafeteria." Shaun, the tubby boy sitting next to her, laughed. Haley couldn't help noticing they both had paint under their fingernails.

"Now, some of you may have seen the despicable vandalism that has defaced the south side of the Hawks' gymnasium. If not, I encourage you to do so at some point today, as it will be gone by tomorrow morning." Harriet Winslow, the school secretary, approached the podium and whispered something in Principal Crum's ear. "Apparently the pressure washers are not available until this weekend. I'm told there's even a chance we might have to repaint the gym. Which means Secretary Winslow here is probably not going to get her holiday bonus this year. How does that make you feel, students? Because it doesn't make me feel good. And it darn sure doesn't make Secretary Winslow feel good." Ms. Winslow shook her head in an emphatic no.

"Now, as I was saying, students," Principal Crum continued, "graffiti is not something we take lightly here at Hillsdale High. Effective immediately, the number of hall monitors will triple. We have also hired an extra night watchman to patrol the grounds during evening and early-morning hours and also on weekends. His name is Mr. Gunter, and he comes to us from the mall parking lot in Paramus. Mr. Gunter, please stand up." A short elderly man in an olive green uniform was slumped over in his chair next to the podium. Ms. Winslow nudged Mr. Gunter awake and he scrambled to his feet, eliciting scattered applause from the student body.

"Aw, he's sort of cute," Haley heard Whitney whisper.

"Of course, students," said Principal Crum, "part of Mr. Gunter's salary will have to come out of the budget for this year's homecoming dance. So now we will be having a DJ instead of the band Rubber

Dynamite." A group of football players began chanting, "Band, band, band," before Principal Crum raised an eyebrow, and the students settled back down.

"No way, I love Rubber Dynamite," Coco whined.

"Look, kids." Principal Crum pushed up his sleeves and casually leaned on the podium, accidentally brushing his tie against the microphone and sending out another blast of feedback. As deafening as the noise was, Haley thought Principal Crum's wild geometric tie was louder. The pattern was something only a Russian figure skater could love.

"I don't like being the heavy here," he said. "You know I want Rubber Dynamite just as much as the next guy. But maybe this is just the price we have to pay to find the person or persons who defaced our school property and threatened our Hawk spirit. So how 'bout it, kids? Who's going to help me track them down?"

"It was me! I did it!" someone yelled in an exaggerated high-pitched voice. This was followed by a series of maniacal giggles. Haley could tell from the sound of the voice as well as the general direction of the laughter that it was coming from Spencer Eton. When he popped up red-faced and a helium balloon suddenly sputtered through the air, deflating, her suspicions were confirmed. Somehow, though, Principal Crum remained clueless.

"Who said that?" Principal Crum demanded, scanning the bleachers with squinty eyes. He stopped and nodded at Johnny Lane, who appeared to be snoozing in his gorgeous nonchalant way.

"Mr. Lane, do you find me boring?" Principal Crum asked.

"Yes," Johnny said, without even opening his eyes. "Extremely."

The student body cracked up with laughter.

"I'll see you in my office after convocation," Principal Crum said, flustered. "This is not a joke, people. Until one of you comes forward with some information about the vandalism every one of you is a suspect. Now get back to class. I want you all out of my sight." Principal Crum left the podium.

"I'm going to the ladies'," Whitney announced as the assembly began to disperse.

Sasha looked at Coco.

"I know, I know," Coco said. "Someone has to escort Preppy la Puke."

As Haley waited for everyone to climb down from the bleachers, she noticed a purse left under the bench where Coco and Whitney had been sitting. *It must belong to one of them,* she thought, wondering if she should track them down in the restroom or head to her next class.

● ● ●

Why in the world would a "surfboard chest" like Coco De Clerq invent a game called Spot the Padded Bra? Coco knows a padded push-up can be a lifesaver during formal occasions or picture week.

Then again, people tend to hate in others what they most despise in themselves.

So will Coco ever evolve and reach a higher state of consciousness? Is she even capable of genuine compassion for another human being? Or can the students of Hillsdale High expect to be tormented by her at every turn during the next two years?

'Tis the season to celebrate All Hallows' Eve and All Saints' Day, so why not do it with a self-canonized saint? Annie may seem a little too Goody Two-shoes to be true, but underneath all that kiss-up charm, is there a bad girl waiting to come out?

There are a lot of options open at the moment. What will it be for Haley?

If you think Haley should keep poking around and learn more about Irene before jumping to any conclusions about the vandalism, go to page 178. To head to the bathroom to find Coco and Whitney and deliver the purse, flip to page 194. Otherwise, accept Annie's offer and hit the mall (page 189) to search for a Halloween costume.

HAP'S DINER

When did food
become the enemy?

"I'm starving," Sasha Lewis said as she and Haley breezed through the door at Hap's. They had just finished a grueling two-hour practice with their soccer coach and history teacher, Travis Tygert. After showering, they had come out to Hap's Diner to refuel.

At first, Haley had been skeptical about joining the soccer team, but now that she and Sasha were becoming friends, she was thrilled to be playing. Especially since they were spending time together off the field now too. Dressed in tan cowboy boots, a white sweater and faded jeans, with her hair still damp,

Haley followed Sasha past the red vinyl booths and up to the counter.

"It's your first time here," Sasha explained, "so you have to follow an old Hap's tradition." Haley was about to ask "What tradition is that?" when Sasha suddenly grabbed the microphone next to the register and announced, "We have a challenge!"

Haley began to turn red as some of the diner patrons and a few waitresses gathered around her, whistling and clapping. Suddenly, a big-bellied cook dressed in grease-splattered whites emerged from the kitchen. Sasha nudged Haley forward. "Go on," she said.

Hap, the cook, whose plastic name tag was pinned to his stained V-neck T-shirt, began circling Haley. He rubbed his stubbly beard while looking her over and finally said, "Three hot dogs, a Hap burger, two shakes and an order of curly fries." And with that, he returned to the kitchen.

One of the waitresses raised an eyebrow at Haley's slim figure and said, "I don't know where she's going to put it." Haley wasn't quite sure what she meant.

"What was all that about?" she asked, following Sasha to one of the booths.

"You'll see," Sasha said cryptically. "I'll just have my usual," she added to one of the passing waitresses.

"Don't I have to order?" Haley asked.

"Nope," said Sasha. "Taken care of. Trust me."

Just then, Coco De Clerq and Whitney Klein entered the diner and headed straight for Sasha and Haley's table. Coco was dressed in a tiny tennis skirt, tank top, and hoodie, though from the looks of her immaculate outfit, she hadn't hit a single groundstroke all day. Whitney, meanwhile, was wearing a pink spandex leotard that hugged every inch of her generous curves under a light jacket. She, too, seemed to be sweat-free and perfectly coiffed.

"So here you are," Coco said, marching up to Sasha with her bony hip cocked. "We've been looking for you everywhere."

"Are we interrupting something?" Whitney asked.

"We just finished soccer practice," Sasha said. "You know the routine."

"Mind if we join you?" Coco asked, already shoving her way into the booth next to Haley. Coco looked over at the waitress and flagged her down as Whitney sat next to Sasha.

"I would like a bottled water, please," Coco demanded.

"For the hundredth time, kid, all we got's tap," said the waitress.

"Fine. Then bring me a diet soda with lemon," Coco said, settling in. "And don't try to use any of those shriveled slices that've been sitting behind the counter for days," she warned. "I want to see you slicing that lemon before it touches my glass."

"And will Her Highness be having anything to

eat today?" the waitress asked. "Or will she just chew on her straw per usual?"

Coco forced a smile. "Improve your sanitation grade and maybe I'll consider letting some of this slop pass my lips."

"What about you?" the waitress asked, turning to look at Whitney. "You bingeing or fasting today?"

Whitney forced a chuckle. "Just a ginger ale for me, thanks."

When a busboy arrived at their table seconds later, balancing an enormous tray of hot plates, Coco nearly screamed.

"Who ordered all this food?" she demanded. Whitney's eyes bulged as plate after plate was set down in front of Haley.

"I didn't order it, I swear," Haley said, staring at the smorgasbord.

"It's a Hap's challenge," said Sasha matter-of-factly.

"That's disgusting," Coco replied. "Don't tell me you're going to try to eat all of that?" The sight of all that grease was making her turn green.

Whitney snatched a fry from one of Haley's plates. Coco caught her and kicked her under the table.

"What's a Hap's challenge?" Haley finally asked, still befuddled by the half dozen plates that were spread out in front of her.

"If you eat everything Hap orders for you, your meal is free," said Whitney, now openly and defiantly snitching Haley's fries in front of Coco.

"How would you know?" Coco asked, glaring at her.

"Um. My dad used to bring me here when I was little?" Whitney said, obviously manufacturing an excuse for why she knew so much about the Hap's binge.

"So I have to eat everything?" Haley asked, her eyes wide. "By myself?"

"Don't worry. Hap doesn't challenge you with anything you're not capable of," Sasha said, diving into her own burger.

"It's a good thing you're playing soccer now, Haley," Coco warned. "Otherwise, those curly fries would be cellulite by next week."

"I don't understand why you come here if you don't eat, Coco," Sasha said as she took another bite of her burger.

"To see and be seen," Coco said in all seriousness. It was at that moment that Haley recognized table after table of Hillsdale High seniors scattered around the diner. *Great,* she thought. *As if there's not already enough pressure here, I get to look like a pig in front of upperclassmen.*

"So what are you up to this weekend? Now that you two are best friends and all," Coco asked, timing her question perfectly with Haley's somewhat reluctant first bite.

"Just pace yourself," Sasha whispered to her.

Haley tried to chew and swallow her bite of chili-drenched hot dog, gulping her shake to wash it all down. "I think we're going to Sasha's," she said, watching Sasha wince. "Or maybe not," she added, trying to undo the damage. Clearly, Sasha didn't want Coco to know their plans. "I don't know," Haley improvised. "My mom said something about taking me to the mall to shop for a Halloween costume."

"You don't have to lie, Haley," said Coco. "I'm not at all hurt that Sasha didn't invite me to her sleepover. Are you, Whitney?" Whitney didn't say anything, so Coco kicked her under the table again.

"Owww! Quit doing that!" Whitney whined.

"Let me guess," said Coco, looking at Haley. "You two kids are going to stay up all night, painting each other's toenails and practicing kissing on your hands?"

"That sounds like fun," Whitney said, eating another french fry.

"Whitney, do you want half of my burger?" Haley offered. "There's no way I'm going to finish all this." Whitney smiled and reached across the table for the burger, but Coco smacked her hand away.

"I think you've had enough trans fats for one day," Coco said sharply. "Since you two seem to be intent on eating your way through Bergen County," she added, looking at Sasha and Haley, "we'll leave you to your *snack*. Whitney, come on." And just like that, they paraded back out of the diner.

Haley looked down at her Hap's meal and found she'd suddenly lost her appetite. The word *cellulite* was still rattling around in her head.

"Don't mind them," said Sasha, trying to cheer her up. "They just can't stand to see anyone else have a good time. And they *really* can't stand to see anyone eat." As Sasha took another bite of her burger, Haley shrugged and finally bit into her own.

"Mmmmm," she suddenly groaned after tasting the deluxe burger with special sauce, lettuce and melted cheese. "This is the best thing I've put in my mouth!" Haley exclaimed.

"See," said Sasha. "I told you you'd love Hap's."

Whatever negative effect Coco had had on Haley's appetite suddenly vanished. And while Haley wasn't about to win any Hap's challenges that day, she did come close to cleaning at least two of her six plates. A couple of seniors swooped in and polished off the rest.

● ● ●

Why is it that every time Coco comes around, Haley starts to feel miserable about herself? In fact, if there's such a thing as a toxic person, Haley's pretty sure Ms. De Clerq fits the bill, since nearly everyone Coco comes into contact with gets infected with her self-loathing and doubt.

Sasha, on the other hand, is totally easygoing and fun to hang out with. And even though she has it all—money, good looks, great clothes and any guy she wants—she doesn't flaunt it, like *some* people at Hillsdale.

So why does Sasha tolerate Coco? Is it simply a case of old habits die hard? Or is Sasha more like Coco than Haley's willing to admit?

If you want Haley to take Sasha up on her invitation to spend the night at the Lewises', turn to page 182. If you think hanging out with Sasha is a bad idea since it will always involve Coco in one way or another, send Haley to shop for a Halloween costume on page 189.

Like it or not, friends often come as a package deal. You either have to accept them as a group or cut all of them out of your life.

Sometimes people-watching
is more fun than
the main event.

"Thanks, Mrs. Armstrong," Haley said politely while getting out of the gray minivan in her jeans, a white tank top and her baby blue ballet flats. Mrs. Armstrong was working with Haley's mom at an environmental law firm in Hillsdale, and over the weekend, she had offered to give Haley a ride to the swim meet.

"Have a great time, girls," Mrs. Armstrong said, leaning through the window to give Annie a kiss on the cheek.

"Okay, Mom. Enough. Bye," Annie said, shooing her mother away.

"I'll pick you up at six," said Mrs. Armstrong, pulling out of the parking lot.

Meanwhile, Spencer Eton and some of his old prep school friends were standing on the sidewalk, staring at Haley and Annie. "Sweet minivan," Spencer said as the other boys laughed.

"Hey, Annie," Haley said, loudly enough for Spencer and his friends to hear. "Don't you think it's weird the way these private school boys come to our swim meets? Just to see a few girls in bathing suits? I mean, who could be that desperate?" She paused, checking their reactions.

"Then again," Haley added, "maybe they come here to see the guys. Rock-hard bodies. Speedos. I've heard the guys' team waxes from head to toe." Haley could see that her strategy was having the desired effect on Spencer's snobby friends. A thin blond boy was shifting uncomfortably.

Annie played along. "Well, Sebastian Bodega *is* pretty hot," she said.

"Totally," said Haley. "I mean, if I were a guy, I'd hook up with him."

That did it. One of them punched Spencer's arm. "Hey, man, I thought you said we were only here to pick up some weed," he said.

Haley took Annie's hand, brushed past Spencer

and his friends and headed toward the indoor pool. Along the way, she spotted a figure in a hooded sweatshirt riding by on a bicycle. "Who is that?" she asked.

"I don't know," said Annie. "Wait, isn't that . . . Irene?"

"Why is she dressed like that?"

"Hello? It's Irene," said Annie. "Total outsider? Weird dresser?"

"Right."

"You can't even really feel bad for her," said Annie. "She's so anti everything. With her, it's like reverse snobbery."

"Do you think she's coming to the swim meet?" Haley asked as they stood in line to buy tickets.

"Are you kidding? Irene doesn't believe in sports. She thinks she's too evolved for it. I bet she spends her weekends reading Satre and smoking clove cigarettes."

Haley watched as the bicycle coasted out of sight. "I wonder what she's up to."

Annie frowned. "I wouldn't be surprised if it had something to do with that graffiti Principal Crum is so upset about," she said, suddenly craning her neck to get a better look at Mrs. Shope standing in line in front of them. "Mrs. Shope, Mrs. Shope," Annie called out to her, waving enthusiastically.

The Shopes were playing host family to Sebastian

Bodega, the exchange student on loan for a year from Seville, Spain, thanks to a program for student athletes. Not only had he earned himself the nickname Bodacious Bodega, but he was also the best swimmer on Hillsdale's competitive team. Rumor had it that he might be competing for Spain in the next Summer Olympics.

"Hi, girls," Mrs. Shope said. "I'm glad you came. I know Sebastian will appreciate the support."

"We wouldn't miss seeing him swim for anything, would we, Haley?" Annie said.

Just then, Coco De Clerq, Whitney Klein and Sasha Lewis walked through the pool entrance and headed toward the stands without bothering to buy tickets. No one stopped them. In fact, for some reason, everyone, including parents, got out of their way. The stunning trio glided past the boy taking tickets, smiling and winking, and took three of the best seats in the house.

"How come they don't have to pay?" Haley asked.

"That's Ricky," Annie said, pointing to the dazed boy who'd just let them pass. "He does odd jobs for the De Clerqs. His father, Jorge, is their groundskeeper. Coco never has to pay when she comes to the swim meets: Ricky's in love with her, and she knows it. I hear she even leaves her curtains open in the afternoons while she's changing, just to taunt him with what he can never have."

"Who's that she's talking to?" Haley asked.

"One of Spencer's old boarding school buddies. Supposedly, she lost her virginity to him this summer, and now he barely speaks to her. But I don't buy it. Coco's an ice queen. She'll never give it up."

"Are you serious?" Haley asked. With Annie around, it was impossible not to get wrapped up in the soap opera that was Hillsdale High.

Haley and Annie entered the pool area with their tickets and sat down close enough to Coco and the other girls to observe.

"So what's Spencer Eton's story?" Haley asked in a whisper, dropping any pretext of being uninterested in the popular crowd.

"Pretension is his name. Suspension is his game," Annie said. "He's been kicked out of three boarding schools for drinking, dating teachers . . . you name it, he's done it."

Spencer was wearing a corduroy blazer, T-shirt, and jeans.

"Frat boy in training," Haley said, marveling at the way Spencer was simultaneously flirting with three girls in the stands while massaging Coco's shoulders.

"I know. He thinks he's pretty much guaranteed admission to Princeton just because his entire family went there. But it's a lot tougher than it was during Daddy Eton's days." Annie had a smirk on her face. "Boy, is he in for a rude awakening."

"So if he's such a jerk, why's he so popular?"

"Money. And his parents are never in town. Oh, and he started this secret gambling ring with some of his friends from boarding school."

"Really?"

"Yeah, that's SIGMA. The trouble is the password always changes and so does the location."

"So how do you get in? Who gives out the password?"

"Not who. What. One of the founders is a computer genius. Every month he hacks into a different Web site and embeds the password in the text. Last month, it was inside a travel agent's site for an eating tour of Tuscany."

"Why would anyone go to all that trouble?"

Annie shrugged. "What else is there to do in Hillsdale?"

Looking at Spencer, Haley said, "Well, I can't imagine why anyone would bother for a party thrown by him. He's awful."

"Awfully perfect for Coco, you mean," said Annie. "Only she doesn't know it yet, since she's too busy chasing after Reese Highland."

"Coco and Reese?" Haley asked. "But I thought . . ."

"What's the matter?" Annie asked.

"Nothing." Haley shrugged it off. "So are they like a couple?"

"I'm not sure if they're together this week or not. Even I can't keep track. Of course Reese is too good for her, but let's face it, she's Coco. She tends to get what she wants."

A whistle blew to signal the start of the meet. The opposing swim team began to file out of the locker room wearing red swim caps, black swimsuits and white and red warm-up jackets. "Hello Hawk" by Superchunk played on the sound system as the Hawks began running warm-up laps around the pool, getting pumped up by the crowd's applause.

"Wow," Haley said as they took off their blue and gold jackets. "They're in really good shape." In particular, she was eyeing Sebastian, who was bending over and shaking out his quads, trying to loosen up the rippled muscles in his legs.

"Um, you think?" Annie said sarcastically.

"Will the owner of the license plate 'Etouthree' please come to the front desk? Your car is being towed," said a voice over the loudspeaker. As inconspicuously as possible, Spencer got up from the stands and headed out to the parking lot.

"Spencer can drive?" Haley asked Annie.

"Not until he's seventeen, just like everyone else in New Jersey. But that doesn't stop him from occasionally taking his parents' cars out for a spin."

Haley noticed that Coco didn't seem concerned about Spencer's car being towed. She was too busy ogling Sebastian, like every other girl in the room.

"Check out the dude from Spanish class," Haley overheard Whitney say. "He's totally hot."

"Sweetie, why do you think we come to these swim meets?" Coco responded. Her silver cell phone rang and she answered it. "What do you want? Well, is it my fault you parked in a tow zone when you don't have a license? And why should I do that for you? Fine. But you owe me. Big-time." Coco hung up the phone. "Come on," she said to Whitney and Sasha. "I have to call my dad to bail out Spencer." The three girls got up from the stands and sauntered out of the poolhouse, clicking across the concrete floor in their dainty heels.

"Swimmers, take your positions," the ref ordered through a bullhorn. Sebastian put on his goggles and stepped up onto the blocks with the other swimmers for the 100-meter butterfly. All eyes were on the pool.

A siren sounded, and the swimmers dove into the turquoise water, popping up after a few meters. Sebastian stayed underwater longer than anyone else, for almost half the length of the pool. When he finally came up for air, the other swimmers were already in his wake.

The Shopes waved their EN FUEGO! GO SEBASTIAN! poster in the air as the crowd cheered. Sebastian pumped his arms, gliding through his lane.

"He's amazing," Haley said while watching him outpace everyone in the pool.

After he'd won the race, Sebastian stood on the

coping, letting the water drip from his washboard stomach. As he toweled off, he scanned the crowd and waved to Haley. Or at least she thought he did.

"What are you doing for Halloween?" Annie asked, snapping Haley out of her daze.

"I don't know. Do you think Sebastian celebrates Halloween?"

Annie shrugged. As they got up to go, Haley noticed something in the bleachers where Coco and her friends had been. It was a leather bag, which Haley recognized as Whitney's. But just as she was wondering whether or not she should return it, she caught a glimpse of Irene through one of the windows near the pool. She was carrying a heavy backpack and furtively looking over her shoulder. *What's she up to?* Haley wondered.

● ● ●

The whole town seems to have turned out for Hillsdale's big swim meet. And really, who can blame them, when the price of admission includes a look at Sebastian in his swimsuit?

But does Sebastian have real feelings for Haley? Or is he just being flirtatious? Will he follow up with her or flake? And does she really want to get involved with a guy who's going back to Spain in a few months?

Irene Chen is definitely hiding something in that backpack of hers, but what? Does she have something to do with the graffiti Annie mentioned? Or is she just an overly secretive loner? If Haley befriends, will she stop acting so strange?

And what about Annie? She and Haley certainly seem to be getting along, though all they do together is talk about Coco De Clerq. Is it healthy to live so vicariously? Or should Annie and Haley get lives of their own?

Speaking of Coco, does Haley secretly harbor a desire to hang out with the popular crowd? Or is she content to just whisper about them from the bleachers?

If you think Haley is in her comfort zone with Annie, have them go pick out Halloween costumes together on page 189. To investigate Irene and the school vandalism, turn to page 178. Finally, to return Whitney's bag to her at school the following week, go to page 194.

Three very different fates await Haley. Will she become a queen bee, a wannabe or the school busybody? It's up to you.

**Spy unto your neighbors
as you would have them
spy unto you.**

"Haley? Sweetie?" Haley's mother said, knocking on the locked bathroom door.

Inside, Haley stared at her "new and improved" reflection in the mirror. There were two black spiders where her eyes should have been, thanks to the heavy eyeliner and mascara Whitney had applied. Her hair had been hot-rollered and teased. And her lips were bright pink. Haley hardly recognized herself. Slut or poodle was right.

"What?" Haley asked.

"Everything okay in there?" Joan asked.

"I'm fine, Mom," Haley said, picking up the bar of soap and rubbing it between her hands. The thick layer of foundation Whitney had caked on Haley's face had begun to irritate her sensitive skin, and she could already feel the breakout coming on.

Haley's mother knocked again, softly.

"A little privacy, please?" Haley said, her face now covered in soapsuds.

"Okay," Joan said. "I just want you to know I think you're beautiful without any makeup." Haley rolled her eyes as she heard her mother head back downstairs to finish fixing dinner.

"Android invasion!" Mitchell shouted outside the bathroom door. "Open up. Or my laser gun will stun you with its rays," he said in his robot voice.

"Go away, creep!" Haley yelled.

"I have to pee," he said. "I will self-destruct in ten seconds if I do not. Ten, nine, eight . . ."

"You have a bathroom in your own room," Haley said, exasperated.

"The toilet," Mitchell said. "Will eat me."

"So use Mom and Dad's!"

"Dad. Is in the shower. Seven, six, five . . ."

Haley had had it. "Then go pee in the backyard!" she screamed. "You're not getting in here!"

"It is. Too cold," said Mitchell. "My laser. Will freeze. Four, three, two . . ."

Haley scrubbed the last of the makeup off her face.

"One . . . Oh no. I am. Self-destructing." Haley heard a thump as Mitchell fell to the floor.

"Congratulations!" Haley said, storming out of the bathroom and stepping over him. "You've just won the Most Annoying Little Brother in the Universe award." She headed for her room and slammed the door behind her.

Haley flopped down on the chair in front of her computer and logged on to her family's joint e-mail account, looking at her buddy list to see if Gretchen, her best friend from California, was online too.

Ever since Haley had moved to New Jersey, the three-hour time difference had made it impossible to keep up with her old friends. By the time her West Coast pals got home from school, Haley was eating supper. By the time they finished their homework, she was getting ready for bed.

Thinking back to the good old days, Haley remembered how she and Gretchen used to instant-message for hours about everything—crushes, mean girls in their classes, what they were wearing to school the next day, their favorite books and magazines. Now Haley was lucky to get one or two e-mails a week from her supposed best friend.

Haley began typing out a message.

```
Today was SUCH a disaster!
   Gretch, I wish you were here.
Or I was there. Or we were both
```

in . . . what's in the middle?
Chicago?

I HATE not being able to talk.

And the people here are AWFUL.
I hung out with these girls from
school today that everyone
secretly, and not so secretly,
wants to be friends with. And for
some reason, they asked ME to be
in their study group. Which, I
know, probably means they just
want me to take notes for them
and do their homework. And that's
fine, I get it.

So I go to this one girl
Coco's house after school. And
it's, of course, like the biggest
thing you've ever seen.

Anyway, after we finished
"studying," which was basically
me flipping through my Spanish
book, Coco and Whitney decided
to give me a . . . makeover. And
silly me, I let them. I mean,
what was I thinking? All they
wanted was for me to be less like
me and more like them. And for a
second, even I thought that was a
good idea.

But they made me look like a
TOTAL SKANK. And then I come home
and, well, Mitchell's being a
freak. As usual. And I can't even
call you. And there's no one here
who understands. And I'm never
leaving my room again. Ever.
    Miss u. Haley

As Haley pressed Send, a light flashed on her
screen. At first, she thought it was Gretchen miraculously signing on. But when Haley pulled up
her buddy list to see who was there, Coco's IM
popped up.

C: Gotcha.

Haley panicked, then calmed down when she
realized there was no possible way Coco could have
read her e-mail to Gretchen.

H: Hey.
C: Meet us in Whitney's chat
   room?

Haley was torn. She wasn't exactly dying to talk
to either Coco or Whitney. But they knew she was
online, so it would be rude not to respond. She
logged on to the site.

H: I'm here.

W: Hi ho.

C: I just wanted to tell you that
   you looked totally awesome
   tonight:)

H: Um, thanks.

W: Yeah, just wait till the guys
   in our grade c u tomorrow!
   They'll totally freak out!

H: I don't know. I'd feel sort of
   weird wearing Coco's clothes
   to school.

W: But you just HAVE to!

C: Don't be silly. It's not like I
   recycle the same outfit ever. Ew.

H: No offense, Coco. But the new
   "look" . . . it's just not me.

W: But it's so TOTALLY you! You
   couldn't possibly look any
   hotter!

C: Whatever. So is Reese home yet?

Haley felt all the air rush out of her lungs. So that
was why they were bombarding her. She lived next
door to Reese.

H: Why?

C: No reason.

W: I can't believe u 2 live nx

```
door to each other. U could
like put up some tin cans with
string n play telefon or
something.
C: So is he there or not?
H: How should I know?
C: Can't you see his room from
yours?
H: My shutters are closed.
C: So open them. Just see if his
light's on.
W: How cool. . . . I feel like a
Bond girl!
```

Haley didn't respond.

```
C: What's the matter? Are you
scared?
H: I'm not scared.
C: Are you sure? I dare you.
```

What's she up to? Haley wondered. And yet now that the prospect of spying on Reese had been put into her head, Haley could think of nothing else.

● ● ●

There's nothing like hiding in your bedroom after an awkward moment, especially one as unbearable as a makeover gone awry. Too bad IM can find you even there. :(

Hillsdale's queen bee, Coco De Clerq, isn't going to let go of her newest drone just yet. She's already trying to make Haley spy on Reese. If Haley gives in, what's next?

Should Haley take the dare? Would Reese really be so upset if he knew Haley was admiring him from a distance?

Then again, how could Haley ever face Reese again if he caught her looking at something more than him studying at his desk?

If you think Haley should peep and dish with the girls, turn to page 157. If you think there's nothing playful about spying, go to the next page.

Watch and learn has always been Haley Miller's motto. However, this time, what she'll watch, and what she learns from it is all up to you.

Being gullible is a
form of self-abuse.

H: Nice try, Coco. What were you
   going to do, wait until Reese
   was naked and then call him
   up to tell him his neighbor's
   spying on him? If you want to
   know what Reese Highland is
   doing in his bedroom after
   dark, I suggest you find a
   ladder, a tall tree and a good
   pair of binoculars.
C: Fine. If that's how you see

```
     it, enjoy your life as a
     social outcast.
W:   W/ zero friends . . .
C:   Except maybe the freaks and
     geeks from the Floods.
H:   No offense, but if it's a
     choice between the freaks and
     geeks and you two vipers, I'll
     take the freaks and geeks.
```

Haley signed off without even waiting to read Coco's reply.

She heard at school the next day that Coco had tried to convince Reese that Haley was spying on him. Fortunately for Haley, Reese didn't buy it.

Unfortunately, though, Haley was indeed on Coco's blacklist. And the only people who would dare risk talking to her were . . .

● ● ●

To send Haley off with the freaks, turn to page 119. To pair her off with the geeks, turn to page 137.

No worries, it's only a temporary banishment. And it was worth it to stand up to Coco. Haley will still be able to find fun, fame and fortune at Hillsdale. You'll just have to be extra careful where you send her looking next time.

**Some things in life are just
too tempting to resist.**

Haley tentatively pulled the shutters back from her window and glanced next door. Reese's light was on, but she didn't see him through the window. She moved her desk closer to the window so she could watch while she typed.

```
H: His light is on.
```

Coco waited a moment before responding. To Haley, it seemed like an eternity.

```
C: His bedroom light?
H: Yes.
C: Good. What's he doing?
H: I don't know. I can't really
   see.
C: Tell me exactly what you see.
```

Haley peered out of her window. Just then, Reese walked by with his shirt off. Haley ducked down and typed.

```
H: He just walked by.
C: What's he wearing?
H: Jeans, I think.
C: What else?
H: Um, not much.
W: What?!
C: So his shirt is off.
H: Yes.
C: Good. What's he doing now?
```

Haley peeked through the window again. Reese lifted his right arm high in the air and . . . smelled his armpit.

```
H: He seems to be . . .
C: What?
H: Sniffing his armpits.
```

```
W: Gross!!#%*
C: Now what?
```

Haley looked again. Reese took a red towel out of his drawer and threw it on the bed. He walked into the bathroom that adjoined his bedroom and flicked on the light. Then Haley watched as he turned on the shower. Her heart was racing.

```
W: Well?!?
H: I think he's about to take a
   shower.
C: Good. Has he gotten undressed
   yet?
H: No.
C: Tell us when he does.
H: I don't know. I don't think
   this is such a good idea.
C: Come on, Haley. Why stop now?
   What color are his boxer
   shorts?
H: You can't be serious.
C: If you don't tell us, Whitney
   and I will tell the whole
   school what we already know.
H: And what's that?
C: That you have a massive crush
   on Reese. Winstead. Highland.
```

His middle name is Winstead? Haley thought.
How can I like a guy whose middle name is Winstead?

```
H: You wouldn't.
W: Oh, yes she would. Trust me. :(
```

Haley couldn't believe it. Coco was cruel, but
could she possibly be downright evil, too?

Haley looked through Reese's window again. He
was unbuttoning his jeans.

```
H: Fine. They're blue. Satisfied?
C: So his pants are off.
H: Yes.
C: What about the boxers? On or
   off?
H: On. But probably not for long.
C: What's he doing now?
H: Brushing his teeth. So listen,
   I'll just see you guys in
   school tomorrow, okay?
C: If you sign off now, Haley, by
   tomorrow afternoon, you'll wish
   your family had never moved to
   Hillsdale. Now, is he naked yet?
```

Haley peered through the window as Reese
picked up the towel from his bed and slung it over
his shoulder. He stretched, yawning, and patted his

stomach lazily. Then—Haley couldn't quite believe it—he turned away from her, slipped his boxers off and let them fall to the floor.

```
C: Well?
```

His butt wasn't nearly as tan as his upper back. Haley watched, her heart racing, waiting to see if he'd turn around.

```
C: Haley?
H: They're off.
C: What's he doing?
```

Reese started to turn around and head toward the bathroom, but something stopped him.

```
H: I don't know.
C: Well, look harder.
```

Haley leaned up against the window. He was walking across his room and reaching for something.

```
H: I can't tell . . . He's . . .
   picking up the phone . . .
   He's turning around . . .
```

Reese suddenly wrapped the red towel around his waist, marched over to the window, looked directly up at Haley and pulled down his shades. By the time Haley realized what had happened and returned to her computer, there was one last message waiting for her from Coco.

    C: Busted . . .

● ● ●

Ooooh, how could Haley have not seen that one coming? There are few situations in life more mortifying than getting caught spying on your crush. Leave it to Cruella De Clerq to come up with such a nasty trick.

Worst of all, Reese is never going to speak to Haley again. By tomorrow morning, the entire sophomore class, make that the entire school, will have heard that Haley Miller is a voyeuristic perv.

Haley Miller is socially dead. Nothing to do now but hang your head and start over. Go back to page I.

Fitting in and standing out don't have to be mutually exclusive.

As Haley dressed for school that morning, she couldn't get Coco's voice out of her head. She pictured Coco frowning at every article of clothing Haley owned. Somehow, nothing in her closet seemed right.

Exasperated and frantically looking at the clock, Haley suddenly had an idea. She picked up a pair of scissors and began hacking away at the hem of an old knee-length jean skirt she hadn't worn since sixth grade. In a flash, she threw on her new mini along with a blue, long-sleeved oxford shirt of Mitchell's her mother had accidentally included in her pile of clean laundry. The shirt was so snug, Haley could barely fasten the buttons, which meant it plunged to a deep V and made her boobs stand out, but that was sort of the point.

"Hurry up, Haley! You'll be late for school!" she heard her mother call from downstairs as she quickly pulled her hair back into a ponytail and slipped on her only pair of high heels, the black pumps her parents had bought for her to wear to a piano recital the previous year. Without any makeup of her own, Haley improvised, using her mom's lipstick for rouge.

Not bad, she thought, catching a glimpse of her reflection in the mirror. *Not bad at all.*

Downstairs in the kitchen, Haley's mother wasn't so sure. "Haley, is that you?" she asked incredulously as Haley breezed through the room, sniffed the bowl of oatmeal her mother had set out for her, put it back down and grabbed her books.

"No time for breakfast, Mom," she yelled, already halfway out the door.

"But, Haley, what about your lunch!" her mother called after her, holding up a brown paper bag as Mitchell dumped Haley's bowl of oatmeal on the table, spreading the goo around with his butter knife.

By the time lunch rolled around, Haley was beginning to rethink her decision to skip breakfast. With her stomach rumbling, she strutted through the cafeteria in her short skirt and high heels. Every-one stopped to stare. From one half of the sophomore class, Haley was inspiring lusty looks, and from the other half, jealous glares. The boys, it seemed, couldn't get enough, while the girls wanted to claw her eyes out.

Not bad, Haley thought. *Not bad at all.*

"Who is that?" Spencer Eton asked, scoping Haley out as she walked by.

"That's . . . That's . . . H-Haley?" Reese Highland stammered. He seemed to hardly recognize his new neighbor.

"Dude, you know her?" Spencer asked. "Hook me up."

"No way. Don't even think about it, Eton," Haley heard Reese say. "That girl is way too sweet and in-nocent for you." At that moment, Haley bent down to grab a lunch tray, giving both boys a good look at her stems. She stood back up, flipped her hair, looked over her shoulder and gave Reese a sexy smile.

"Innocent?" Spencer added. "She looks ready, willing and able to me." Even Reese couldn't help noticing there was something different about Haley. And he wasn't quite sure if he liked it.

"Haley, over here," Coco called to her from across the cafeteria. It was as good as a statement to the rest of the sophomore class: Haley Miller is now one of us.

"Of course," Haley heard Spencer say to Reese.

"Coco's already trying to adopt her. She keeps her friends close and the pretty girls even closer."

"Hey, hot stuff," Whitney said as Haley approached the table. "Love the outfit."

"Edgy preppy. I like it," said Coco. Even though the table was round, it felt as if Coco were sitting at the head, flanked by Sasha on her left and Whitney on her right. "Whitney, move down a seat to make room for Haley?"

"But—" Whitney started to protest, but Coco gave her one of her withering do-as-I-say gazes, and Whitney meekly got up and switched chairs. It was a demotion that was not lost on the rest of the lunchroom.

"Thanks," Haley said, tucking in next to Coco and setting down her tray, which held a toasted bagel slathered with cream cheese.

"So you're certainly the new flavor at Hillsdale," Coco said to Haley. "How does it feel to have every guy in the room sweating that hot little bod?"

"Are they?" Haley asked, taking a sip of her bottled water. "I hadn't noticed."

"Girls, she's a natural," Coco said.

"Seriously," Whitney added with conviction, taking a huge bite of her turkey-and-bacon club sandwich. She followed that with a handful of potato chips and several gulps of her full-calorie soda.

Coco took a single bite of her carrot stick and

chewed it slowly and deliberately, while Haley bit into her bagel.

"Is that real cream cheese?" Coco asked.

"Yep," Haley said, taking another bite.

"A moment on the lips . . . ," Coco warned.

Sasha rolled her eyes and took a bite of her chicken salad. "As if Haley needs to watch her weight," she said. "Face it, Coco. If you just exercised a little more you could eat whatever you wanted too."

Coco angrily took another bite of her carrot. "What, and be a soccer jock like you? When I exercise, my thighs get thick. You know that."

"Your thighs could use a little thickness if you ask me," Sasha said under her breath.

"My soon-to-be-stepmonster and I saw a model when we were shopping in SoHo last weekend," Whitney announced. "She was wearing this ratty T-shirt and shades, but I so recognized her from all the September issues."

"Wow, caught her in her natural habitat," Sasha said sarcastically.

"What do you mean?" Haley asked.

"Whether U.S. born or naturalized, models are indigenous to a twenty-block radius in lower Manhattan." Sasha sipped her lemonade.

"You should know," Coco said, seething. To Haley she added, "Sasha was recruited by a modeling scout last year."

"Yeah, only she turned them down," Whitney said, causing Sasha to blush. "How can models be indigenous?" Whitney asked. "Don't they make, like, a thousand dollars a day?"

"Not indigent. Indigenous," Sasha corrected her. "It means native to."

Turning to Haley, Coco said, "Whitney, poor thing, is dyslexic."

The color was slowly draining from Whitney's face. "I don't feel so good."

"What is it, hon? Did you eat too much again?" Coco asked knowingly. Whitney suddenly stood up and without a word headed straight for the restroom.

"Is she all right?" Haley asked.

"Who, Whitney?" Coco formed her hand into the shape of a gun and pretended to pull the trigger. "Nothing a little alone time in the stalls won't fix. Just in case, I think I'll go check on her."

"Just don't encourage her," Sasha said as Coco left the table.

"I get the impression that those two don't exactly have the best relationship with food," Haley said, finishing her bagel.

"Why do you think their nicknames are No Eat and Repeat."

Haley wrinkled her nose. "Ew."

"So what are you up to this weekend?" Sasha asked.

"Why?" Haley raised an eyebrow.

"I've got a stash of eighties movies and a freezer full of ice cream, and you know Coco and Whitney won't enjoy it."

"Yeah, what good is a chocolate-covered eighties fest if you don't have someone to share it with?"

"Exactly." Sasha downed the last of her cookie and lemonade. "So what do you say?" she asked, getting up from the table. "You, me, John Hughes, rocky road, Saturday night?"

Just as Haley was about to answer, she noticed Whitney's leather pocketbook still slung over her chair and wondered if she should try to find Coco and Whitney in the bathroom.

"I'll let you know after school," Haley said as Sasha headed off to her next class.

● ● ●

For a healthy California girl like Haley, eating disorders are about as foreign as the New Jersey Turnpike. Thank goodness there is at least one other normal eater in the group.

Sasha Lewis, fortunately, seems more content to kick soccer balls than count calories. But is Sasha really as laid-back as she appears to be? Or is her aloof demeanor masking something else?

And what about Coco and Whitney? If you are what you eat, they're what they don't eat—as in empty. But are these girls simply products of their too competitive environments? Will Haley's sweet disposition be a good influence on them? Or will their unhealthy attitudes toward food—not to mention boys, clothes, parties and homework—rub off on her, too?

If you're already fed up with the food issues, have Haley spend some quality time with Sasha on page 182. To have Haley go find Whitney and Coco in the bathroom, turn to page 194.

Trying on old clothes is
a bit like trying on
other people's lives.

"Cool jacket," Irene said, leaning over Haley's shoulder as she pulled an army green bomber jacket off a rack of used clothing.

Haley looked it over and then handed it to her. "You try it," she said. "It'd look better on you anyway."

"I thought we came here to shop for you," Irene replied, dropping her book bag on the floor.

Jacks was Irene's favorite vintage store, which was why she had suggested it as stop one on their mission to find Haley some new fall clothes. Not only did

Jacks have variety, from lace Victorian slips to sixties minidresses to faded blue jeans, but they sold clothes by the pound, so everything was dirt cheap.

Haley sifted through a stack of beaded cardigans and said, "I'm more of a . . ." as she searched for the best way to describe her own style.

"Preppy New Wave meets boho California chic," Irene said, finishing Haley's sentence.

"Something like that," said Haley. "I guess I'm still figuring it out."

In the packed Jacks warehouse, hints of body odor, old leather, cigarette smoke, powdery perfume, mothballs and cedar chips culminated in the olfactory experience peculiar to thrift stores.

Irene held up a funky polyester shirt with a floppy butterfly collar and dizzying geometric shapes. "Good times," she said. Haley stared at her. "What? I like the pattern."

"Come on," Haley said skeptically. "It's a little chaotic, don't you think?"

"Well, you'd never find anything like it at the mall. Who wants to show up for school looking like Coco De-freaking Clerq? And besides, it might work. For something. Sometime."

"Like Halloween?" Haley added, taking the shirt from Irene and hanging it back on the rack. "Now, these, on the other hand, these you could live in," she said, pulling out a pair of buttery soft blue jeans.

172

"Wait until you see what they have upstairs," Irene boasted as she rummaged through a huge basket of miscellaneous T-shirts, pawing around in the rainbow of faded cottons until she found one from an old Kinks concert. "This would look good with them," Irene said, and tossed it to Haley before picking out a shirt for herself that read, THINK ANIMALS. BECAUSE ANIMALS THINK.

"Thanks," Haley said, slinging the shirt over her shoulder and holding the jeans up to her thighs. Just as she suspected, they were exactly the right length.

"I remember when I found my first pair of Jacks jeans," Irene said wistfully. "It was like they'd been made for me."

Just then, Haley's cell phone began beeping with a new text message.

"Wow. It's Gretchen," she said, surprised.

"Who's Gretchen?" Irene asked.

"A friend from California," said Haley. "I was just thinking about how much she would love this place, and then she texts me. That's so like her."

"Creepy," Irene said. "You should call her back." She lifted a derby off the shelf, tried it on and wandered off to another part of the store, leaving Haley alone to read the text message.

"Just checking in . . . ," Gretchen's text began. "Lydia now going out with Steven. Can you believe? Call me. Gretch."

Haley happily allowed herself a moment to think about San Francisco. Between the road trip across country and moving to the house in New Jersey and starting a new school, Haley had been so busy for the last few months, she'd hardly had a chance to catch her breath. But now, standing in the middle of Jacks, she suddenly realized just how much she missed her old life, her old friends and her family's farmhouse in Marin.

"So what's the latest from the West Coast?" Irene asked, reappearing behind a pair of white sunglasses with huge lenses.

"Oh, nothing," Haley said. "She's just filling me in on the gossip."

"Well, here's some gossip for you. The guy behind the counter is totally checking you out."

"Seriously?" Haley asked, suddenly self-conscious.

"Yep. And. He asked about you."

Haley tried to get a look at the store clerk. Peeking through the racks of clothing, she saw a cute, shaggy-haired skater boy.

"His name is Devon. He's a photographer. And he's into eighties New Wave," Irene whispered in Haley's ear.

"Girls. Get. A load. Of this." Coco De Clerq's voice came out of nowhere and was followed promptly by the appearance of its impeccably dressed owner. When Haley turned around, she saw Coco staring at her, with Sasha Lewis and Whitney Klein dutifully standing next to her. All three Cocobots were carrying shopping bags from the mall. "We aren't interrupting anything, I hope?" Coco asked.

"What are you doing here?" Irene demanded.

"Well," Whitney began babbling, "there's this Halloween party at Richie Huber's house, and we went to the mall to get our costumes. But they didn't have white rabbit fur so—"

"Klein, cool it," said Coco. But Haley's ears had already perked up at the word *party*.

"Funny," said Irene. "I thought Coco spent all her time after school consulting with plastic surgeons about that boob job she's been dreaming of."

Whitney gasped. "Who told you?" Coco glared at Whitney, then Irene.

Irene allowed her white oversized sunglasses to slide forward on her nose so that Coco got a good look at her eyes.

"Irene, you're like an elephant provoking a sniper," Coco warned.

"It figures a De Clerq would use a poacher analogy, seeing as how your daddy the big-game hunter has single-handedly managed to endanger entire species."

"Whatever," said Coco, turning to Haley. "Now— Haley, is it?" Haley nodded. "You're new here in Hillsdale, so I'll give you some advice. Be careful who you associate with. For a girl like you, it matters a lot more than you think."

"Thanks for the advice, Coco," said Haley, collecting her pile of maybes. "I'll take it under advisement. Now if you'll excuse us, I think we're ready to try on."

And with that, Haley pulled Irene toward the dressing rooms, leaving Coco, Whitney and Sasha standing among the old T-shirts and torn jeans.

● ● ●

Let's face it, you can't miss Coco De Clerq when she walks into a room. Then again, you don't really miss her after she's gone, either.

Even though Haley has seen enough to know that Coco is just a bully in better clothes, could she still be the least bit curious about the popular girls? If they invited her to join their clique, would she accept?

As for Irene, she's, well, different. A friendship with her will put certain limits on Haley's social life. So what happens when Haley suddenly wants more than one-on-one afternoons at Jacks and the Golden Dynasty? Will there still be room for Irene in her life, once Haley's circle has widened?

And what about this cute new photographer Devon? If Haley sticks close to Irene, will she finally get to meet him? And isn't he just the sort of excitement Haley's been craving in her life?

To have Haley continue her friendship with Irene, go

to page 199. If you think all this playing dress-up has put Haley in the mood for Halloween, turn to page 205.

Vintage clothes are a uniform for Irene, but nothing more than a costume for Coco. So how will they fit on Haley? And will that dictate how she fits in at Hillsdale?

If curiosity kills the cat,
what does it do to the
nosy new sophomore girl?

Haley had begun following Irene after school, making sure to keep a safe distance behind her as she tailed Irene on her bike, from school to the art supply store to work at the Golden Dynasty to the Chens' split-level ranch house near the Floods.

So far, a lot of little clues were adding up to a pretty incriminating picture for Irene. There were her paint-splattered fingernails and sneakers, which were dotted in colors identical to those used in the mural. Then there was the way she crosshatched lines and used shadowing in her doodles, effects that, Haley noticed, matched elements of the graffiti on the gym. Haley had also caught a glimpse of the words *The Hedon* in Irene's closely guarded sketch-book, and the lettering was very similar to the vandal's tag.

I swear those almond eyes in the graffiti belong to her, Haley thought, watching through a pair of binoculars as Irene took a sack of garbage out to a Dumpster in the Golden Dynasty parking lot. After Irene went back inside the restaurant, Haley snuck over to the Dumpster and lifted the lid, almost gagging at the smell of old sweet-and-sour pork and sesame shrimp. Squeamishly, she held her nose and used a stick to poke through the bag Irene had just hoisted into the Dumpster. Unfortunately, all she found was a pile of crushed fortune cookies, some old menus and a couple of singed napkins.

Still, Haley wasn't discouraged. Irene's frequent disappearances during class and the fact that she often lingered in the parking lot after school had only given Haley more reasons to be suspicious. If anything, she was more determined than ever to track down the vandal, or at least find out exactly what Irene knew.

During the school day, Haley tracked Irene's every move. She took notes as Irene watched Garrett "the Troll" Noll doing flip tricks on his skateboard, or met up with her friend Shaun, a stocky kid with a blond mullet who wore motorcycle boots. She even noted the number of times Irene visited her locker, the restroom or the cafeteria.

But Haley still hadn't found any hard evidence linking Irene to the crime. Once, she thought she caught Irene heading back to school after dark on her bike. But when Haley finally reached the Hillsdale parking lot, Irene had been nowhere in sight. By the time Haley pedaled back home, she had broken curfew. That stunt had cost her phone privileges for a week.

In fact, all the snooping was beginning to take its toll on Haley. She was starting to have trouble waking up on time for school in the mornings. Her grades were slipping. People were avoiding her in the halls. But despite the lack of tangible evidence and the dark circles under Haley's eyes, she was still convinced that Irene had to have tagged the back of the gym. *But why?* Haley wondered. *And if she did do it, what am I supposed to do? Turn her in?*

It was especially troubling, since Irene Chen had been nothing but nice to Haley since she had moved to Hillsdale. Granted, Irene could sometimes be difficult, even tough, but Haley was sure that deep down, she was a good person. She certainly didn't deserve to be ratted out by one of the only girls at school she actually considered a friend.

And yet, Haley thought, if Irene wasn't confronted soon, would she keep tagging and get caught on her own?

Lately, each time Haley thought about the graffiti or Irene, her head hurt and she felt stressed. The only thing she did know for sure was that she would have to do something, and soon.

● ● ●

It seems as if Haley has some convincing evidence pegging Irene to the graffiti. But what should she do about it? Trust Irene? Or turn her in?

Is Irene really the type of person who would deface school property? Or is Haley reading too much into the clues?

To have Haley go to a teacher and ask for advice, go to page 249. To have Haley stay loyal to Irene and forget about the vandalism, go to page 232.

A little skepticism can be a good thing. But suspicion and paranoia? Not so much.

A pretty face will open
doors—just don't be
surprised if a few
skeletons pop out.

"**W**ow, you can almost see the city tonight," Sasha said, pointing to a faint luster of lights in the distance. Haley could just make out a twinkling tower that might or might not have been the Empire State Building. It was hard to tell with the glare of traffic lights in the foreground.

"Great view," Haley said, peering through the wall of glass in the living room. Sasha's dad's condo was perched on one of the highest peaks in Hillsdale.

"Which freeway is that?" Haley asked, pointing

to a line of cement that stretched out to meet the horizon.

"Not freeway. Parkway," Sasha corrected her.

"Right. I keep forgetting."

"Come on, Cali girl," Sasha teased. "You're in Jersey now."

"All the smokestacks, swampland and shopping malls your heart desires."

"Now you're talking," Sasha said. "So, sundaes for supper?"

"Won't your dad care that we haven't had any real food?" Haley asked.

"Are you kidding? To him, ice cream is a basic food group. Besides, he probably won't be home until late tonight." Sasha fluffed the square cushions on the sofa, though it didn't do much good. All the furniture in the Lewises' house had severe, geometric lines, and most of the pieces were just as uncomfortable to sit in as they looked.

"Does he work a lot?" Haley asked.

"Hm?" Sasha asked absently. She seemed to have drifted. "Sure," she added. "He puts in crazy hours at the office."

"So does my dad," Haley confided. "He's teaching at Columbia. That's why we moved here, actually."

"Which department?" Sasha asked.

"Filmmaking, documentaries."

"That's so cool."

"It's not exactly Hollywood," Haley explained. "His latest effort is about the growth cycle of deciduous trees. What does your dad do?"

"My dad?" Sasha repeated. "He works in . . . finance."

"In the city?"

"No. . . . Around here," Sasha said, straightening the photos of her and her dad on the mantel. Haley didn't see any pictures of a Mrs. Lewis around the house and thought it best not to ask. If Sasha wanted to reveal something about her mother, Haley would let her do it in her own way.

Sasha headed toward the kitchen in her green camouflage miniskirt and off-the-shoulder cream cashmere sweater. "Pick your poison," she said, opening the freezer door. They looked inside and found all the telltale signs of a bachelor pad—a hoard of TV dinners, economy-sized bottles of vodka and gallons of ice cream. Haley counted no fewer than six different flavors.

Haley went for butter pecan. Sasha started with rocky road, piling scoop after scoop into two bowls and drowning them in dark chocolate sauce. Finally, she held up a can of whipped cream and sprayed the sundaes with white fluff.

"Is that good?" Sasha asked.

"Sure. We don't really eat refined sugar at my house," said Haley, "except on birthdays, and that's only four nights a year."

"To the den," Sasha commanded, picking up the overflowing bowls of ice cream and heading toward the one moderately comfortable room in the Lewis condo. Haley followed her down two short steps into the sunken TV room and plopped down next to her on the black leather sofa.

Sasha tossed her a blanket and grabbed the remote for the projection TV.

"So, eighties movie marathon? We've got *Ferris Bueller*, *Fast Times*, *Pretty in Pink*, *Valley Girl* and finally, *Fresh Horses*."

"Awesome," said Haley. "I love the backwards progression of a genre."

"I know, right? By the time you start dozing off, you don't have to worry about missing anything."

While Sasha loaded the DVD player, Haley scanned the far wall of the den. A display case full of sports memorabilia—baseballs signed by New York Yankees, framed New Jersey Devils Stanley Cup pennants and a Nets basketball with a handwritten note from Jason Kidd was next to a wet bar with a few dusty shot glasses and, above it, a *Sports Illustrated* calendar autographed by one of the swimsuit issue cover models.

On another wall, there was a series of framed photographs with political and entertainment luminaries, all posing with one recurring face: Sasha's father, Jonathan Lewis. The only other common denominator in the pictures was that they were all taken inside or in front of casinos. From Reno to Las Vegas to the Cayman Islands to Atlantic City, there he was, with a winning smile, a cigar, a pretty lady and a Hollywood, Washington or New York mogul.

"Are you going to the big Halloween party at Richie Huber's next weekend?" Sasha asked.

Haley shrugged and leaned back on the couch pillows, snuggling under her blanket.

"I'll give you the address," Sasha said, picking up her bowl of ice cream. "If there's one thing at Hillsdale that's not to be missed, it's the house parties."

"And if there's one classic from the eighties that's not to be missed, it's *Bueller . . . Bueller . . . Bueller.*"

"Ah," Sasha sighed dreamily. "Why can't the boys our age be more like Ferris?"

"I know." Haley paused. "I bet if Ferris went to Hillsdale, he'd have his own podcast."

"What, like 'Inside Hillsdale'?" Sasha asked.

"You know it?" said Haley, flabbergasted. "Inside Hillsdale" was a live podcast that a sort of geeky guy in their Spanish class, Dave Metzger, had started out of his bedroom the previous year.

"Sure. I listen to it sometimes. Dave's a little weird and all, but on the air, he's actually pretty funny."

"He wants to interview me for the show," Haley revealed, looking at Sasha to gauge her response.

"No way!" Sasha said. "That's so cool! You should totally do it."

"Really?" Haley asked. "I was under the impression that everyone thought Dave was, well, a dork."

"You'd be surprised. He's developed a cult following, and not just in Hillsdale. I heard someone called in from Florida the other day."

"Really?" Haley said. "Maybe I will do it."

"I would," said Sasha, settling into the sofa and pressing Play. "You only live once."

● ● ●

Well, Sasha clearly has a much more complicated life than Haley realized. Though there do seem to be some perks to living with a bachelor dad. For starters, there's that mountain of ice cream in the freezer. And what a cozy night for sundaes and a movie marathon without any parents around.

But then, isn't there something missing in the lovely Sasha's life? What happened to her mother? Why are there no pictures of her on the walls? And why does Sasha never mention her?

Sasha's dad sure seems to have a thing for casinos. But why was Sasha so cryptic about his job?

If you think Haley has found a kindred spirit in Sasha, send her to the house party at Richie Huber's on page 205. If you think Haley should accept the offer to be interviewed on Dave's podcast instead, turn to page 252.

With two appealing options, Haley faces a tough choice. A little exposure for the new girl never hurt anyone, right? Then again, if Haley turns down Sasha's invitation to the Halloween party, will the two girls still be friends?

Mall rats come in all
shapes and sizes.

"This mall is the size of a small town," Haley said wearily, dragging her feet after the third hour of shopping with the unrelenting Annie.

"As you know, Haley, New Jersey is the mall capital of the world," Annie reminded her.

"Aren't you tired yet?" Haley asked.

"Come on, we can't stop now," Annie said. "I want my costume to be epic this year."

"Well then, make up your mind already." Haley was becoming increasingly annoyed. Ever since her mother had started working with Annie's mom at an environmental law firm in Hillsdale, the two girls had been thrown together for shopping excursions, study dates and sleepovers, usually without Haley's prior approval. "Can't we at least take a break?" she said.

"I guess." Annie sighed as they sat down on a bench. "But only for five minutes. We can't afford to waste any time."

"Right," Haley said, closing her eyes. "I just need a minute to relax."

"Ooh, ooh, ooh, guess what?" Annie said, practically bouncing out of her seat.

"What," Haley said flatly.

"I was searching online last night, and I think I've found out where the next SIGMA is going to be."

"Wow. You're officially obsessed," said Haley.

"Wouldn't it be so cool if we could break the code together?" Annie asked.

"It can't be that hard. Freshmen have gotten in."

"What's that supposed to mean?" Annie challenged.

"Just that it's a silly gambling ring. You shouldn't be so worried about it. I'm sure if you did get in, it wouldn't even live up to the hype."

At that moment, Coco De Clerq, Sasha Lewis and Whitney Klein appeared, their arms loaded with shopping bags. Annie tugged on Haley's shirtsleeve and pointed them out, as if Haley couldn't spot the popular trio on her own.

Haley assumed they would breeze right by, but to her surprise, Coco seemed to be headed in their direction.

"Hey, Haley, Annie," Sasha said warmly.

"What are you doing here, Headstrong?" Coco asked.

"Haley and I were just shopping for our Halloween costumes," Annie said breathlessly. "What are you guys going to be this year?" She leaned toward them, trying to get a peek into their shopping bags. Whitney frowned and pulled hers away.

"I loved last year's idea. That was genius," Annie continued. She explained to Haley, "They always dress up as a group. Last year, they were the wives of Donald Trump. Coco was Melania, Sasha was Ivana and Whitney was Marla Maples. Oh, and Spencer dressed up as the Donald. He even had a toupee. How funny is that?" Annie, Haley had noticed, always babbled when she got nervous. And right now, her lips were practically quivering. "So what's it going to be this year? Charlie's Angels? Chick superheroes? Coco, you'd make such a great Elektra, by the way."

"What are you going to be for Halloween, Haley?" Coco asked, blatantly ignoring Annie's barrage of questions.

"I don't know yet," Haley said. "That's why I'm still shopping, obviously." Haley was determined to cancel out Annie's fawning with her own indifference.

"Interesting," Coco said, sizing Haley up from head to toe. "You know there's a party at the Hubers' this weekend. Maybe we'll see you there?" And with that, Coco, Whitney and Sasha went on their merry way.

"Did that really just happen?" Annie said after they were out of earshot. "Coco De Clerq did not just invite us to the Halloween party at Richie Huber's! Now we've really got to find something to wear." Annie pulled Haley to her feet.

As she grudgingly trailed after Annie through the mall, Haley didn't have the heart to tell Annie that the invitation hadn't been extended to her.

● ● ●

Well, that was certainly an unexpected turn of events. Coco is suddenly courting Haley, inviting her to an upperclassman's party and possibly even into the popular sophomore clique. But does Haley want to join? Or does she see right through Coco's manipulative little tricks?

And what about Annie? Is her obsession with the popular crowd becoming an illness that even Haley can't cure? Will Annie's neediness continue to test Haley's patience and destroy their shot at being friends? Or will Haley find a way to help Annie be more content?

Getting into SIGMA seems to be all Annie thinks about these days. That is, when she isn't obsessing over Richie Huber's Halloween party. So will Annie be able to break the SIGMA entry code with Haley's help? Or will Haley end up ditching her to go to the Halloween festivities with Coco instead?

If the idea of Halloween with the popular clique is intriguing, go to page 205. If you'd rather have Haley help Annie figure out the SIGMA password, go to page 216.

Sometimes pretty
isn't worth the price.

"Whitney, seriously, we don't have time for your turkey club to make the return trip today. We'll be late for class." Coco knocked on the bathroom stall again as Haley walked in carrying Whitney's purse.

Whitney feebly answered, "Be right out."

Haley held up the bag. "I think this is Whitney's," she said.

Coco looked at her, then stood in front of the mirror and perfected her sleek ponytail before reapplying her sheer nude lip gloss. She passed the tube to Haley when she was finished. "Sometimes I think

Whitney spends more time in that stall than she does in her classes."

Haley dabbed a little of the gloss on her lips while staring at their dueling reflections in the mirror. "That color's great on you," Coco added without ever breaking her own narcissistic gaze.

Whitney flushed one last time and emerged from the stall with ruddy cheeks and tossed hair.

"There she is, Miss America," Coco said sarcastically.

Whitney smiled weakly in Haley's direction and, purely for her benefit, said, "Must have been something I ate."

"Yeah, like half the freakin' lunch counter," Coco snarled.

Whitney splashed water on her face and leaned against one of the wall-mounted sinks, taking the bag from Haley and pulling out a toothbrush and toothpaste.

"Haley, what are you doing for Halloween?" Coco asked innocently, watching Whitney's face to gauge her response.

"I don't know yet. I may have to take my little brother trick-or-treating," Haley said.

"Thrilling," said Coco, arching one eyebrow.

"But that's not definite," Haley quickly added. "Why?"

"There's a party at Richie Huber's house," Coco said. "Do you know him? He's a junior."

"Sure," said Haley. "I mean I think so. He lives down the street from me."

"You should come," Coco added. "I mean, if you're not . . . trick-or-treating." Whitney jealously eyed Haley.

"What are you doing later?" Whitney suddenly asked.

"Whitney, you know I'm going back to the dentist today. I'm still not happy with the color of my teeth," Coco said, still preening in front of the mirror.

"I wasn't asking you. I was asking Haley." Whitney had a satisfied look on her face.

"Oh." Coco frowned.

"I don't know yet," Haley said. "Why?"

"You should come over," Whitney said.

"You actually think she'd want to hang out at Dysfunction Junction?" Coco asked, bemused.

Whitney's neck almost snapped. "What's wrong with my house?" she demanded.

"Well. It's not the house so much. It's the people who live in it."

Whitney took a vial of mint breath spray out of her handbag and squirted some into her mouth. "Well, at least my house isn't full of spooky dead animals."

"Take it back," Coco said through gritted teeth. "Now."

"Hey," said Haley, hoping to distract them both before they clawed each other's eyes out, "did you guys know that there's a kid in our class who can read backwards?"

"Whatever," Coco said, scowling as they entered the hallway. However, the minute she spotted Spencer Eton heading toward them, her frown turned into a radiant, if artificial, smile.

"Ladies," Spencer said, linking arms with Whitney and Coco. "It's confirmed. Huber's parents are out of town. Accordingly, we're burning green on Halloween." He looked right at Haley, flashing her a smile. "Your friend should come too," he said before sailing off down the hall.

Whitney looked at Haley and said, "Spencer totally wants you."

Coco smiled. "Before we're finished with you, Haley Miller, everybody at Hillsdale will."

● ● ●

Wow, is Coco ever promising a lot with her claims of turning Haley into the next big thing at Hillsdale. But are her powers really that extensive? Can she simply snap her fingers and make Haley appealing enough to get any boy she wants?

And what will happen if Coco succeeds? Will she be able to handle all the attention Haley gets? Or will her jealousy sabotage Haley's new life?

Whitney, poor thing, should have nothing to worry about. She's rich, popular and one of the prettiest girls in her class. And yet something fairly ugly seems to be troubling her. So what's eating Whitney Klein? And more importantly, why is she eating everything in sight?

If you think Haley should be a friend to Whitney and find out why she's bingeing and purging, go to page 224. If Whitney's problems are too heavy to handle, then have Haley dress up for Halloween on page 205 instead.

**The best way to get to
know a person is to spend
a little time in her room.**

"**W**ow, have you really read all these?" Haley asked,
looking up at the massive bookshelves in Irene's bedroom. The walls were lined with literary classics and
nonfiction volumes on Buddhism, fauvism, cartogra-
phy and nineteenth-century French poetry.

"Not even close," said Irene. "But I can't help it. I
walk into a bookstore and I have to buy something."

"You too?" Haley asked, knowing exactly what
she meant. Haley scanned the shelves and noticed
one book in particular, an old leather volume with a

spine that was almost falling apart. "What's the . . . *I Ching*?" she asked.

"You sure you want to know?" Irene asked.

Haley nodded.

Irene pulled the book from the shelf, dusted off the cover and switched on a row of Chinese lanterns hanging above her desk.

"It's *The Book of Changes,*" she said. "It's an ancient Chinese oracle dating back to about one thousand BC. This was my grandmother's copy."

"So what's it about?" Haley asked.

"Everything and nothing. It's how the universe tells your fortune," Irene said.

She opened the old book and blew a cloud of dust into the air, where it twinkled in the pink light given off by the lanterns. As she flipped open the cover, Haley noticed a pencil sketch of a pair of hypnotic eyes, and her mind flashed back to the wall of the gymnasium at Hillsdale High, which had recently been defaced with an elaborate graffiti mural. The pair of eyes in the *I Ching* was a perfect match with a pair on the wall.

Irene hastily flipped to the next page. "Now. Ask a question," she ordered.

"What kind of question?" said Haley.

"Any kind of question," Irene said. "Except—"

"What?"

"Just be careful you don't ask the oracle something trivial, or it won't cooperate."

Did Irene vandalize the school? was the only thing Haley could think of, but she knew she couldn't ask that.

"Here," Irene said, handing Haley a piece of paper and a pen. "Write it down, and I'll tell you if it's trivial or not."

Haley quickly thought up an alternate question and dashed out, "Who is my soul mate, Devon or Reese?" on the piece of paper. Irene took the note, read it and brought out a small silk pouch that contained three solid gold coins. "Now," said Irene, handing them to Haley. "As you toss the coins, empty your mind and focus on the question."

Haley put the coins in her hand and blew on her fist for luck.

"You're not gambling," Irene corrected her. "Focus." With a flick of her wrist, Haley cast the coins onto the floor. Two were faceup. One was facedown. Irene began to draw lines, some broken, some unbroken. "It's auspicious," she said when she had finished.

"What is?" asked Haley anxiously.

Irene read, " 'The truth is as you suspect.' "

"I don't get it."

"It means you already know the answer to your question."

Haley quickly passed the coins back to Irene. "Here, your turn."

Irene picked up the coins, held them in her hand

for a moment and, without opening her eyes, tossed them onto the ground. Each one landed faceup. Looking at the symbols, Irene sketched out some more lines. " 'The superior man discriminates between high and low,' " she said, reading her own prediction aloud.

"What the heck does that mean?" Haley asked.

"Well, for that"—Irene smiled—"you would need to know my question. And I'm not telling."

A tiny dog began barking on the other side of the door. Irene closed the book and put it back on the shelf before letting her white Maltese into the room. Haley picked up the puppy and nuzzled it.

"You're so lucky you get to have pets," she said. "My parents don't trust my little brother with anything that has a pulse. What's his name?"

"Falcon."

"The Maltese Falcon. Hi, Falcon." Haley let the puppy lick her chin.

"Yeah, my parents are kind of old-Hollywood freaks. They learned to speak English by going to the dollar theater and watching Humphrey Bogart and Cary Grant movies. *The Maltese Falcon* was one of their favorites. So, apparently, was *The Awful Truth*. I'm named after the actress Irene Dunne."

"Well," Haley offered, "look at it this way. At least you're not named after a comet."

"Good point," said Irene.

"Haley," Irene's mother called from down the hall. "Your father is here to pick you up."

"Thanks, Mrs. Chen," Haley responded, picking up her book bag.

As Haley gathered her things, Irene said, "Johnny's band the Hedon are finally playing next week at the station. From what Johnny says, they've gotten pretty good. You should come."

"Yeah, I heard," Haley said.

"Oh," Irene said. "Guess I'll see you there then."

"Sure," said Haley, noticing a framed drawing on Irene's wall that featured some of the same strange symbols as the graffitied wall at school. Smiling brightly as she headed out the door, Haley couldn't help wondering if maybe Irene was hiding something that even the *I Ching* couldn't reveal.

● ● ●

First things first, is Devon Haley's soul mate or is it Reese? Or is there someone else out there who will soon catch her eye?

As for Irene, the writing, or rather, drawing on the wall is clearly pointing to her being the Hillsdale vandal. So what is Haley going to do about it?

If you think Haley should talk to a teacher about the vandalism, flip to page 249. If instead you think Haley should take a step back from Irene and go check out the rock show, where Reese is likely to be, turn to page 238. Or, if you want Haley to stand by her friend no matter what, and maybe also get to know a certain cute photographer a little better, go to page 232.

The farther Haley gets into the school year, the more weight each decision carries. Based on the choice you make here, Haley could end up miserable and alone, or with everything her heart desires.

**Wear a mask long
enough, and you'll forget
what your face looks
like underneath.**

The day before Halloween, Haley received a text message from a private cell phone instructing her to dress up as "Autumn" for the party Richie Huber was throwing. She knew it was from Coco.

At first, Haley was reluctant to oblige. She didn't like being told what to do. But at four o'clock on Halloween, when the only other alternatives for the night seemed to be taking her little brother trick-or-treating or sitting at home and handing out trail mix and sugarless candy to a bunch of disappointed neighborhood kids, Haley reconsidered.

She walked the four blocks to 157 Oakwood Lane wearing her homemade costume, a dark brown leotard and olive green tights with aubergine, crimson and terra-cotta felt leaves pinned strategically to her hips and chest.

Haley knew she looked like an overgrown six-year-old. *I hope this party's worth the embarrassment,* she thought, ringing the doorbell as a floor lamp came sailing through one of the windows facing the street.

Great, Haley thought, wondering if perhaps this wasn't just a little too *Animal House* for a Montessori kid from Marin County, California. After all, the "entertainment" at the last party she'd been to in San Francisco was a three-piece folk band from UC Berkeley. Not exactly stuff that would provoke the neighbors to call the cops.

Haley considered turning around and heading back home. But then the front door opened and she was sucked into the crowd of upperclassmen.

As she made her way through the living room, scanning the sea of painted faces in search of anyone she knew, she realized she would've been thrilled to see even weird Shaun or squirrelly Dave Metzger from her Spanish class. Any sort of life raft would do.

Just as she was about to give up hope of finding anyone her own age, Haley spotted Sasha Lewis on the stairs near the formal dining room. Richie had her pinned against the wall and was whispering something in her ear, and from the look on Sasha's face, she didn't exactly like what she was hearing.

"Haley!" Sasha called out. "Over here."

Sasha's "Spring" costume was composed of a scoop-neck ivory leotard with a pale pink tulle skirt. A thin garland of rosebuds, gardenias and lilies was draped over her arm, and her blond hair was pinned away from her face by a halo of forget-me-nots. *She looks like Venus in the Botticelli painting,* Haley thought, suddenly self-conscious about her own hastily constructed costume.

"Have you met Richie?" Sasha asked Haley. "Richie Huber, Haley Miller."

"Hey, how's it going?" Richie screamed a little too loud, in order to be heard above the stereo. Haley was nearly knocked out, not only by his deafening voice, but also by the pungent smell of Kentucky bourbon on his breath.

"Here, let's get you something to drink," Sasha said, grabbing Haley's hand and pulling her away from Richie and toward the safety of the kitchen.

"What's the rush?" he slurred. "I'm thirsty too." Richie took a few steps after them, but Sasha swiftly navigated through the crowd, and Richie was too wasted to keep up.

"Thanks. You saved my life!" Sasha said to Haley when they'd finally lost him.

"Not before you saved mine," Haley fired back. "I don't know anyone here."

"Yeah, Richie throws a great party, but he often expects a price of admission from sophomores and freshmen, if you know what I mean. What are you having?" Sasha asked, opening the fridge. "We've got imports, domestic, some sketchy blush wine in a box, sparkling water and peach liquor."

"Just water for me," said Haley.

"Me too," Sasha agreed. "I never drink on Halloween. Too many crazies in the house. You make the perfect Autumn, by the way. Those colors are great with your hair."

"Really?" Haley asked. "I feel like nobody has any idea what I'm supposed to be."

"Trust me, once Coco and Whitney get here, there won't be any need to explain."

"Looks like they already are here," Haley said, pointing to Coco's sister's convertible parked in the middle of the front lawn.

"Well, well, well," said Sasha. "Come on. We'd better find Summer and Winter before Richie tries to teach them about season change." She led Haley out the back door of the kitchen and through the side yard, which was filled with costumed kids huddled around a keg.

Whitney Klein was also surrounded—by a handful of sturdy jocks who were hanging on her every word. As Whitney unfastened the tie of her Hawaiian-print kimono, the guys tried not to seem too eager. She opened the robe and flashed them, revealing her summery red string bikini underneath.

"See," said Whitney.

"I still don't get it," one of the guys said.

"You're a flasher?" another one guessed.

"I'm not a flasher!" Whitney exclaimed. "I'm Summer! Come on, guys. You know, of the four seasons? Like the hotel chain?"

"Let me see," Spencer Eton said, holding open Whitney's kimono and staring at her massive chest spilling out from the tiny triangle top. "I don't know, that's a tough one."

"I know what you mean," another guy said. "I like the whole tropical theme, but I just don't know if it says 'summer.' "

"Of course it does," Whitney sulked. "Look harder."

"Hey," Spencer said, "you know what might help? If we could see your tan lines."

"Okay, break it up," said Sasha, butting in and closing Whitney's kimono for her. "Summer is going to get frostbite if you two don't leave her alone."

"You're no fun!" someone yelled.

"Hey, Sash, are you going to let me come on spring break this year?" another one of the boys asked.

"Show us your Easter Bunny!"

"Bite me," Sasha said.

"I'd love to," Spencer said, sandwiching himself in between Sasha and Haley. He leaned in and whispered, "Next week, I'm hosting the biggest SIGMA to date. I want you both to be there since I'm . . . seriously interested in gambling my allowance."

"You'd better tell me the SIGMA password, too!" Whitney called out at high volume, forgetting that they were surrounded by what Spencer called undesirables.

"Come on, seasons," said Sasha. "Let's go find Coco." She led Haley and Whitney through the sea of beer guzzlers and back toward the house.

"Ugh, when did all these people get here?" Whitney whined, suddenly shivering.

"Didn't you bring a jacket?" Sasha asked. Whitney shook her head.

"You don't wear jackets in summer, Sash. Everyone knows that."

Haley was the first to catch a glimpse of Coco, who was standing on the back steps of the house, wearing a white satin bodysuit trimmed in white rabbit fur. She had on tall white fur boots and was carrying a white muff. It was total ski bunny meets *Dr. Zhivago*.

Wonderful, Haley thought. *She looks like a goddess, and I get to be the pile of yard debris someone's about to torch.*

"Aw, look at all of you. So cute," said Coco dismissively.

"If it isn't the fairest of the seasons," Sasha replied.

"Haley?" Reese said, stepping out from behind Coco. "Is that you? What are you doing here?"

"We needed a fall, baby," Coco said, snuggling closer to him. "She was the only redhead I could think of."

"Hi, Reese," said Haley, checking out his Scottish golfer costume. He was in plaid pants, a bright green polo and a red beret, and his golf club had a knit yellow pom-pom cover. Despite the silly duds, he still looked hot. "Great costume," Haley offered.

"Thanks," said Reese.

"And I'm his hole in one," Coco said, patting his chest.

"I saw *Caddyshack* last week," Reese explained, untangling himself from Coco. "It sort of put me in the mood."

"Hey, look, her leaves are falling," Coco said as a felt leaf from Haley's costume floated to the ground.

Haley shrugged. "Last-minute costume. Anyone know where I can find a ladies' room around here?"

"I'll show you," Reese offered.

Coco, annoyed that she no longer had Reese's full attention, said, "Aw, Reese honey, look. It's so cute. I think Haley stuffed her bra to impress you."

Haley tried to laugh it off, but Coco reached out and gave her chest a quick squeeze. Mortified, Haley pushed past her and ran into the house. Reese tried to follow her, but Coco tightened her grip on his arm.

"Leaving so soon?" Coco said, but Reese pulled himself free.

Inside the kitchen, Haley slipped on the beer-drenched floor. She scrambled back to her feet and thought, *Great, total humiliation is now complete.*

"Have a nice trip, see ya next fall," said one of the participants in the drinking games Olympics that was going on in the Hubers' kitchen.

Just ignore them, Haley kept telling herself as she hunted for the bathroom. The first door she opened turned out to be the laundry room, where a shirtless couple was making out against the washing machine.

"Sorry," Haley apologized. They stared at her blankly, and then the guy went back to shoving his tongue down the girl's throat.

Haley closed that door and then tried the next one. Bingo. The bathroom, and miraculously, it was free. She locked herself in to compose herself.

How could I have been so stupid? she wondered. *That's the last time I take orders from Coco De Clerq.*

Someone began knocking at the door.

"Just a minute," Haley said, splashing cold water on her face. When she finally emerged, Reese was standing there, waiting for her.

"Hey," he said.

"Hey," she answered, looking down at her beer-stained shoes. Another crimson leaf drifted to the floor at Reese's feet. He picked it up and reattached it to her shoulder, then brushed her hair away from her face.

"You know, fall's my favorite season," he said. It wasn't much, but it was enough to make Haley smile.

"Really?" she asked.

At that moment, the front door swung open and a motley crew from the Floods entered the living room, led by Johnny Lane, who was, not that surprisingly, dressed as himself.

"Hey, man," Johnny said to Reese while eyeing his costume. "Nice threads." He looked at Haley and added, "Is she your leprechaun?"

"Something like that," Reese said, putting his arm around Haley protectively. "Hey, I hear you guys are playing the Station next week?"

"Yeah, man. You coming?" Johnny's eyes were drifting, and Haley sensed what, or rather who, he was looking for.

Sasha Lewis was standing on the other side of a pair of double glass doors, and when Johnny finally spotted her, he started heading that way.

"Dude, I'm there," Reese said. "And let's hoop it up soon." He took Haley by the hand and led her through the party in the opposite direction, introducing her to everyone as if she were his date. At eleven, when she said she needed to go, he walked her home. After she checked in with her parents, Reese and Haley stayed up for another hour, talking on her porch.

"You shouldn't let Coco get to you," Reese told her.

"I know, but it's hard. I don't really know that many people here. And she practically runs the school."

"Well, you met a lot of people tonight."

"Yeah, but how many of them are going to talk to me once word gets out that Coco hates my guts?"

"She doesn't hate you," Reese said.

"Right. Publicly humiliating people is just her way of showing affection."

"Well, if you ask me, Coco's the one who needs to be stuffing her bra. Not you." Haley blushed.

Haley's father dimmed the lights on the porch twice, giving her the household's signal that it was time to come in.

"That means bedtime," she said, waiting, hoping Reese would kiss her goodnight. Instead, he stood up and squeezed her arm.

"Haley," Reese said.

"Yeah?"

"I'm . . . really glad you moved to Hillsdale." He let go of her arm.

"Me too," she said as Reese jogged across the lawn to his house. And for the first time, Haley actually meant it.

This is torture! The better Haley gets to know her new neighbor, the more she appreciates all his good traits. He's solid, stable, well mannered and, let's face it, ridiculously cute. Even when he is dressed up as a Scottish golfer. But come on, when is he going to make a move?

Coco, on the other hand, may just be the meanest person Haley has ever met. Coco De Clerq so clearly only wants what she can't have. And right now, that just happens to be Reese. So if Haley and Reese start spending more time together, will Coco keep trying to ruin Haley's life? And at some point will she finally succeed?

Wouldn't Haley just be better off avoiding Reese altogether as long as it means keeping Coco at bay?

If you think Haley shouldn't worry about what Coco wants, and want her to try to see Reese again at the Hedon's rock show, turn to page 238. If you think Coco isn't the type of person Haley should mess with, have her go to SIGMA, the private gambling party at Spencer Eton's house, on page 260.

It's party season in Hillsdale, and for Haley Miller, the invitations just keep rolling in. The only trouble is deciding which dates to keep and which ones to tear up and toss out with the trash.

Sometimes the only way
to get what you want
is to be willing
to walk away.

"What do you think it means?" Annie asked, holding up a copy of an e-mail that had been passed around at school that day.

"I don't know. Maybe it's some sort of code," Haley said, staring out the window in Annie's bright yellow bedroom, her mind someplace else.

"But all the clues we need to figure out the location and the password for SIGMA are supposed to be right here," Annie said. "So why can't we figure it out?"

Because maybe we're not supposed to, Haley felt like saying to her.

For as long as Haley had known Annie—in other words, since the first day of school—Annie had been babbling on about SIGMA and how great it would be if they could just get in. At this point, Haley didn't mind if she never heard the word *SIGMA* again.

Of course, things had only gotten worse after Richie Huber's Halloween party. Annie had dressed up as a unicorn and turned up at Haley's house, begging her to take her. But the last thing Haley wanted to do was crash an upperclassman's party, with a guest, when she wasn't even officially invited. So she'd lied and told Annie she wasn't feeling well. And ever since, Annie hadn't let her hear the end of it.

Missing out on one of the biggest parties of the year had made Annie that much more determined to gain entry into SIGMA. So while Haley just wanted to forget that the club existed, she knew Annie wouldn't stop nagging her about it until they'd figured out the password.

"Maybe we should ask Dave Metzger for help?" Haley said, looking at Annie. "He's pretty good at solving riddles."

"No way," said Annie. "I'm not asking him over here. And I'm definitely not going to his house. His mom creeps me out."

"Have you ever listened to his podcast?"

"You mean 'Inside Hillsdale'?" Annie said with a raised eyebrow. "Try inside Dave's bedroom. That's where he broadcasts from."

"I think he's funny. I like the show," said Haley. She had gotten used to listening to the podcast after school.

"But he has the worst guests. Can you believe he once had my florist on the program?"

"He's asked to interview me," Haley said tentatively.

"What?" Annie demanded, sitting up on her bed. "Dave and I have gone to school together since kindergarten, and I've never once been asked to be on that show."

"I thought you didn't even like—" Haley tried to interject.

"And after two lousy months here, he picks *you,* just like that? Ugh! I never get to do anything! Not Richie Huber's Halloween party, not SIGMA, not the podcast!"

Wow, Haley thought. *She's obviously a bigger fan of "Inside Hillsdale" than she lets on.*

"You're not going to do it, are you?" Annie asked.

"I don't know. I haven't really thought about it yet," said Haley. Reluctantly, she picked up the SIGMA e-mail and began scanning it for clues. If there was one thing that could take Annie's mind off the podcast, it was the password for SIGMA. "It says here, 'For fifty-four vision . . . ,' " said Haley.

"Like that makes any sense," Annie complained. "My dad's an optometrist. There's no such thing as fifty-four vision. Believe me, I asked him."

"Well, what if it's, like, a fifty-dollar buy-in, and the game is on the fourth of this month?" Annie sat up. Haley studied the e-mail for a moment and then read the cryptic message aloud. " 'Trim the fat before trying to ante. It's a Texas Hold 'Em, without the toast.' "

"See! It's useless!" Annie cried, throwing herself back down on her bed.

"No, listen."

"Face it, Haley, we might as well just plan on heading to the mall with all the other losers that night."

" 'Trim the fat,' " Haley repeated absently.

"Just once, *once!* I would like to be able to come to school on Monday and feel like I actually *did* something over the weekend."

Haley pulled up a chair and sat down at Annie's computer. "Annie, how do you trim the fat?" she said as she began typing.

Annie frowned at her. "Find a good butcher?"

"Sure, that's one way. How else?" Haley asked, still typing.

"Liposuction?"

"Annie, come on. How do you trim the fat?"

"Well." Annie thought hard. "Diet and exercise?"

"Bingo," said Haley, pulling up a search engine

and cross-referencing dieting Web sites with the word *SIGMA*.

"Yeah, right," Annie scoffed. "I highly doubt the password for SIGMA is going to be buried in some food pyramid."

Haley paid no attention but kept combing through the sites until she landed on one about a low-carb diet. "Hold the toast," Haley said knowingly. Her eye was suddenly drawn to one column on the page. Something about the formatting didn't seem quite right. And suddenly, she knew why. Right there in the middle of a paragraph about refined starches was an encrypted sentence, printed upside down and in a peculiar font.

"Here it is," Haley said. " 'Seriously Interested In Gambling My Allowance.' That's it. SIGMA. It's got to be. And look, there's the address. Six-nineteen Bell Court. Twenty-one hundred."

"That's Spencer Eton's address," Annie said. "What's twenty-one hundred?"

"Nine o'clock," said Haley. "That's what time it starts. What did I tell you?"

But Annie just stared blankly at the screen. "I don't buy it," she said finally.

"What?" Haley gasped. She couldn't believe that after all Annie's whining about wanting to go, here was the SIGMA password right in front of her, and she was turning her nose up at it. "But it's right there!" Haley said.

"Yeah. That's the problem. It's too . . . obvious."

"So obvious that three minutes ago you were ready to give up the search?"

Annie began typing away at the keyboard. "Let me try something," she said, pulling up the search engine again and typing "Hillsdale, NJ," "Texas," "toast" and "SIGMA" in the search line. The first entry that popped up was for Adam's Steak House in downtown Hillsdale. Annie clicked through and discovered an interesting message filed under customer reviews.

The post was titled, "Supper Is Gross, Mr. Adams," and it read, "I ordered the sirloin strip the other night and asked the chef to trim the fat, but my steak still came to the table marbled with gristle. The only thing I could eat on the plate was the Texas toast. And even that was burned. We won't be coming back.—Herb Stanley, 619 Bell Court, Hillsdale." The time and date of the post was the fourth of November at exactly nine o'clock, nearly two days into the future.

"That's it," Annie said.

"Come on, that's not it," Haley said. "Talk about too easy."

"You just moved here. You didn't even know what SIGMA was until a few days ago. Trust me. This is the one I think we should try." Annie was firm. "We missed Halloween because of you. I heard Coco, Whitney and Sasha dressed up as the four seasons with Cecily Watson. Cecily Watson! I'm definitely not missing this."

Maybe Annie does have a point, Haley thought. *After all, she has been tracking SIGMA for almost a year. But then why hasn't she gotten in yet?* Haley also found it hard to believe that a simple engine search would yield the information they were looking for. She looked at Annie, then at the computer screen, then back at Annie, trying to figure out what to do.

● ● ●

SIGMA, the secret gambling party at Spencer Eton's house, is easily the event with the highest stakes of the semester at Hillsdale. So why is Haley so bored with the idea of it? Annie's hounding may have taken the fun out of finding the password, but if Haley does go to the party, will she surprise even herself and have a good time?

Speaking of, what's Haley's best shot at getting in? Should she just give up and let Annie use the password she found on the Internet? Or will Haley insist on using hers instead? And if they don't get into SIGMA, will Haley be able to put up with Annie's complaints?

There's still one other option on the table for Haley. She could forget about SIGMA entirely and take Dave Metzger up on his invitation to be interviewed on the podcast. It may not seem like the most glamorous option, but then again, with a little exposure, Haley could end up experiencing a whole different side of life "Inside Hillsdale."

Before Haley can be inducted into the secret gambling society, you're going to have to roll the dice. If you think Haley has found the right password, go to page 260. If instead you want to try Annie's luck, go to page 273. Alternately, to go to the Metzgers' to be interviewed, turn to page 252.

Whatever direction Haley goes in here will alter her life at Hillsdale considerably. Whether she's welcomed into the fold of the popular crowd, or she becomes locally famous after Dave's Web chat, you can be sure this will be the last afternoon Haley and Annie spend alone, moping around in one of their bedrooms.

Those who think money will buy anything often do anything for money.

"Jer-ree," Trisha moaned from the upstairs balcony of the Kleins' palatial home, her nonfat grande extra foam, half-caf cappuccino in hand.

"Is she always this testy?" Haley whispered as she and Whitney headed for the safety of Whitney's room.

"You should see her when she's having one of her low-blood-sugar attacks," Whitney said.

Trisha had just come back from one of her "privates"—i.e., a one-on-one Pilates session with a personal trainer—and she was still wearing her tight mint green leggings and matching Lycra tank top.

"But you promised," Trisha whined, showcasing her cleavage as she leaned over the pine balustrade.

Whitney frowned, looking at the off-white cardigan tied around Trisha's tiny waist. "That's my sweater," she said.

Downstairs, Jerry raised a finger to let Trisha know that he'd be another minute. "I don't want to hear it," he yelled sternly into the phone. "How many times do I have to explain to you the difference between peppermint and spearmint?" Jerry paused to listen, then shouted, "I'm in the breath spray business! Of course it matters!"

"Jer-ree," Trisha whined again, stomping her foot.

"I said I'd be right there!" Jerry called, polishing off his vodka and club soda.

"Fine!" Trisha pouted, stomping into the master bedroom and slamming the door behind her.

"To think, that woman might actually end up married to my dad," Whitney said once she and Haley were behind closed doors.

Compared to the basic layout and plain oak furniture in Haley's room at home, Whitney's bedroom seemed like a showroom at a department store. On the pale pink walls hung impressionist replicas. A champagne-colored velvet settee sat near the picture window, and across from the enormous canopy bed was a French country armoire, which housed, of all things, a flat-screen TV.

Only Whitney would defeat the purpose of owning a plasma screen by storing it in an armoire, Haley thought.

"Trisha as stepmother. That's a scary thought," Haley said.

"You have no idea," said Whitney, taking a candy bar from her backpack and gnawing on the chocolate nougat center. "Imagine if your dad had an affair, kicked your mom out of the house, froze all her accounts, and before the divorce was even final, asked a twenty-one-year-old waitress from the country club to move in with him?"

"I'd dye my hair blue and stop speaking to adults," Haley said.

Whitney took another bite of the candy bar. "If only blue was a good color on me," she sighed.

"If it makes you feel any better, Whitney, the statistics aren't in their favor. After five to seven years, twenty-one percent of couples who live together still aren't married. And forty-six percent of couples who live together before they get married end up getting divorced."

"See. You're so smart, Haley. Why can't I be more like you?" Whitney took another bite of her chocolate. "My dad would pay me if I brought home your grades. And I bet he wouldn't be dating a woman like *her,* either. Do you know how lucky you are?"

"Lucky to be ignored by my mom and dad, who've put me on the equivalent of parenting autopilot? I'm beginning to think being 'gifted' isn't such a gift."

Whitney sighed. "Face it, Haley. Nobody wants us."

"Whatever. There are only, like, thirty football players who would give up their spot on the team to go out with you." Haley paused and added, "Except for maybe Shepherd Smith, who I hear is gay."

"Who, Shepherd? Totally. We shop together on the weekends." Whitney polished off her candy bar. "I don't know what's wrong with me, Haley. I'm just not that into football players."

"Really?" Haley began. "I thought you were definitely a quarterback kind of girl."

"No way. Guys my age? Not my thing."

"So who do you like, then?" Haley asked.

Whitney sat down. "Well. Promise you won't tell?" Haley nodded. "I sort of have this thing for . . . older men."

"Like how old?" Haley asked.

"Like . . . forty-two."

"Whitney!"

"What? It's not like I'm seeing him. He's my dad's business partner. He has dinner over here once a week. Uh, and he's sooo cute. He has this salt-and-pepper hair and he wears these glasses and pinstriped suits that are just . . . adorable."

"I guess," Haley said, plopping down on the bed. "It just seems weird is all, especially since your dad's dating Trish." At the mere mention of Trisha's name, Whitney jumped up, ran to her closet and began compulsively sorting through her drawers.

"Um, are you okay in there?" Haley called out.

"Yeah, I just have to do a periodic closet check after I stay with my mom. You know, to see what Trish has stolen." Whitney emerged a few seconds later. "I knew it."

"What is it?"

"She took my favorite pair of white jeans!" Whitney cried. "That skank. Now if I ever get them back I'll have to burn them."

Whitney's purse suddenly began to vibrate and then started chirping out the latest boy band anthem. "Haley, would you mind getting that?" Whitney said. "I'm too upset to talk to anyone."

Haley grabbed the fringed white leather bag and dug around for the ringing phone.

"If it's Spencer, remind him he hasn't given us the details for SIGMA yet."

"What's SIGMA?" Haley asked.

"You'll see," Whitney said cryptically.

Haley looked at the pink bedazzled phone. "It's . . . Drew Napolitano," she said, reading the varsity quarterback's name and number on the screen.

"Don't pick it up!" Whitney warned.

"Okay," Haley said, setting the phone on Whitney's nightstand.

"That's, like, the fifth time he's called me today,"
Whitney said. "He won't leave me alone."

"Five times? Wow. He must really like you."

"Whatever."

"Jer-ree!" Trisha called out from the balcony
again.

"Ugh," Whitney groaned, turning on her stereo
and scanning the satellite radio stations to drown out
Trisha's voice. "I'd even listen to talk radio if it meant
not hearing Trish."

"Speaking of, what do you think of 'Inside Hillsdale'?" Haley asked.

"You mean that weird podcast?" Whitney said.

"Yeah."

"It's sort of creepy, don't you think? Some nerdy
kid in his bedroom, commenting on football games."

"He does interviews, too."

"That's even weirder, if you ask me," Whitney
said. "Sitting alone with him in his bedroom to talk
about what, his crush on you? Ew."

Haley decided now wasn't exactly the best time
to mention that Dave Metzger, the host of the podcast, had recently asked her to be interviewed on the
program. Somehow she sensed Whitney wouldn't ap-
prove.

While putting away a stack of clean laundry the

housekeeper had left on her dresser, Whitney freaked. "Oh my God. She took my purple lace thong? I can't believe that woman hooks up with my father wearing my underwear. That's it," she said. "I'm calling my mom."

Whitney tossed her ivory silk nightgown, a pair of jeans, a yellow tank top, a sweater and the contents of her bathroom counter into a small leather carrying case. She picked up her cell phone, turned to Haley and said, "Come on. We're leaving."

"Sure," Haley said, relieved to be escaping the Klein household. For once, she realized, Coco had been right. It *was* Dysfunction Junction at the Kleins'. Of course, Haley still hadn't met Mrs. Klein.

Whitney's mother Linda took yet another drag off her cigarette as she drove the aging yellow luxury sedan back to her apartment. "So," she asked. "Has your father lost any more weight?"

"Mom!" Whitney pleaded. Her mother had mercifully held her tongue for the first ten minutes of the car ride, but now she was practically bursting with questions.

"Well, is he on that diet again or what? I bet he still farts at the dinner table, doesn't he?"

"I refuse to talk about Daddy and his fiancée with you."

Linda Klein simultaneously slammed on the brakes and the gas, throwing Haley against the backseat.

230

"So they're engaged now?" she asked as Haley buckled her seat belt. "Is that it?"

"I don't know," Whitney said, lowering her gaze. "He bought her a ring."

"And you were afraid to tell me? What for? You don't have to worry about me, Whitney." Her mother laughed nervously. "I'm fine. Just fine."

"You know what the doctor said, Mom. Stress isn't good for you."

"Yeah, well, what the hell does he know?" her mother asked as she crossed the train tracks, revved the engine and headed toward her shabby apartment complex in the Floods.

What have I gotten myself into? Haley wondered.

● ● ●

Well, no wonder Whitney is such a mess. Her home life has all the stability of a shaken-up can of soda. The question is, will Haley stick around to witness the inevitable explosion?

Then again, Haley's friendship might be a good influence on Whitney. That is, if Whitney's chaotic life and bad habits don't corrupt Haley first.

If you think Haley should distance herself from such a mixed-up girl, have her make an audio cameo appearance on "Inside Hillsdale" on page 252. If you want Haley to continue to be a friend to Whitney, send her to SIGMA at Spencer Eton's house on page 260.

From barely friends to
thick as thieves.

On the day a kid from the Floods nicknamed the Troll was falsely accused of vandalizing the school, Shaun turned himself in to Principal Crum.

"Dude may be a freak, but I can't let him take the fall, or should I say credit, for my work," Shaun had said to Haley and Irene as they walked him to the principal's office.

Crum ended up going easy on Shaun because he said coming forward showed "character." Of course, in Shaun's case, no one was ever sure if what he had was weird personality character or strong moral fiber character, but either way, he only got a week's detention and two Saturdays helping the janitors pressure-wash the school.

Devon, Shaun's neighbor and a photography student at an art school in New York, who worked at Jacks, the local thrift store, came to document the masterpiece before the sandblasting commenced. Irene and Haley were there too, since they had volunteered to help. The four of them managed to scrub the wall clean in a single afternoon.

"Seems like such a waste, doesn't it?" Haley said once the graffiti was gone.

"Why?" said Irene. She watched as Shaun rinsed the last of the paint down a storm drain.

"Well, why not just paint on canvas?" Haley asked.

"Maybe he wasn't looking to make a permanent statement." Irene wandered over to where Shaun was cleaning their wire scrub brushes and said something that made him laugh. He squirted her with the hose, then rinsed the paint and grime from her feet.

Suddenly, Haley got it. She couldn't believe she hadn't realized it before. What Shaun had painted on that wall was a declaration of his feelings for Irene, along with the frustrated conclusion that her heart already belonged to someone else. And that someone, Haley knew, was Johnny Lane.

On the walk home, Devon took pictures of bridges, stop signs, moving cars, traffic lights, birds, dandelions on the side of the road, even Shaun and Irene. Mostly, though, he took pictures of Haley.

"So is that thing attached to your face?" Haley finally asked, pointing to the camera.

Devon lowered it, letting the 35mm hang by its strap. He was cuter than Haley remembered, maybe even cuter than Reese Highland, her next-door neighbor and sometime crush. Devon had long, wavy hair, full lips and firm, tanned biceps that stretched the sleeves of his bright blue T-shirt. Haley felt herself becoming nervous. She almost wished he'd start taking pictures again so they wouldn't have to speak.

"How did you get into photography?" she asked, distracted by the awkward sound of her own voice.

Devon kicked a rock, sending it skipping across the road. "I don't know. My mom told me I took a camera apart when I was four, just to see how it worked."

"It's good you know what you want to do," Haley offered. "I wish I did. Had a hobby, I mean."

"I'm sure you'll figure it out."

Great, Haley thought. *Now he thinks I'm an immature idiot without any interests.*

Devon looked at her and asked, "Irene said you just moved here?"

"Yeah, from California," Haley said, trying to sound breezy.

"Really?" said Devon. "I lived in Portland until last year."

"No way!" Haley grabbed his arm a little too enthusiastically. Letting go, she added, "We were just north of San Francisco. My parents used to take us camping in Oregon every year."

"Do you miss the West Coast?" he asked.

"Sometimes," Haley said. *Yeah, like always,* she thought. "So what do you do with all those pictures?"

"It's mostly for school," said Devon. "But I've published a few."

"Really? Where?"

"You ever heard of *The Mission*?"

"Get out!" Haley gasped. "I love that magazine."

"I sent something in during fall open submissions last year. They've been doing this thing where if they publish your stuff, you get a pair of tickets to San Francisco."

Haley had stopped listening after the phrase *pair of tickets to San Francisco.* It had been months since she'd seen Gretchen and all her friends out West. The thought of a free trip to her old hometown was almost too much to bear. "Are they still doing that?" she asked.

"Sure. The deadline for submissions is next week."

Next week, Haley thought. *Maybe there's still time.*

"Hey, are your parents home?" Devon asked Shaun as they caught up to him and Irene.

"Nah, man. They're at the lake," Shaun said.

"Well, you thinking what I'm thinking?" Devon asked.

"I don't know, brother. Are you thinking about a banana-and-mayonnaise sandwich?" Shaun put his hands on his substantial gut and growled. " 'Cause I sure am."

"Who's up for a dip in Shaun's pool?" Devon asked, looking specifically at Haley.

"Sure," Haley said. Irene shrugged.

Shaun led the way onto a tree-lined street and up a long, sloping driveway. As they reached the last bend in the drive, Haley glanced up and saw a large modern house with a flat roof, Asian-inspired land-scaping and entire walls made of glass.

"Shaun, you live here?" she asked, gaping at the pristine grounds.

"Let me guess. You thought he was from the Floods?" said Irene.

"Kind of," Haley admitted.

"Last one pulling water gets no banana mayo," Shaun said, peeling off his shirt.

"Only Shaun would think that was a punish-ment," Devon said, taking Haley by the hand and leading her toward the pool. With her hand securely in Devon's, Haley momentarily forgot about San

Francisco and Gretchen. And she definitely forgot all about Reese.

• • •

It's a good thing Haley and Irene gave up their Saturday to help Shaun. What's a little hard labor when you've got a cute photographer by your side?

Now that Haley and the talented Devon have bonded over their West Coast roots, what's next for these two? With Devon in the picture, not to mention taking Haley's picture, will she finally forget about her unrequited crush on Reese? Or will her neighbor keep her from letting Devon or anyone else in?

And what about that contest in *The Mission*? Will Haley figure out a way to win those tickets to San Francisco? Will she do whatever it takes to be reunited with her old friends? Even if it means endangering new friendships in the process?

If Devon and San Francisco are too tempting to resist, turn to page 279. If you think winning that contest is a long shot and, anyway, think Haley is better off with Reese, send her back home to page 294.

Haley's being pulled in different directions right now. It's up to you to figure out the right path for her.

Guys are just
more appealing when
they've got an instrument
in their hands.

"Hey, Haley. Awesome boots," Sasha said when they bumped into each other in the will-call line at the Station.

"Thanks," Haley said. She was wearing the cowboy boots she'd picked up on her family's summer cross-country road trip, with a short corduroy skirt and a slouchy cardigan. Since she'd slept in braids the night before, her long auburn hair was full of loose curls.

Sasha was also looking very bohemian, in vintage jeans, a halter top made from a printed silk scarf, and a mohair shrug. "I'm dying to finally see these guys play," she said.

"Me too," Haley agreed. "With Johnny in the band, how could they not be good?"

The Station, Sasha explained while they waited in line, had formerly been Hillsdale's train depot. The building had remained abandoned for more than a decade until a couple of recent college grads had thrown up some lights, new wiring and a stage. Now hipsters from all over the tristate area made the once-a-week trek to the Station's Localpaloozas, a revolving showcase of emerging indie rock bands.

As they reached the front of the line at will call, Haley caught a glimpse of the girl taking tickets. "Irene?"

"You're not on the list," Irene said, suspiciously eyeing Haley.

"Lewis plus one," said Sasha, grabbing two tickets and handing one to Haley. "Come on," she said, taking Haley by the hand and dragging her toward the entrance.

Haley looked over her shoulder and shrugged at Irene. "See you inside," she called out, but Irene didn't seem to care.

"You want something to drink?" Sasha asked once they were inside.

"Sure. Like a soda?"

"Or like a beer." Sasha waited for Haley's reaction.

Haley looked at the bouncer standing near the door. "Won't someone see us?" she asked.

"If it seems sketchy, we dump them."

"Okay," Haley said as Sasha left in search of booze.

The lights dimmed and kids began pushing toward the stage. Haley glanced up at the high ceilings and the wooden rafters crisscrossing overhead. From behind the black velvet curtains hiding the stage came the sound of buzzing amps, electrifying the room.

Sasha finally reappeared, carrying two plastic cups, and handing one to Haley. "Just in time," Haley said.

● ● ●

If you think Haley should drink, keep reading below. If you want her to stay dry, go to page 245.

● ● ●

Haley took a sip of the frothy cold beer. She wasn't impressed. *Why does everyone make such a big deal about beer?* she wondered.

The curtains rose and a deep bass line burst forth from the stage. Layered over it was one screaming guitar, then another. Finally the drum beat kicked in. Johnny and the band were silhouetted onstage by a blinding white light behind them. Sasha started to dance uncontrollably. Haley felt herself swaying too, as Johnny's voice rose above the music.

"We are the Hedon!" he screamed, and the crowd erupted.

The lights turned purple, and the band, dressed in their signature fitted white collared shirts and skinny black ties, were fully revealed, writhing onstage. Johnny thrust his head toward the mike, belting out lyrics as he stomped his foot in time to the beat. Before Haley knew it, she had finished half her beer.

"Hey, isn't that Reese?" she asked Sasha, pointing to a head in the crowd.

"Yep, Natural Highland," Sasha said.

"What do you mean?" Haley asked.

"Didn't you know? I thought everybody did. Reese doesn't drink."

He approached them, smiling—that is until he saw the blue cup in Haley's hand.

"You been here long?" Haley asked.

"Nah, I just got here," he said, still eyeing Haley's cup.

"You okay?" Haley asked.

"I should go say hi to Coco and Whitney," he said. "I'll catch up with you guys later." Reese made his way through the crowd toward Coco, who was only too happy to see him. Haley watched as Coco wrapped her arms around Reese. He didn't exactly pull away.

*　　*　　*

Ninety minutes later, Johnny and the band disappeared from the stage. Sasha grabbed Haley's arm and led her through the crowd. "Come on," she said. The audience was still cheering for an encore.

Haley looked around for Reese, and finally saw him walking out the front door, holding hands with Coco.

Crushed, Haley reluctantly followed Sasha downstairs to the pit, a charmless room in the basement, where Toby, the Hedon's dark-haired drummer, was busy packing up bags, while Josh, the pale, lanky bassist, took a swig from his whiskey bottle.

"Hey," Johnny said, looking up at Sasha.

"We'll be right back," Sasha whispered to Haley as Johnny took her hand and led her to a back room.

Great, Haley thought. *I gave up Reese Highland for this?*

"Great set," she said, trying to make conversation with the remaining band members.

"You thirsty?" Josh asked, holding up his whiskey bottle.

"No thanks," said Haley. "I've had enough for tonight."

At that moment, Irene pushed through the door carrying a case of bottled water. "Here," she said, dropping the water on the table with a thud. "I'm covering for Shaun tonight." On her way out, Irene gave Haley a dismissive look. Haley heard her mutter "Groupie" as she headed back up the stairs.

What's her problem? Haley wondered.

Luke, the second guitarist and—Haley thought—the second-cutest member of the band after Johnny, was sitting in the corner, smoking. He was tall and blond, with piercing green eyes.

"What are you getting into tonight?" he asked, looking at her.

Haley shrugged. "I've got school tomorrow. We just stopped by to say hello."

"That's too bad," Luke said, still staring at her.

Sasha suddenly reemerged from the back room. "We have a soccer game after school on Friday. You guys should swing by," she announced, grabbing a bottle of water and dragging Haley back upstairs.

"See ya," Luke called out, as Haley stared over her shoulder at him.

● ● ●

Unfortunately, Haley seems to have really blown it with Reese. He clearly wasn't impressed with her antics at the Station. In fact, Haley's drinking seems to have driven him straight into the arms of Coco De Clerq.

So has Haley lost Reese Highland for good at this point? Is she better off just forgetting him and distracting herself with someone like Luke? Maybe an older guy is just what Haley needs right now. Then again, Luke doesn't exactly seem mature.

To see if Haley can repair her friendship with Reese,

go to page 294. If you think Haley and Sasha should stick with the rocker crowd, turn to page 285.

A lot can happen when you pair good girls and bad boys. But before you send Haley off in search of trouble, you'd better make sure she's ready to handle it.

STAY DRY

Just because you're at a rock show doesn't mean you have to party like a rock star.

"Here you go," Sasha said, coming back with two plastic cups of frothy cold beer.

"I think I'll pass," said Haley. "It's a school night."

"Sure," Sasha said. Suddenly, she squealed as Spencer snuck up behind her. "Spencer, you can't do that!"

"Is that for me?" he said, reaching for one of the beers and gulping it down in a single chug. Haley saw that Coco and Whitney had just arrived and were pushing their way to the front of the crowd.

"Ahhh, the great refresher," Spencer said after polishing off the beer. "Come on, Sash, we've got to get refills before the show starts. You don't need anything, do you?" he asked Haley, looking at her empty hands. He clearly preferred not to associate with people who weren't in the drinking club.

"No thanks," Haley said. "I'll meet up with you later," she said to Sasha.

"Totally," Sasha said, holding Spencer's hand and heading backstage.

Left alone, Haley made her way through the crowd and back to the ticket booth, where Irene was just hanging up the SOLD OUT sign. Haley could hear the sound check and knew she didn't have much time. She knocked on the glass.

"Hey there," she said. "You done yet?"

"What are you doing?" Irene said, though she did seem vaguely happy to see Haley. "I thought you were off turning into, like, a Sasha Lewis clone."

"You mean like this?" Haley asked, lifting an imaginary glass to her mouth and pretending to chug.

"So they're getting wasted when they could be listening to the making of a legend?" Irene said, locking the register drawer. "That's a travesty."

"Haley?" a guy's voice asked.

Haley turned around to find Reese Highland standing behind her. Surprised, she felt her cheeks growing warm.

"I've been looking for you," he said.

"Figures," Irene mumbled.

"Hey, Irene," said Reese.

She nodded at him. "Look, the show's about to start. You two should go inside. You don't want to miss it."

"You're coming with us, aren't you?" Haley asked. Irene seemed surprised that Haley wanted to include her, especially now that Reese was around.

"Yeah," Reese said. "Come on."

Irene looked skeptical.

"Here, follow me," she said finally, opening the side door of the ticket booth. Reese took Haley's hand and they followed Irene through the booth and up a spiral staircase. At the top, high in the rafters, was a crow's-nest with two of the best seats in the house.

Irene sat in one chair and Reese sat in the other and patted his knee, offering Haley his lap. As Haley took her seat, snuggling up against Reese, the curtain rose, and she felt that no matter how Johnny and the Hedon played, this was going to be a perfect night.

● ● ●

Sometimes what you want falls right into your lap. And then other times, you fall into the lap of someone you want. Reese Highland just redefined the term VIP seating.

Haley certainly scored big in this round. But what happens next? If Haley and Irene continue to be friends, will Reese just as quickly fall back out of Haley's circle?

If Haley chooses Reese instead, will that mean the end of her friendship with Irene?

If you think Haley's bond with Irene is more important than her crush on Reese, go to page 279. If you think Haley cares more about Reese than Irene, turn to page 289.

Unfortunately, friends and boyfriends aren't always a natural fit. Choosing to spend time with one may take you away from the other. So what's it going to be in this round, love or loyalty?

The road to the principal's office is paved with good intentions.

At first, Mr. Von had asked Haley only a few gentle questions about Irene. He wondered how Irene was doing in her other classes and if his was the only one she regularly skipped. But before Haley knew it, his questions grew more complex, and she was suddenly unspooling all the evidence against her friend in a few guilty breaths.

Haley regretted what she had said almost instantly. Mr. Von just patted her on the arm and reassured her that she had done "the right thing." He said he didn't believe that Irene was responsible for the vandalism either but added that it was his duty as a teacher to go to Principal Crum.

Haley wanted to die. She couldn't believe she hadn't at least gone to Irene first to ask her about the graffiti before mentioning it to Mr. Von. And now, of course, it was too late.

Irene would be questioned. Her parents would be called. She might even get suspended. And almost certainly, she would never speak to Haley again.

Haley spent the first two periods that day hiding out in the girls' bathroom. By the time she screwed up the courage to come out and face Irene, it was nearly lunchtime and Irene was nowhere to be found.

Over the course of the day, thanks to gossiping classmates, Haley was able to piece together what had happened. When Principal Crum had questioned Irene, she had refused to say anything, even after her father arrived from the Golden Dynasty and pleaded with her to defend herself.

Eventually, Principal Crum had decided it would be best if Irene gave some thought to the severity of the charges against her. She was instructed to go home and not come back to school until she had something to say about the graffiti.

It only took until one o'clock that afternoon for Shaun to come forward, and he said the only reason it took that long was that he'd fallen asleep in study hall and hadn't heard until after lunch that Irene was in trouble.

Shaun took Principal Crum to his locker to show him his sketchbooks and the early drawings he had made when he was composing the mural. He then told Principal Crum where he could find the cans of leftover spray paint.

After Shaun finished confessing, Principal Crum's only question was "Why?"

"Hey, man, why does the lion roar?" Shaun had said. "There's that little itch in the back of your throat, and you just gotta scratch."

Because Shaun had turned himself in, and because he promised Principal Crum that he would never again deface school property, he received a relatively light sentence, including helping the janitors pressure-wash the building on two consecutive Saturdays.

Even after Irene was vindicated, she still didn't come to school for the rest of the week. Haley knew it was to prove a point.

When Irene did finally come back to class, she asked Mr. Von to move her to the other side of the art studio so that she was no longer sitting anywhere near Haley Miller.

Haley tried to apologize, but it was no use. For the rest of the semester, as far as Irene Chen was concerned, Haley Miller didn't exist.

● ● ●

Way to kill Haley Miller's chances at a social life. Maybe you can do better on your second try.

Hang your head and go back to page 1.

Some of us only get fifteen seconds of fame.

Dave faded out the volume on the Pixies' "Here Comes Your Man" and said softly into his mike, "Welcome to the podcast. This is 'Inside Hillsdale,' and I'm your host, Dave Metzger. I have with me this morning a mystery girl you may have noticed passing you in the halls in the past few weeks. New student in the Hawks' sophomore class Haley Miller is here.

"Haley moved to the great Garden State with her family back in August. She comes to us from California. Her father is an adjunct professor in the film department at Columbia University, and her mother is with Armstrong & White, a legal firm specializing in environmental issues.

"Haley's favorite color is blue. She is a Gemini. And she enjoys sailing, go-cart racing and long walks on the beach.

"She also just happens to be the girl who sits next to me in Ms. Frick's third-period Spanish class.

"Good morning, Haley. Or should I say, *hola*?"

"Hi, Dave," Haley said, leaning into her mike. She felt a little weird being alone with Dave Metzger in his bedroom. Maybe that was because Dave's mother had insisted on leaving the door cracked and demanded that they "keep one foot on the floor at all times." Whatever that meant.

"Haley, tell us. What was your first impression of Hillsdale?"

Haley tried to recall. "Um, my family drove cross-country to get here, so we'd been in the car for two and a half weeks. I wasn't exactly in the best shape to be forming first impressions."

"Take us back to that moment, Haley. How did you feel?"

"Um, I guess I felt sweet relief? Followed by the sneaking suspicion that Hillsdale's one of those towns that's too perfect for its own good."

"Interesting," Dave said, stroking his chin. "You think we've got secrets."

"All I'm sayin' is, what's the mayor hiding under

that heavy tweed coat?" She raised an eyebrow at Dave.

"Don't be so suspicious of heavy fibers, Haley. You haven't lived through an East Coast winter yet."

Haley was surprised by Dave's on-air transformation. Normally, he was what you'd call squirrelly. But the minute he picked up his mike, his voice lost some of its tinny nervousness and his whole body just seemed to relax. For once, Haley noted, Dave actually looked somewhat comfortable in his own skin, and maybe even, she thought, kind of cute.

"You Jerseyans with all your talk of 'ice storms' and snow chains—you don't scare me," she said.

"One word for you, Haley. *February*. You'll be turning tail and goin' back to Cali in no time."

"That's big talk for a kid with an inhaler strapped to his belt," Haley replied.

"Oh, she's saucy. I like it," Dave said. "We've got Haley Miller for the hour, folks. But first, a brief message from one of our sponsors."

Dave picked up a stack of blue notecards on his desk, cleared his throat and began reading. "Is your room a disaster zone? Does it seem like the lawn is growing faster than you can mow it? Are your parents after you to take out the trash . . . again? Well now you, too, can get your chores done on time without burning precious daylight. For a mere six dollars an hour, freshman Ryan McNally will tackle all of your household duties for you. Why spend your after-school free time washing cars and windows, when you could be playing video games, hanging out with friends or talking on your cell phone? Ryan is available weekdays from three p.m. to five-thirty p.m., meaning parents who work normal business hours will never be the wiser. So make your mom and dad proud. And call Ryan McNally, 201-666-0306."

Dave set down the cards. "We're back, coming to you live from Casa Metzger with sophomore Haley Miller. Haley, before we continue, I'd like to ask you my version of Marcel Proust's infamous questionnaire."

"Shoot," Haley said.

"If you could invite any six people at school to sit with you during lunch, who would they be and why?"

"Tough one. I guess I'd start with Sasha Lewis, because she's got such great style. Then Annie Armstrong, the best campus guide a newbie could ask for."

"Amen to that," Dave said, leaning into his mike.

"Next, my neighbor, Reese Highland. He actually says hi to me in the halls, so I could be reasonably sure he'd show up. Then the large and in charge senior Darla and her ninety-eight pounds of freshmeat, Russ Tweeter." Haley added in a conspiratorial whisper, "I'm sort of sickly fascinated when they make out on the bus." She paused for a second to gather her thoughts. "And finally, I'd add the mature perspective of history teacher slash soccer coach Travis Tygert."

"Haley, you arrange that lineup and 'Inside Hillsdale' is there," Dave said, taking a sip of water before continuing. "What would you most like to change about yourself?"

"Remember how you told me to be here at nine-thirty and I showed up at ten-oh-two?"

"Ten-fifteen, but go on."

"I have a tardiness problem. But I'm working on it."

"Real-life hero?"

Haley's tone became serious. "That would be my mother, Dave. And if you're listening, Mom, I'm sorry about that window in the garage. I swear I wasn't trying to sneak out."

"Qualities you look for in a friend?"

"Loyalty, courage and the ability to tell a good story."

"Qualities you look for in a boyfriend?"

"A sense of humor, a great music collection and, of course, dancing skills."

"We're streaming audio live from Casa Metzger with sophomore Haley Miller. And we'll be taking your calls, right after this message from our sponsor."

Dave picked up the stack of blue cards and began reading again. "Flunking out of English, even though English is your first language? Need help on a term paper that's due . . . tomorrow morning? Don't sweat it. Thanks to a new exchange program with Ridgewood Academy, papers for all grades and subjects are now available for purchase, starting at a mere nineteen ninety-nine. Not only are these essays untraceable on the Internet, but they're from a prep school, and you know what that means. So if you're in need of an eleventh-hour thesis on the politics of G. B. Shaw's plays, or a thoughtful exploration of John Donne's religious sonnets, call Ryan McNally at 201-666-0306. Please note, some editing required. The views and opinions expressed here are not necessarily those of this podcast."

When it was all over, Haley couldn't believe she'd actually been dreading her interview with Dave. There were certainly worse ways to spend a Saturday.

The thing that surprised her most was how many people had phoned in during the hour to ask questions. But that was nothing compared to the next morning, when she opened her e-mail in box and saw forty-seven new messages. On Monday at school, she was approached by dozens of people she'd never even met before, all to congratulate her on the podcast. *Who knew so many people tuned in to the*

Internet? she marveled as yet another boy asked for her number.

In light of all the attention she was getting, Haley felt she should do something for Dave in return. *But what?* she wondered. And then she remembered the yearbook photo of Annie Armstrong taped above Dave's desk. And the comments he'd made before the podcast started about Annie's "uncanny ability to multitask."

Maybe there is something I can do for Dave, Haley thought as she fished around in her bag for Annie's number.

● ● ●

Haley's gone from new girl to It girl overnight, and now she's got half the boys at Hillsdale trailing around after her. With that kind of following, anything is possible. Haley could end up with everything she's ever wanted: the right invitations, the right guy and more friends than she can count.

Of course, she owes at least some of her good fortune to Dave Metzger.

Dave has clearly got a thing for Annie Armstrong. But unfortunately, he's too shy to ever make a move. If Haley leaves it up to chance, Annie and Dave will likely never get together. And if ever there were two people who deserved each other . . .

So should Haley take a moment to return Dave's favor by calling up Annie on his behalf? If so, send

Haley to page 319. If you think fame is fleeting and want Haley to enjoy the attention while she can, turn to page 289.

Sure, it's fun when everyone knows your name. But what's the point of popularity if you don't use your powers for good?

You can't change the hand you're dealt, but sometimes you can stack the deck in your favor.

On the night of the fourth, a horde of kids descended on Spencer Eton's house on Bell Court. Haley stood in line, directly ahead of Annie Armstrong, who was blatantly eavesdropping on conversations around them, trying to overhear some clue that would tell her which of the passwords they'd discovered online was the right one.

"What's the code?" Annie finally asked a boy standing in front of Haley.

"Why would I tell you?" The kid laughed and turned away abruptly.

"How many times have these idiots copied my homework or cheated off me in a test? And the one time I need the answer, this is what I get?" Annie said, seething.

She tapped the boy on the shoulder. "Remember math class? You owe me. What's the code?"

"Sorry," he said. "There's a little more at stake here than square roots, Annie."

"Come on," she begged. But he shook his head as they advanced one more place, putting him at the front of the line.

Spencer paused for a moment. "Password?" he asked, pointing at the boy.

"Seriously Interested In Gambling My Allowance," he whispered. And with that, the door opened and he entered the house.

"I'm waiting," Spencer said, as Haley stepped up. She repeated the phrase, and Spencer waved her inside. As she walked past him, she overheard Annie say, "Supper Is Gross, Mr. Adams."

"Sorry, folks, maybe next time," Spencer said, hanging a sign on the door that read, SIGMA CLOSED. So Annie Armstrong had used the cutoff phrase, Haley thought, glad to have made the SIGMA cut. Spencer shut off all the lights on the landscaped grounds and everyone on the lawn began to scatter. They knew they had less than five minutes to clear off the property before the Etons' two pit bulls started patrolling grounds. Besides, any hope of getting in next time would be dashed if Spencer or one of the other hosts caught them loitering now. Such was the power of the hosts of Hillsdale's highly exclusive gambling ring.

Haley felt a tickle in the back of her throat as she followed Spencer into the smoke-filled basement. The room had wood-paneled walls and ceilings, Moroccan carpets strategically scattered around the room, and a bunch of prep school boys in rumpled polo shirts and khakis sprawled out on leather couches with cigars in hand. A sampling of Hillsdale High's jocks, hipsters, divas and math geeks rounded out the mix.

Haley stood quietly, not sure where to place herself in the crowd.

"Oh, dude, sorry," a slit-eyed Matthew Graham, one of Spencer's many boarding school chums, apologized after dumping his bourbon and ginger on the antique rug.

"Don't worry about it," Spencer said, lounging in his leather armchair. "Ryan McNally's coming tomorrow. He'll clean it up."

"Right on," Matt said. "Freshman slave."

Spencer motioned for Haley to come over and join his inner circle of friends, who were seated around the flat-screen TV. It was muted and paused on a college football game, the winning play frozen just as the pigskin was about to land in the wide receiver's hands.

"Dude, just hit Play already."

"It's beautiful," Spencer said, admiring the game-winning moment preserved on the TV like a piece of fine art.

Haley had heard about this habit of Spencer's. He would freeze frame just as a ball was about to land in a player's hands, thus delaying gratification. His friends were constantly threatening to stop watching major sporting events at his house. But who were they kidding? Where else could they go that would have multiple flat-screens on hand, open bars, next-day maid service and not a parent in sight?

"Mad Max," Spencer called out, chewing the end of a Cuban cigar.

"Reefer keeper," Max answered, sipping his bourbon on the rocks. "What do you say we fire up that bowl again? This room is starting to stand a little too still."

"Ask and ye shall receive," Spencer said, packing another bowl. After firing up his lighter, he put the pipe to his lips and pulled in a puff of smoke as deeply as he could, holding for a count of six. His expression went slack. Coco, who had just arrived with Whitney and Sasha, walked into the room and said, "So, Spencer, is that the face you make after you hook up? Complete and utter boredom?"

Spencer sat back in his chair and passed the bowl to Max. "Join me upstairs and find out."

"Keep dreaming," Coco said.

Haley, meanwhile, was practically mute. This was about as far from the cake-and-ice-cream socials she'd been to in California as she could get.

"So where's Reese?" Coco asked.

"Natural Highland?" Drew Napolitano said. "I think he's studying for some exam." Haley felt a knot in her stomach. Reese wasn't coming.

"No, that's okay, don't get up," Coco said, clearly annoyed that the boys weren't hailing her arrival.

"Marsh man, turn the music down," Spencer called out. His laptop was linked to the house's surround-sound speakers, and he was streaming satellite radio into the house. Spencer shoved a wooden folding chair toward Coco with his foot, a clear invitation for her to sit next to him. She didn't accept.

Even though Spencer had never looked hotter—he was in his scruffy old blazer with his shirttails untucked, his blond hair ever so slightly askew—Coco wasn't about to let him play her.

"Spence, this is killer weed," said Todd after taking a huge hit.

"Is that so?" Sasha asked.

"Sure, man. Weed keeps me loose."

"Yeeaaahh. Suuuurrrre. Riiiiggght," said Sasha.

"Dude, quit talking like that! You're freaking me out."

Shaun, a stocky kid with a blond mullet who wore combat boots, shoved aside some of the others and barreled toward a table, carrying a small jug of paint thinner. When someone offered him a drink, he said, "Nah, man, I'm good."

"Just how many people did you let in this time?" Coco asked, put off by what she considered less than desirable guests.

"Who cares? We're here," said Whitney, sipping on a heavily diluted gin and juice. As long as there was some sort of process of elimination and she was on the right side of the dividing line, Whitney was happy.

"Dude, he's got to let in the skanks and the shanks, else who's gonna lose?" asked Todd.

"Todd, how much money did you bring last time?" Sasha asked.

"Two hundred bucks."

"And how much did you owe Spencer when you left?"

"Sixty. But man, I'm feeling it tonight."

"Ladies and gentlemen, congratulations on your entry into SIGMA this evening," Jake Hutchins announced. He put on his dealer's visor and emptied out his book bag of playing cards, poker chips and assorted gambling paraphernalia on the six card tables Spencer had set up around the room.

"You know how it works," Spencer explained. "It's a fifty-dollar buy-in, tournament style. Winner at each table takes all."

"Just the way I like it—Hillsdale Hold 'Em," said Drew.

"Sweet," said the boy who'd gotten in behind Haley.

"Good to see you, man." Jake and Drew smacked and slapped hands in one of those complex hand-shakes that only professional athletes and twelve-year-old boys think are cool. "Sit here," Jake said, directing Drew to a spot between Coco and Whitney, who were already claiming their seats.

"By the way, we'd like to thank Spencer Eton for hosting tonight," Jake said. There was some obliga-tory but faint applause. "Remember to kick some money into the jar at the bar if you're drinking. And now, without further ado, let the games begin."

Spencer came over to Haley, guided her to his own private table and had her sit between him and Sasha. The other tables quickly filled up. Cards began shuffling and chips were doled out to players.

"Do you want some help?" Sasha asked, noticing the confused look on her face.

"You leave her to me," Spencer said protectively. "Haley, right? Why don't we play the first few rounds together, until you get the hang of things?" he said, putting his arm around the back of her chair.

"Benedict has the high card," said Spencer. "All right, Max, you're the button." Spencer handed the deck of cards to Max, who shuffled them as if he'd spent half his young life in a casino. Max let Sasha cut the deck and then suavely fanned them out in front of her. She clearly wasn't impressed.

After Sasha matched the blind and Spencer checked, everyone at the table slid the first round of chips into the center, forming the pot.

Then came the flop. Max burned a card, putting it in the discard pile, and flipped three communal cards faceup in the middle of the table.

"Two bucks," Spencer raised.

Matthew called it and raised again.

"I have the worst luck," Sasha said, and dropped her hand on the table, frustrated.

"Huh, just like the old man," said Matt. Spencer shot him a withering look.

"Cool it, man," he said.

"What's that supposed to mean?" Sasha asked defensively.

"My old man, he's lousy at cards," Matt said, and chuckled.

At the next table, Whitney was concentrating on her cards, as if staring at them would improve her hand. "Playing two," she said, placing two chips neatly on the table.

Raising the stakes gave Jake a rush of adrenaline, and he started bouncing his leg under the table. Coco placed two more chips in the pot.

"I'm always up for another round," said Coco,

locking eyes with Spencer at the other table. He broke the stare first. Straightfaced, Coco tapped her index finger on the table twice. "Check."

Back at Haley's table, Max stared at everyone, trying to get a read on their cards.

"Dude, cut it out," said Todd. "You're totally mind-raping me." He shivered and twitched. "Ecchh."

"I'm in," Max said.

Spencer paid one more chip with no comment. He didn't really have anything, but no one had any idea he was bluffing as long as he kept wearing that smug smile. Looking at Spencer's hand, Haley was more confused than ever.

"Four bucks," Drew raised.

"Making the call," said Spencer.

Over at her table, Whitney was trying as hard as she could to look serious, but her expression was so contrived, she looked like she was even less of a threat.

"Is it my turn?" she asked innocently. "I check," she said.

The whole table chuckled.

"You can't check when the person before you just raised," Coco explained harshly.

"Match it or fold," said Jake.

"And then when you fold, can you get me a beer?" Spencer called out from the other table.

"Get it yourself," Whitney said, coughing up four more chips. "I'm gold-digging."

"Per usual," said Coco, checking her cards. "In."

"You know, if I had to date a card, I think I'd date the king of diamonds," Whitney said, staring off into space.

"Of course you would, Whitney," said Coco. "He's got white hair and his own kingdom."

"Don't forget the diamonds," Whitney added.

Max raised again at his table. Spencer looked at Haley, then at their junk, and folded. "We'll get 'em next time," he said, winking at Haley and squeezing her shoulders before heading for the bar. Coco watched the way Spencer was acting with the new girl, and the look on her face made it clear she was jealous.

Todd was out too, along with all the others. The round had ended and the mountain of chips belonged to Max.

Over at Coco's table, she checked for the third time, staring greedily at the pot. But after looking at Spencer, she suddenly laid her cards facedown on the table and said, "On second thought, I fold."

Coco followed Spencer to the bar, came up behind him and whispered something in his ear. Haley watched from across the room. As Coco linked her arm with Spencer's and walked him back to the tables. She knew they'd been talking about her from the look on Spencer's face.

"*H-u-s-t-l-e-r,* hustler," Jake said, and went in with all his remaining chips. "Thirty-one bucks."

Drew paused. "All right, I'll call you," he said,

and pushed all his chips into the center of the pile. He stood up and walked away from the table, exhaling loudly, too nervous to sit and watch it unfold. The excitement was palpable at the sight of more than two hundred bucks in the pot.

"I'm all in," Whitney said proudly.

Coco smirked.

"Okay, flip 'em," Jake instructed.

Everyone watched to see what the cards held, while Whitney continued staring at Coco blankly.

"Queen high flush," Jake said confidently.

"I won!" Whitney yelled, and flipped over her cards. "King, queen, ace, two, three—all in a row, all the same color!"

"Maybe you go both ways, Whitney," Jake said, "but the ace of hearts doesn't."

"What do you mean? When did the rules change?" Whitney asked, devastated.

"Um, never?" Coco said as Drew walked back to the table and flipped over his cards.

"Oooohh . . . a boat," Jake said. "That hurts. Nicely done."

"Wooohooo!" Drew yelled.

"You'll get 'em next time, De Clerq, and then you'll give me some of that booty," Spencer joked, turning to walk back to the bar.

"You wish, Eton," Coco yelled back at him.

"Awww, yes!" the kid Haley had been in line

with screamed from another table, pumping his arms in the air. "I'm rich!"

"An orgiastic junket, man," Jake said to Spencer. The two guys high-fived as Spencer tossed Max a bottle of beer and came back to sit next to Haley.

"So, you want to go upstairs and get high?" he asked her, running his finger down the length of her arm. Haley looked at him. The attention was flattering. He was cute, rich, popular. Spencer had it all. And yet, something about the thought of going upstairs with him frightened Haley.

He brushed the hair away from her face and whispered in her ear, "Come to my room with me," insistently. His breath was warm on Haley's neck, and she caught a whiff of his aftershave.

● ● ●

Funny how the seedy underbelly of Hillsdale can be found in the nicest house on the best block of the most desirable street in town.

Haley seems to be in a bit over her head here, though. What exactly was going on between Coco and Spencer Eton at the bar? Was that just harmless flirting? Or were they really talking smack about Haley?

And what about Reese? Where was he tonight? Will Haley ever figure out a way to get closer to her neighbor?

To send Haley back to school in search of Reese,

go to page 289. To go upstairs with Spencer, turn to page 276. Alternately, you can send Haley home for a little down time with her family on page 294.

Now that the Hillsdale school year is well underway, it's time to decide whether Haley should partake of certain extracurricular activities. Of course, some of them won't exactly help Haley's transcript.

It's agonizing to watch someone try harder than they should.

As Annie and Haley reached the front of the line at Spencer's house, Spencer opened a latch and peered through a small window in the heavy oak door.

Haley watched as Annie rattled off their chosen password. "Supper Is Gross, Mr. Adams," she said confidently.

"That's it, folks. SIGMA is officially closed for tonight," Spencer announced. "Sorry, people, we've reached maximum occupancy. Better luck next time." He closed the window and turned off all the lights on the landscaped property, leaving the remaining crowd of rejects hanging out in the dark.

"Who said the cutoff phrase?" a guy wearing a black skullcap demanded. "Who the hell said, 'Supper Is Gross, Mr. Adams'?"

Haley watched the mob in fear, waiting for them to turn on Annie and her.

"We should fight back," Annie yelled, addressing the group. "It's a corrupt system!"

Haley tugged on Annie's sleeve, trying to get her to be quiet. But Annie took this as a sign of encouragement.

"Heck no, we won't go!" Annie shouted, pumping her fist in the air and climbing on top of a garden urn. At first no one joined in, but Annie persisted. "SIGMA, SIGMA, SIGMA!" she chanted, and the group of kids began to chime in. What had been an orderly line up the front walkway had morphed into an unruly mob of outraged teenagers scattered all over the Etons' property. As angry slurs were shouted at the house, the group seemed to be teetering on the brink of a full-blown riot.

"Down with Spencer Eton!" Annie exclaimed as if she were ready to lead the coup d'etat single-handedly.

● ● ●

After hearing the rebellious commotion on the usually quiet street, neighbors began peering through their windows. One by one, their outdoor lights switched on.

No one ever found out which neighbor called the police first, but the Hillsdale sheriff was notified that a riot was brewing in Hillsdale Heights.

When the cops arrived, Spencer was arrested, and though he later pleaded to lesser charges, thanks to Mr. Eton's connections with a local judge, Spencer was eventually shipped off to boarding school in Switzerland. SIGMA was suspended indefinitely. And everyone at Hillsdale blamed not only Annie Armstrong, but her new best friend, Haley Miller.

Time to start over. Hang your head and go back to page 1.

Smoke signals only work if there's someone looking for a sign.

Spencer led Haley up to his bedroom, which had navy blue walls, hardwood floors, and flannel linens on the bed. As soon as they were inside, he grabbed the dictionary on his nightstand. The innards of the book had been hollowed out, forming a secret compartment where a marbled glass pipe and a quarter bag were hiding.

Spencer packed a bowl for Haley first, then coached her through taking the first few hits.

"Nice, isn't it?" he asked.

"Yeah," Haley said, coughing profusely. Her throat and chest were on fire. "It's strong."

Haley lay back on the feather pillows and zoned out as Spencer packed himself a bowl, smoked it, then packed another and finished that. She was beginning to feel a bit dizzy when he finally curled up next to her, stroking her arm. More than anything, though, Haley felt weird.

"It's good, isn't it?" he asked, pressing himself up against her. He kissed her. His hands were all over her, creeping up her blouse, caressing the back of her neck, squeezing her thigh. Haley felt light-headed. None of it seemed real.

What did seem real, however, was the fist that kept pounding on the bedroom door. "Open up," a booming adult voice said. It was then that Haley realized that her shirt was nearly off. She fastened as many buttons as she could while Spencer threw the bowl and his bag of pot back into the hollowed-out dictionary and opened the window to air out the room.

"Open the door," the voice commanded. It didn't matter, though, since a uniformed policeman burst into the room.

"Who let you into my house?" Spencer demanded. "This is a private residence, and as far as I'm concerned, you're trespassing."

"Mr. Eton, we've had complaints from the neighbors," the officer said. "There are alcoholic beverages being served to minors on the premises. We found drug paraphernalia in the basement. I'm afraid I'm going to have to ask you to come down to the station."

"I'm not going anywhere with you. Don't you know who my father is?" Spencer said, reaching for his cell phone. Haley, on the other hand, was petrified at the thought of the call she would soon have to make.

• • •

When Haley's parents found out that Spencer Eton had been arrested for drug possession, underage drinking, serving alcohol to minors and, on top of all that, hosting an illegal gambling ring, Haley had some serious explaining to do. She tried to talk her way out of it pleading wrong place, wrong time, but Joan and Perry didn't buy it. Haley was grounded, not just for a couple of weeks, but for the rest of the semester.

Even worse, Haley's mother did some digging and uncovered all the major players in the SIGMA secret society. She even tracked down Mr. and Mrs. Eton, who were traveling in Peru, to let them know what their son was up to. SIGMA was suspended indefinitely and Spencer was shipped off to boarding school. In Geneva. Switzerland.

Haley, meanwhile, had to remain at Hillsdale with her new reputation: "The random stoner girl Spencer was having sex with when he got busted by the cops, whose mom turned everyone in."

Haley deserves another chance, doesn't she? Hang your head and go back to page 1.

278

THE MISSION

**Not every artist craves
public recognition.**

Haley tried to forget about *The Mission* magazine's
contest and its prize of two round-trip tickets to San
Francisco. But once Devon had mentioned it, it was
all Haley could think about. Not even a swim in
Shaun's infinity pool could clear her head.

She thought of the Golden Gate Bridge and the
scent of eucalyptus trees on the road to her old
house. Haley imagined taking Irene to visit Gretchen,
her best friend on the West Coast. It had been months
since Haley and Gretchen had seen each other. If she
and Irene went to San Francisco, they could all

finally hang out together and do the things Haley and Gretchen loved best, like going to Stinson Beach, taking the boat to Alcatraz, eating clam chowder from sourdough bread bowls at the pier and, of course, vintage shopping on Haight Street. Haley knew Irene would love that.

She just had to figure out a way to win that contest. *But how?* she wondered. Her fingers were starting to prune, so she climbed out of the pool and toweled off, leaving Shaun and Irene in the deep end. Devon had gone inside to get some lemonade, so Haley was alone on the patio. As she was wrapping herself up in a white terry-cloth bath towel, she noticed Irene's backpack sitting unattended. Her prized black sketchbook was peeking out of the top of the bag.

Haley, unable to control herself, lifted the sketchbook out of Irene's bag. *I'll just take a quick look,* she told herself. But for reasons that remained fuzzy to Haley for days afterward, she did much more than look. She tore out the best drawing she could find, a portrait of Johnny Lane, put it in her bag and then returned the sketchbook to Irene's backpack before anyone had noticed.

"You had enough?" Devon asked, carrying a tray of drinks through a large glass sliding door.

"I was starting to shrivel," Haley said, holding up her wrinkled fingers. "Besides, it's getting late. My mom'll start to worry." She gathered up her things.

"I can't tempt you with some lemonade?"

"Thanks, but I've got a big math test on Monday. I should really go home and study."

"It's Saturday, Haley," Devon said.

"I'm not really feeling well. Tell the others bye for me?" Haley asked, grabbing her bag and dashing through the door, before Devon could object.

First thing the next morning, Haley had Irene's drawing matted at the local art store so that it wouldn't be damaged en route to the magazine.

Irene is too modest to ever get published on her own, Haley told herself. *I'm doing her a favor,* she thought, repeating this mantra right up until the moment she addressed the padded manila envelope and dropped it in the mail.

Two seemingly endless weeks later, a package arrived in the Millers' mailbox addressed to Irene Chen, care of Haley Miller. Haley tore it open, her eyes scanning the page for any indication Irene had won.

Haley had to sit down. Irene's drawing had been selected for publication in the next edition of *The Mission.* Two open tickets to San Francisco were enclosed, and the letter said the issue would hit newsstands in a matter of weeks.

Haley was elated. Irene was good enough to be published. She was a real artist, and finally, her work would be recognized.

Not only that, but Haley and Irene would soon be on their way to San Francisco. Haley's two best friends would get to meet, and they could finally all hang out. She could hardly wait to e-mail Gretchen.

And then suddenly, Haley's excitement morphed into panic. *How am I going to tell Irene?* she wondered. More ominously, she thought, *What have I done?*

The next day at school, Haley took pains to avoid Irene in the halls. She skipped every class they had together and locked herself in a bathroom stall during lunch hour. Haley knew she couldn't disappear forever, but she needed time to figure out what to do.

Unfortunately, Irene and Haley were supposed to meet up with Shaun and Devon that afternoon after school. Haley found herself dreading the bell at the end of the day. As her last class drew to a close, she waited for the other students to leave before she gathered up her books, and then took extra time at her locker, stopping to ask a teacher about a homework assignment. When she couldn't stall any longer, she headed to the parking lot.

"Hey," Irene said when Haley finally arrived. "Where have you been?"

"Around," Haley said, unable to look Irene in the eye.

"I missed you in art class today."

"Oh, I had this thing."

Irene frowned. "What sort of thing?"

"A meeting with a college counselor," Haley lied. She scuffed the pavement with her low-top sneakers. "Irene, how come you don't show your artwork? I mean to someone other than our teachers."

"Not interested," Irene said matter-of-factly.

"But you're so good at it. I bet you could get a scholarship."

"Don't need one."

"Well, wouldn't it be cool to just share it with people? Like in a gallery or a magazine?"

"Absolutely not." Irene stared at Haley. "That would not be cool."

"Gotcha," Haley said. What she thought was, *This is going to be even harder than I thought.*

● ● ●

Poor Haley. In her own misguided way, she really had convinced herself she was helping Irene by submitting that drawing to *The Mission*. But in reality, Haley's main concern was the free trip to San Francisco. Now that she's recognized her own selfish motives, she feels awful. But that doesn't change the fact that she still has to deal with Irene.

If Haley tells Irene what she's done, will Irene ever speak to her again? If Haley doesn't tell her, won't Irene find out anyway? Is there any possible way out of Haley's current predicament?

If you think Haley should fess up and tell Irene about *The Mission*, turn to page 331. If you think Irene will never forgive her, and that Haley should tear up the tickets and pray Irene never lays eyes on a copy of *The Mission* instead, turn to page 304.

Sometimes, the worst thing that can happen to you is to get exactly what you want.

THE VAN

There's a reason parents are suspicious of vans in empty parking lots.

On the Thursday before homecoming, Haley and Sasha emerged from the locker rooms freshly showered and changed after winning their home soccer game and walked out of the building.

"See ya, Coach," Sasha called out, waving as Travis Tygert drove out of the parking lot, wearing his worn leather jacket and aviator sunglasses.

It's criminal for a teacher to look that good, Haley thought.

"Great job today, girls," Mr. Tygert said. "I'd stay and chat, but Annabelle's waiting."

Haley had met Mrs. Tygert a few times during practice. She was a pretty, petite blonde, and had been Coach Tygert's high school sweetheart. In Haley's mind, Mrs. Tygert was also one of the luckiest women on earth.

As Sasha and Haley reached the far end of the parking lot, they spotted the van that belonged to Luke, the second guitarist in Johnny Lane's band. He and Johnny were sitting with the doors open, listening to the stereo.

"Look who it is," Sasha whispered, nudging Haley.

Luke began to applaud. "Well," Luke said with a cigarette dangling from his bottom lip. "I never would've pegged you two for soccer stars, but I must say, you looked pretty good out there."

"And what did you think?" Sasha asked Johnny.

"I saw that last goal," he said.

"Nice work," Luke added, congratulating Sasha on scoring the winning point.

"Thanks to Haley's pass," Sasha said, giving the credit to her friend. Haley blushed and looked away, diverting her gaze not so much because of Sasha's compliment, but because Luke was staring at her.

"We can't stay," Johnny said.

"Where are you off to?" Sasha asked.

"Toby strikes again," Luke said, shaking his head. "He booked us for a house party."

"Let me guess. Spencer Eton's?" Sasha said.

"Yeah, some going-away thing for one of his old boarding school friends," said Luke.

Sasha smiled. "Either that or he's secretly hosting another SIGMA."

"He's one of the SIGMA hosts?" Luke asked, flicking his cigarette onto the pavement.

"You know about it?" Sasha asked.

"It's a nice little club for the kiddies. I prefer the real deal. Atlantic City."

Haley saw her dad circling the parking lot. Fortunately, he hadn't spotted her yet, as he wouldn't exactly have been psyched to see her hanging out with Johnny and Luke next to a shady van.

"We're going down there on Saturday to meet with a manager," Luke said. "Why don't you two come with us?"

"Saturday's homecoming," Haley said.

"You're not actually going, are you?" Luke asked.

"I'm kind of on the court," Sasha said sheepishly.

"I bet little Haley here has never even been to Atlantic City. Am I right?"

Haley shrugged. "It's like a boardwalk and a bunch of amusement park rides and stuff, right?"

"More or less," said Sasha cryptically.

Luke added, "So what do you say? We'll pick you up here at ten a.m.?"

Haley and Sasha looked at each other. The Millers' station wagon was now headed right for them.

"What's the matter?" Luke taunted. "You're not scared of taking a little ride down to the shore, are you?"

● ● ●

Here comes trouble with stubble. To these guys, SIGMA seems like child's play. But then, when you take weekend jaunts to the casinos in Atlantic City, you learn the difference between the big leagues and the little leagues of gambling pretty fast.

Sure, Haley seems intrigued by Luke. But is she interested in him because of his talent or because of his bad-boy rocker edge? Is Haley secretly longing for a little danger in her otherwise buttoned-up life? Or could there be a softer side to Luke she hasn't discovered yet?

And what about Sasha? Coco might call her connection with Johnny slumming, but is he Sasha's idea of Mr. Right? Can these two kids from opposite sides of town find happiness together? Or will their friends keep pulling them apart?

If you think it's a bad idea for Haley and Sasha to go to Atlantic City with Luke and Johnny, send Haley back home to the Miller household on page 294. If you want to go full throttle in the fast lane with Johnny and Luke, turn to page 307.

Remember, when throwing caution to the winds, it's always better to first figure out which way they're going to blow.

THE BALLOT

Life isn't a popularity contest? Yeah, right.

"This week, class, voting will begin to nominate sophomore candidates for the Hillsdale High homecoming court," Haley's homeroom teacher announced at the beginning of the school day. Ms. Lipsky was only thirty-three, but sometimes Haley thought she looked decades older, what with her preference for denim jumpers, sack dresses and thick wool tights.

Annie Armstrong, a Ms. Lipsky in training, sat on the edge of her seat, anxiously awaiting her ballot. When Ms. Lipsky got to Annie's desk, she paused and held on to the piece of paper for a moment. "Remember, class," she warned. "This is not a popularity contest. This is an opportunity to reward the hard work and school spirit of your fellow students. Your homecoming representatives should be the best and brightest among you, not simply the prettiest or the best dressed." She looked at Annie pointedly and set the ballot on her desk.

Haley thought about what Ms. Lipsky had said as she scanned the list of students on her ballot, looking for the most deserving people in her class. When she spotted her own name, she felt a rush. *Can you vote for yourself?* she wondered, then dismissed the notion.

"You have until Thursday to make your selections," said Ms. Lipsky. "The results will be announced on Friday at the end of the school day."

Haley left homeroom, avoiding eye contact with the teacher, and began walking down the yellow hall toward her next class. Homecoming calendars were posted all over the school, listing the Friday night pep rally and bonfire, the Saturday afternoon football game, the homecoming procession and, of course, the big dance.

The dance. Right. Who am I going to go with? Haley wondered as she walked down the hall, catching snippets of excited conversations.

"Cecily, you're going to look awesome up on that stage," a perky brunette cheerleader said to Cecily

Watson, the pretty, chocolate-skinned captain of the cheerleading team.

"Stop. I bet I won't get nominated," Cecily said modestly, before adding, "Besides, talk like that, and you'll jinx it."

Not a popularity contest? Yeah, right, Haley thought.

Next she passed two guys from the football team. "Relax, man," one of them said. "As soon as the game is over, Coach will take off, and we'll have beers on ice waiting in the coolers."

Everyone seemed to have plans for the big night except for Haley.

"Haley Miller!" a guy's voice bellowed from down the hallway. Haley turned to see that Spencer Eton was maneuvering to catch up with her.

What does he want? she wondered.

Like most current or former boarding school boys, Spencer had mastered the art of accidental cool. He was wearing a blue button-down shirt, half tucked, half untucked, and roughed-up jeans that were just loose enough. His "Old Faithful" navy blue blazer was casually thrown over one shoulder.

"Hey," she said, surprised to see him taking such an interest.

"My favorite girl. So who are you voting for?" Spencer asked, pointing at her ballot.

"I don't know. I have to think about it," Haley said. *So that's why he's so eager to talk,* she thought. *He wants my vote.*

"What do you mean, you have to think about it, when there's me, me, me and let's see . . . hmmm . . . me?"

"Oh, right. How could I forget you when you're so modest, charming and self-deprecating?"

"I'm voting for you," he offered.

"Now, why would you do that?" Haley asked. "You're a poker man. You know the odds. New girl in town? Nobody knows her name yet? I'm the exact opposite of a sure thing."

"You never know," Reese said, appearing with a smile on his face and a pen behind his ear. "You've got my vote."

"Cecily, wait up!" Spencer called out, off to continue his version of a listening tour.

"I never shy away from a challenge," Reese said to Haley.

"It's not a challenge, Reese. It's a mathematical impossibility."

"Come on," he said. "Have a little faith."

"Why should I?"

"Because I want the girl I go to the dance with to be on the court."

Haley was flattered. "Who said I was going to the dance with you?"

"That's funny," he said, and squeezed her arm. "You're a funny girl, Haley Miller."

"So they tell me."

"See, a challenge. Love that. That's what's going to get you elected."

Haley shook her head and waved goodbye before she breezed into her next class.

● ● ●

Well, way to go, Haley. Three minutes ago she had zero prospects for a date to the big homecoming dance. And now her crush not only wants her to be his date but also thinks she's got a chance at a spot on the homecoming court.

So what should Haley do next? Does she get ambitious and try to score votes among her classmates with a little self-promotion? Or does she leave her fate to chance and risk not ending up on the court *or* with Reese?

If you think Haley should do everything she can to will herself into homecoming honors, turn to page 299. If you think she'd be better off letting people decide who to vote for on their own, turn to page 313.

Often, when what we want is within our grasp, by reaching for it, we end up pushing it further away.

You only get one family in life. Which is why it's crucial to choose the right friends.

Haley set the table as her father unpacked the take-out bags from Lisa's Pizza, sending the aromas of spicy tomato sauce, oregano, parmesan and mozzarella wafting around the kitchen.

Most nights of the week, Haley's family ate organic chicken or fresh fish, steamed vegetables and whole grains, but on Sundays, Haley and Mitchell got to choose what to order from a stack of takeout menus. Usually, they voted for the Green Burrito or Golden Dynasty. But tonight, they'd gone with Lisa's: one cheese pizza, one sausage and mushroom, a green salad with grilled chicken and garlic bread. Haley couldn't wait to dive in.

"Mitchell, are you feeling all right, honey?" Joan Miller asked, feeling Mitchell's forehead with the back of her hand.

Great, Haley thought. *Just what we need. Another delay.*

"Perry, I think he might have a temperature," her mother said.

"Why do you always baby him?" Haley asked.

"Haley, I don't baby your brother."

"You do too." Haley knew she was being a little unreasonable, but she was starving and she knew if her dad got out the thermometer, dinner wouldn't start for another fifteen minutes.

"Haley, we don't play favorites in this family. Your dad and I love you both exactly the same."

"Yeah, and I feel exactly the same way about New Jersey as I did about California," Haley said sarcastically.

Mitchell sat down at the table and started blowing bubbles in his milk with his straw. Haley did notice that he was being unusually quiet. She suddenly felt guilty. *What if he really does have a fever?* she thought.

"Do you feel bad?" she asked him, whispering so her mother wouldn't hear. Mitchell shook his head.

"Negative," he said quietly, matching Haley's whisper.

"Okay, who wants sausage? And who's going for cheese?" Haley's father asked, doling slices out on plates.

"Cheese for me," Haley announced. Her mother arranged salad next to her slice of pizza.

"Haley, I ran into Mrs. Highland at the market the other day," said Joan. "She said Reese speaks very highly of you. In fact, I think her exact words were 'Our Reese is very taken with your Haley.'"

"She actually said that? Weird."

"Why is that so weird?" her mother asked. "Why wouldn't he be taken with you? Look at you."

"Mom," Haley groaned.

"What about you, Mitchell?" Perry asked. "Are you still a sausage man?"

"Affirmative," Mitchell said in his robot voice. "I will have exactly. One and one half slices of pizza."

"Now my boy's feeling better," Joan said, kissing Mitchell on the forehead. "Haley, do you not like living here?"

"It's okay, I guess. I miss California."

"I don't see why. You have a new boyfriend here—"

"Mom, he's not my boyfriend."

"And a new best friend."

"And who would that be?"

"Annie Armstrong."

"I wouldn't go that far."

"Which reminds me, she called here earlier. Said she was returning your call."

"Good. Now if I could just track down Dave."

"Who's Dave?" her mother asked.

"Promise you won't tell Mrs. Armstrong?"

"It depends."

"Mom," Haley said.

"Okay, I promise."

"A boy in our class likes Annie and I've been trying to set them up."

"That's nice of you."

"Be careful, Mitchell," Perry warned. "That pizza's hot."

"There's nothing nice about it. Annie follows me around school constantly. I'm hoping if I get her a boyfriend, she'll finally leave me alone."

"Who's the boy?" Joan asked.

"Dave Metzger."

"Metzger . . . I think I've spoken to his mother," Joan said.

"What about?"

"She called here once, looking for Dave. It sounded like she was going down the phone list from his homeroom."

"Yeah," Haley said. "She's a little high-strung, that one. So's Dave, actually, which is why I think he and Annie would make a perfect couple."

Joan refilled Haley's glass with water and sliced

lemon. "Well, you'll have to let me know if it works out," she said. Then she turned her attention back to Mitchell. "Sweetie, please don't dissect your pizza."

"I. Am looking. For alien devices implanted in my food."

Haley rolled her eyes at her brother and took another slice of cheese pizza. Oh, how she loved these Sunday-night family dinners.

● ● ●

Haley certainly perked up when her mother relayed that comment from Mrs. Highland. Could Reese really be "taken" with her? And if Reese does like Haley, why is he taking so long to ask her out?

Haley may not have control over her own love life right now, but she does have some influence over Annie and Dave's. If Haley's instincts are right, these two odd ducks are birds of a feather. The hardest part will be getting them to actually go on a date.

If you think Haley should set up Annie and Dave, turn to page 319. If you'd rather have Haley stick close to home with the hope of running into her neighbor Reese Highland, turn to page 325.

While good things come to those who wait, the ones who wait too long risk ending up alone.

ON THE CAMPAIGN TRAIL

There's a reason people don't trust politicians.

By midmorning, Haley was beginning to think that maybe making a play for the homecoming court wasn't such a bad idea. *I am new in town. A little self-promotion might not hurt,* she told herself.

At lunch, homecoming was all Coco and Whitney could talk about. It was a foregone conclusion that they would end up on the court. Haley listened as they discussed the dance's theme, the decorations, who each of the boys in their class would ask. Somehow, as they mapped out the entire night, Haley got the idea that she, too, would be up onstage in a velvet dress with a sash.

By midafternoon, Haley was openly campaigning for a spot on the court, smiling at strangers and flirting with boys she normally would've ignored.

"Hey, Guns," she said to Drew Napolitano in the hall. "Walk me to class?"

"Uh, I'm headed the other way," said Drew, shrugging.

"Hi," Haley said brightly to Jessie, a pale bookish girl from her English class. "I'm Haley Miller. That's *H-a-l-e-y*." The girl ignored her and went back to text messaging on her cell phone.

Haley turned to Dale, a skinny black kid with glasses who sat next to her in couple of classes. "What's up, Darryl?" she asked, mixing up his name.

"I'm Dale," he said. "And I bet I can guess what's up with you. Trying to scare up votes for the homecoming court? How original."

Okay, so maybe this is going to be more work than I thought, Haley said to herself. *Well, I'll just have to try harder is all.*

An after-school trip to the mall netted a pair of tight-fitting designer jeans and sparkly gold dangling earrings, which Haley thought might get her a little more attention on campus. At a boutique near her house, she found a low-cut black velvet dress to wear to the dance. She knew it was a risky move, buying the dress before she even knew if she was on the court. *But,* she thought, *go big or go home.*

Between the jeans, the earrings and the dress, Haley had blown half her savings. *Doesn't matter,* she thought. *It'll be worth it when I'm up onstage Saturday night.*

At school, she continued to annoy everyone in her class with her forced introductions, awkward conversations and superficial compliments. By the time she strutted into homeroom on Friday, wearing a cashmere sweater that had "accidentally" shrunk in the dryer the night before, people were openly avoiding her. In fact, the only person who would talk to her was Dave Metzger, and he was red, blotchy and oozing, thanks to a bad case of hay fever.

"May I have your attention, please?" said Principal Crum's voice over the loudspeaker. The class was hushed—except for Dave Metzger's heavy asthmatic breathing. Haley leaned back in her chair with a cool confidence, looking up at the speaker on the wall expectantly.

"The results of the voting for this year's homecoming court are in. Now, let me first say—"

Several of the students in Haley's class mouthed the words as he said, "This is not a popularity contest."

Principal Crum continued. "I would also like to remind all the candidates what an honor it is to represent your peers. You should take great pride in your school, in your class and in yourself, because we certainly take great pride in you." Principal Crum proceeded to list the freshman nominees.

"Quiet, class," Ms. Lipsky said from behind her desk as he got to the sophomores.

"This year, our sophomore homecoming court consists of . . . Reese Highland . . ."

The students applauded. ". . . Sebastian Bodega . . . Drew Napolitano . . . and . . ."

Haley looked as if she knew exactly what name was coming next.

"Spencer Eton," Principal Crum announced. Haley detected a note of annoyance in the principal's voice. There was lackluster applause scattered across her homeroom.

"And now . . . for the sophomore girls," Principal Crum said. Haley squirmed to the edge of her seat. "You have elected the following homecoming court of ladies to represent your class this year: Coco De Clerq . . . Sasha Lewis . . . Whitney Klein . . . and . . ."

Haley sat up tall, anticipating the sound of her own name ringing through the loudspeakers across the whole school.

"Cecily Watson," Principal Crum said at last, just as Haley was about to leap out of her seat victoriously.

Haley froze, instantly replaying the unbelievable announcement in her head. *He just said Cecily Watson,* she told herself in a state of near shock.

At that point, Haley stopped listening. She didn't hear Principal Crum reading the names of the junior and senior class representatives. Ms. Lipsky glanced up from grading papers just in time to catch a look of crushed astonishment on Haley's face.

● ● ●

Depending on how you look at it, Haley either just got robbed, or she got exactly what she deserved.

So what do you think? Has Haley gone too far this time? Or should she have tried even harder to get that nomination? And better yet, what should she do next?

To have Haley get dressed up and make an appearance at homecoming, even though she's not on the court, go to page 335. If you think Haley has learned a humbling lesson and should lie low for a while, send her to page 325.

Believe it or not, there's still a chance that Haley can salvage what's left of her homecoming. And there's also a chance that she can stumble even further toward complete and utter humiliation.

The truth always manages
to come out.

Haley shifted awkwardly in front of Irene. *I wish she'd quit staring at me,* Haley thought.

"What is it, Haley? You wouldn't have something you're trying to tell me, would you?" Irene asked. Haley just shrugged.

"No," she said defensively. "What do you mean?"

Irene pulled out her sketchbook. "I know there's a drawing missing, Haley, and I've got a pretty good idea why you took it and what you did with it."

"What are you talking about?" Haley asked innocently.

"Did you think I wouldn't notice? An entire page of my sketchbook has been ripped out."

"Are you accusing me of something?" Haley demanded. "What would I want with one of your drawings?"

"Devon told me about the contest, Haley. I know about the tickets to San Francisco. I called *The Mission*. They had a submission from one Irene Chen sent in by Haley Miller."

"Look." Haley began backpedaling. "I just wanted to help. I knew you'd never submit something on your own."

"No, you knew you didn't have the talent to win that contest on your own, so you stole something of mine to make sure you got those tickets. And you know what upsets me most? You didn't even have the guts to tell me."

"It's not like that," Haley said pleadingly.

"Don't tell me you didn't expect to go."

"I just thought—"

"Save it," Irene said. "You've already wasted enough of my time. You can keep those tickets to San Francisco. Go and visit your friends back home, because you sure don't have any here in Hillsdale anymore."

● ● ●

Haley spent the next two weeks trying to get through to Irene, but it was no use. Every e-mail she sent went unanswered. Her phone calls went unreturned. And her letters were sent back unopened. As far as Irene was concerned, Haley no longer existed.

Irene told Shaun and Devon what Haley had done, and they stopped speaking to her too. Word leaked out among the kids from the Floods that Haley was not to be trusted, and soon she couldn't even ride the bus anymore without watching her back.

As for the tickets, Haley couldn't bring herself to use them. And Irene wouldn't take them back, so Haley eventually returned them to the magazine. In the end, Haley was left with nothing. No friends, no trip to San Francisco and most importantly, no self-respect.

Maybe you can do better for Haley on your second try. Hang your head and go back to page 1.

BAD BOYS IN
ATLANTIC CITY

Sometimes you have
to go all the way to
figure out you're headed
in the wrong direction.

Haley knew there was no way her parents would let her go to Atlantic City with an older guy, so she lied and told them there was an emergency soccer practice. Her dad woke up early that morning and drove her to the field.

As he pulled into the parking lot, Perry Miller waved to the school security guard, Mr. Gunter, who was sitting in his white Pinkerton car with his head bowed. Mr. Gunter didn't wave back.

"Should we check on him?" Perry asked. "He looks a little old. And still."

"Nah," Haley said. "He just likes his sleep."

"And this is the guy who's supposed to be keeping our kids safe?" Perry shook his head.

"Bye, Dad. See you tonight," Haley said, giving him a kiss on the cheek and hopping out of the car.

"Honey, are you sure there's practice today?" Perry asked. "I don't see anyone else around."

"I'm just a little early, that's all."

"Do you want me to wait with you?"

"No, really, Dad, I'm okay."

"Well, call us if you need a ride home," Perry said. He drove past Mr. Gunter's car, honking until he startled the old man out of a sound sleep. Mr. Gunter sat up straight and saluted.

But by the time Sasha's housekeeper dropped her off ten minutes later, he was once again fast asleep.

"Hey," Sasha said, setting her overnight bag on the curb.

"How long are we going for, anyway?" Haley asked. She had a sudden urge to call off the trip.

"Relax," said Sasha. "It's just in case."

In case what? Haley thought.

Luke pulled up with Toby, Josh and Johnny in the van, and less than two hours later, they were in Atlantic City. Luke found a space on the parking deck of one of the casinos, and he and Josh proceeded to smoke two joints before they all got out of the van.

"We're in lot four C," Luke said. "Remember that for tomorrow."

"Tomorrow?" Haley gasped, looking at Sasha. "We're not really spending the night, are we?"

"Don't worry," Sasha said. "You can call your parents and tell them you're staying with me. Besides," she added, nodding toward Luke as he stumbled into the elevator, "do you really want him driving us back to Hillsdale in that condition?"

"Come on, people," Luke called out from behind his dark shades. "We're late."

"And whose fault is that?" Toby muttered as he caught up with them after locking the van.

"So who exactly is this manager, anyway?" Sasha asked skeptically as the elevator doors closed and Luke pressed the button for the gaming floor. "And why are we meeting him in a casino?"

"Come on, admit it. You think it's cool he takes meetings at the craps tables."

"Sure, a chronic gambler for a manager," said Toby. "That's not sketchy at all."

"At least Frank can get us better gigs than local prep school parties," Luke shot back.

"We got paid, didn't we?" said Toby.

"We'll never get noticed playing house parties for rich kids."

"That rich kid from last night is the son of an executive at a record label in New York. And you're telling me spending a Saturday in some crummy casino is a better use of our time than that?" That seemed to shut Luke up, at least for the time being.

"Dude," Josh marveled. "This wallpaper is wicked." He ran his hand over the raised red velvet paisley print. When the elevator doors opened on the casino floor, Haley was overwhelmed by the smell of cheap perfume, cigar smoke and gin-soaked carpeting.

"Follow me," Luke said as he made a sharp right turn. The rows of brightly lit slot machines were almost more overwhelming than the casino stench. As they passed the roulette wheels, Haley said to Sasha, "Where are the Russian roulette wheels? I don't know how much more of this I can take."

"It's an adventure," Sasha said, looking at the group of unshaven men and elderly women clustered around the green gaming tables. "A boozy liver-spotted adventure, but an adventure nonetheless."

It took a while to find the craps station, but when they did, Luke asked for Frank.

"Sorry, kid," the dealer said in a husky voice. "Frank was indicted yesterday for defrauding his clients." Luke looked like he'd just been sucker-punched.

"You kids better get outta here," said the dealer. "The gaming commission catches you, our license is toast."

"Wow, this is actually even more of a disaster than I thought," said Haley. "How much worse can it get?"

At that exact moment, Jonathan Lewis, Sasha's

dad, spun around on his stool at the craps table with a soggy cigar in his mouth.

"Daddy?" Sasha said in disbelief. To Haley, this guy looked like a distant cousin of the sharply dressed businessman she had seen in photos at Sasha's house. His expensive-looking suit was rumpled and stained. He had sweat marks on his shirt and what looked like a five o'clock shadow on his face, even though it was only half past noon.

"Sweetie," he slurred. "What are you doing here?" He took a step toward her, but Sasha backed away, grabbing Johnny's hand.

"You told me you were working in the city today."

"I am working, baby. This is the city. I could make your entire college tuition in one night, you know that?" He said it with such conviction, Haley almost believed him.

"Get me out of here," Sasha said to Johnny.

"Wait," Sasha's dad said. "Where you going?"

"For God's sake, Dad, take a shower." Sasha and Johnny headed toward the elevator, followed by Haley and the others. Jonathan Lewis was left alone to nurse the last of his scotch.

Once they reached the parking deck, it was clear they wouldn't be spending the night in Atlantic City after all. Johnny took the keys from Luke and climbed into the driver's seat. Sasha, who had stopped speaking by this point and turned a sickly shade of white, rode shotgun. It was, Haley knew, going to be a long ride home. Especially since Luke was trying to feel her up in the backseat, in plain view of Toby and Josh.

Haley vowed then and there that this would be her last weekend jaunt to the gambling mecca of the Jersey shore. At least as a sophomore, anyway.

THE END

HOMECOMING

**Anyone who says life
gets better after high
school obviously doesn't
know what it feels like
to be prom queen.**

Haley had never been so excited in her life. She fiddled nervously with the hem of her new pink dress, which her parents had bought for her especially for the occasion. Reese stood to her right, looking terribly handsome in his navy suit and crisp white shirt, with a gardenia pinned to his lapel.

I can't believe this is really happening, she thought. *I'm the new girl. We're not supposed to be on homecoming courts, going to dances with boys like Reese Highland.*

Though it wasn't entirely unprecedented, Haley was right—it was unusual for someone so new to Hillsdale to be elected to the homecoming court. But by some fluke of timing, split votes and Haley's sunny disposition, she had won over enough of her fellow sophomores to secure a spot on the court. And now here she was, in a new dress, about to dance the night away with Reese. She felt that at any moment she might wake up from a dream.

In fact, the only thing that convinced her she wasn't dreaming was the performance of the home team. The dispirited Hawks straggled off the field at halftime and disappeared into the locker rooms. They were down twenty-one points, and it was easy to see why. Cecily Watson was leading the cheering squad in a series of halfhearted shimmies that didn't have a chance of revving up the crowd. Haley began to wonder why the pretty dark-skinned sophomore had ever been appointed captain.

"Our cheerleaders are so lame," Whitney said as Drew Napolitano, his hair still wet from a hasty shower, joined her and the rest of the sophomore class representatives at the entrance to the field.

"They don't have to be good. They're hot," Spencer said, eyeing the cheerleaders' short skirts. Coco rubbed her bare arms, an obvious ploy to get Spencer to offer her his jacket. He didn't.

"Hey, thanks for talking me out of that trip to

Atlantic City," Sasha whispered to Haley. "I don't know what I was thinking."

Haley had run into Sasha and Johnny Lane after school the previous week. Sasha had tried to convince Haley to come along with her and Johnny's band on a road trip to Atlantic City that Saturday, but Haley had talked Sasha out of going, reminding her that they were both on the homecoming court.

"Sure," said Haley now. "No problem."

The announcer's voice came over the loudspeaker. "And now, allow me to present to you this year's homecoming court!" A teacher shoved one of the freshman representatives, and their class's awkward little troupe paraded out onto the field.

And then suddenly it was Haley's turn to go. Spencer and Coco led the way, followed by Whitney and Drew, then Sasha and Sebastian. Reese looked at Haley and said, "If I haven't told you yet, you look great." He took her by the arm. "Are you ready?"

Haley walked out in front of the stands packed with fellow students, teachers and parents. They paused at the fifty-yard line to pose for the flashing cameras, as the announcer read their names.

"And there you have it, folks," he said as Haley waved to her parents in the stands. "The sophomore class representatives for the Hillsdale High homecoming court!"

* * *

Due to a slight disaster involving a flood in the gym, the original theme of the dance had been scrapped at the last minute. With only two days to go, Whitney and Sasha had stepped in to salvage the night. For her part, Whitney had "borrowed" dozens of strands of tiny white lights from her soon-to-be-stepmonster's stash of Christmas decorations. As far as Whitney was concerned, they didn't even belong in the house, since the Kleins were Jewish, so it wasn't exactly stealing.

Sasha, meanwhile, had convinced a local fabric store to donate fifty bolts of pale blue jersey to the cause, which Whitney had draped in billowing swags from the ceiling.

For music, Sasha had programmed a list of British Invasion and sixties and seventies hits into her MP3 player and plugged it into the gym's sound system.

Despite the last-minute preparations, it had all finally come together, and as Haley and Reese walked into the gym that night, they heard the dance's theme song, Donovan's "Jersey Thursday," blasting through the speakers.

"Love your dress," Sasha said to Haley as she passed.

Coco and Whitney weren't quite as generous when they saw her. "Pink is so over for evening," Coco pointed out. "What kind of fabric is that, anyway? Polyester?"

"It's silk," said Haley, determined not to let Coco

get to her tonight. Reese took her by the arm and led her to their table.

"Would you like a drink?" he offered.

"Sure," Haley said, smiling.

As Reese headed to the refreshments table, Haley watched the people filing in. Everyone seemed to be in a great mood, buoyed by the Hawks' eleventh-hour win. Somehow, Hillsdale had managed to pull off a victory in the second half of the game, scoring three touchdowns and a field goal while holding the other team to their halftime score.

Haley watched as Sebastian, the Spanish exchange student from Seville, approached Ms. Frick for a dance. She all too willingly obliged, and soon other couples were following them to the dance floor.

"Hope you like punch," Reese said, setting two cups on the table.

"I believe Whitney's calling it Jersey Juice," Haley reminded him. "Whatever that is," she added skeptically.

"Hey, are you knocking Jersey?" he asked. "I know we might not seem like much to a California girl, but Jersey has a lot to offer."

"Like what?" Haley asked. "Shopping malls and industrial parks?"

"I'll have you know we gave the world its first drive-in movie theater. And," Reese said, pausing for effect, "President Grover Cleveland was born here."

"Wow," said Haley. "That is impressive."

Coco was now dragging Spencer onto the dance floor, but, Haley noticed, she kept sending weird looks in their direction. In fact, the longer Coco stared at Reese and Haley having a good time, the more annoyed Coco seemed to become.

"So have I done something to deserve the wrath of Coco, or is she like this with everyone new?" Haley asked.

"Don't worry about her tonight," Reese said, taking Haley by the hand and leading her onto the dance floor for the first slow song of the night.

As Haley and Reese swayed to the music, Coco buried her face in Spencer's neck. She seemed to be giving up on her obsession with Haley's date, at least for the time being. But what did Haley care? She was finally in Reese's arms, and even Coco De Clerq couldn't spoil that.

Yes, after only three months at Hillsdale, Haley Miller had everything her heart desired: the right guy, the right friends, the right dress, the right grades. And for one brief moment, she didn't care the least little bit about what came next.

THE END

Clearly, there's a match out there for everyone.

For weeks, Haley had been trying to trick Annie and Dave into spending more time together after school, but they kept putting her off. In fact, Haley would probably have given up on ever getting the two of them together if Dave and Annie's lists of excuses hadn't sounded so remarkably similar.

So far, Annie's schedule had included a math Olympics practice, a Francophiles club meeting, a model UN rehearsal, a student council meeting, a new students' tour and a badminton match. Dave's list of reasons for not being available: producing his podcast, "Inside Hillsdale," memorizing the Spanish dictionary, applying for a Young Scientists membership and studying for honors economics, a class he didn't need to take for another year.

Haley just knew that Annie and Dave were perfect for each other. All she had to do was get them together. So, on Friday afternoon before homecoming weekend, Haley called Dave.

"It's another beautiful day inside Hillsdale," the outgoing message on his voice mail announced. "I'm currently indisposed, so please leave a message after the beep."

"Hey, Dave," Haley said. "Listen, about the homecoming dance. I know you're working the Snack Shack during the game and all, but I don't have a date for the dance. So I was hoping I could convince you to bring a shirt and tie to change into and come with me? Just as friends. I won't be checking messages between now and then, so don't try to leave any long-winded excuses. I'll just see you tomorrow night, in front of the Snack Shack. Oh, and bring a corsage. I like roses. See ya!"

Haley hung up and dialed Annie's number. Annie's voice mail picked up right away, just like Dave's. *Figures,* Haley thought. *If these two don't fall in love, there's something wrong with the universe.*

"Annie, Haley here. Just wondering if you'd like to crash the dance tomorrow night, just us girls? I mean, who cares if we don't have dates? It'll be fun. Throw on a dress and meet me in front of the Snack Shack after the game. I promise you won't be sorry." With that, Haley hung up the phone, pausing for a moment before she dialed a third number.

"Mrs. Shope, hello. It's Haley Miller." The Shopes were hosting foreign exchange student Sebastian Bodega for the year.

"Oh, Haley, hi."

"Is Sebastian home?"

"Hold on a sec." Haley could hear Mrs. Shope even with her hand covering the receiver: "Do you want to talk to Haley Miller?"

"Hello, Haley!" Sebastian said enthusiastically when he picked up the phone. "How are you?"

"I'm great. Listen, are you coming to the home-coming dance?"

"Haley, how can this be called a dance when no one in America really dances?"

"Sebastian, there will be dancing. I promise. But first, I need your help."

Once Haley had explained her plan to him, Sebastian agreed to do his part by meeting her at the Snack Shack after the game. "Anything to bring more love to my Spanish study group," he said. "It is my mission in life for David to know a great woman. And if a great woman is not available, then there is always Annie Armstrong."

"Precisely," Haley said. "See you at eight."

The Snack Shack stood on the edge of the football field and looked like a brightly painted barn. Haley arrived early, in a green strapless dress she had worn to a piano recital in San Francisco the year before. Dave was so busy restocking the condiment stations, he didn't seem to notice.

Dave, as Haley knew, liked to check, double-check and triple-check all the dispensers before he left for the night, so that everything was stocked to maximum capacity. It was a precautionary measure. As he said, "What if everyone in the stands simultaneously has a snack attack at the start of the next football game? Then where will we be?"

"Hi, Dave," Haley said finally.

"Haley? Wow, you startled me," Dave said, his hands full of catsup and mustard packets.

"David!" Sebastian boomed, entering the Snack Shack. "I am filled with joy thinking of you and what you will experience tonight." Sebastian scooped Dave up in a hug.

"Easy," Dave said, backing away from Sebastian. "What's he doing here?"

Haley suddenly wondered if she'd made a huge mistake. But then Annie walked into the Snack Shack. She was wearing a lemon yellow chiffon dress, and the look on Dave's face told Haley to keep trying.

"What are they doing here?" Annie asked, frowning and looking at Dave and Sebastian.

"Annie, do not be mad," said Sebastian. "It is my fault. I am on this, this homecoming court. But I did not know that this must mean I should go to the dance. Yesterday, I call Haley and ask her to come. But Haley, she tells me that she already has plans. So, I figure that we all go to the dance together. Then everyone is happy, no?"

"I guess," Annie said, suspiciously eyeing Dave.

"Annie," Dave began. "You look—"

Haley gave him a nudge. *"Stunning,"* she whispered. "Say *stunning.*"

"—Stunning tonight," Dave said reverently.

"Don't you have something to give Annie?" Haley asked. Dave seemed confused, so Haley pointed to the corsage that was sitting in a sealed plastic bag on the counter.

Dave handed it to Annie.

"Thanks," Annie said, accepting the red rose with sprays of baby's breath.

"I just ask that you don't open it until you get home tonight." Dave instinctively scratched his arm and loosened the collar of his shirt.

"Right," said Annie. "You're allergic. How could I forget?"

"Well, shall we?" Haley asked, leading the way to the gym. She and Sebastian walked ahead.

"So? Do you think it's a love connection?" Haley asked Sebastian. At that moment, Dave was trying to put his arm around Annie, but she kept shrugging it off.

"I will say this," Sebastian replied. "There is passion between them."

Sebastian led Haley into the Bridge and Tunnel–themed dance as Ms. Frick, their Spanish teacher, called out to them, *"¡Hola!"* They proceeded over the miniature replica of the George Washington Bridge, pausing in the center to have their picture taken.

From the bridge they watched Dave spread his jacket over a puddle of spilled soda near the gym's entrance so that Annie wouldn't step in it. Annie smiled, took Dave's hand and pulled him toward the Tunnel of Love picture booth.

"Haley, you are a true romantic," Sebastian whispered, leading her to the dance floor.

Much later, after she and Sebastian had danced for hours under the twinkling lights, Haley caught sight of Dave with his necktie around his forehead and sweat marking the armpits of his short-sleeved shirt. He was still cutting loose, having a blast with Annie. Haley suddenly realized that in the three months she'd known Annie and Dave, she'd never seen either of them happier. And in that instant, with Sebastian smiling and holding her hand, Haley couldn't help wondering if maybe she hadn't somehow managed to set herself up that night too.

THE END

FOOTBALL GAME
WITH PARENTS

Never underestimate the power of the home-field advantage.

Haley sat in the bleachers with her mother and younger brother, watching Cecily Watson lead the Hillsdale High cheerleaders in a series of hip thrusts, arm shimmies and head rolls. Cecily's routine blended urban street moves, classic dance and acrobatic maneuvers that her squad had picked up at spirit camp over the summer.

"Looks like your dad just paid a visit to the Snack Shack," Joan said. Haley's father was climbing the bleachers carrying a cardboard tray piled high with hot dogs, popcorn and sodas.

"I thought you were only getting snacks?" Joan said as he sat down.

"I was hungry," Perry said, handing the first hot dog to Mitchell.

"It's not exactly the healthiest dinner," Joan said.

"It's homecoming, honey. Slaw and onions for my lovely wife?" Perry said, passing her a dog.

"Is this how you're buying me off?" Joan asked, eyeing her husband slyly.

Down on the field, Cecily was pulling out all the stops to rev up the crowd. Trying to energize fans whose team had a 1–6 record for the season wasn't exactly easy, but Cecily had managed to keep the crowd in the game. Now the score was tied. As the buzzer sounded at the half, the players huddled around their coach, then jogged off into the school's locker room.

After a passable performance by the Hillsdale High marching band, the announcer's voice came over the loudspeakers to introduce the homecoming court. Haley watched as the couples paraded onto the field in pairs, first Coco and Drew Napolitano, followed by Cecily and Spencer Eton, then Whitney and Sebastian Bodega. Finally, Reese walked out onto the field, alone.

That's weird, where's Sasha? Haley wondered. *I wonder what happened? I can't imagine she'd skip without a good reason.*

"Do you know any of those girls?" Haley's mother

asked, taking a sip from a thermos of herbal tea she'd brought from home.

"Sure. I guess," Haley said, looking around at the packed crowd. "They're in some of my classes."

Coco waved to both sides of the bleachers regally, acting as if she had already been crowned. And in a way, she had. Coco De Clerq was obviously going to be holding court at Hillsdale for the next three years.

"And there you have it, folks, this year's sophomore homecoming court," the announcer added.

Haley watched as the three couples walked off the field arm in arm, trailed by the solo Reese. Suddenly, Mitchell tugged on Haley's sleeve.

Ever since he was a baby, Mitchell had shown zero interest in the many new children's books, toys and games his parents bought for him. Instead, he preferred to play with found objects. Flashlights. Microscopes. Discarded cash registers. His current obsession was an old Rubik's Cube Haley's father had recently picked up at a yard sale.

At first, Mitchell had just stared at the thing and carried it around with him in his satchel. After staring at it for an hour one day, he took out a black Magic Marker and drew a series of lines and dots on the colored blocks of each section. By manipulating the configuration of the cube, he could now rearrange the lines and "draw."

Mitchell held up the cube, showing Haley what looked like a lopsided smiley face.

"That's so cool, Mitchell," she said, examining the cube.

"Hey, little man. Hi, Mr. and Mrs. Miller," Reese said, suddenly appearing in the stands and tousling Mitchell's hair. "How's it going?" he said, looking at Haley.

She was trying not to stare, but Reese looked so adorable in his navy suit and crisp white shirt, she couldn't help it.

"It's good to see the whole family out for the game." He looked at Haley again and smiled.

"What happened to your escort out there?" Haley asked.

"So you noticed," Reese said. "We're not really sure, actually. Sasha called up Coco about an hour ago saying she was in Atlantic City with Johnny Lane and his band and some girl named April Doyle."

"Weird," Haley said.

"Anyway, I just stopped by to see if you'd reconsidered about coming to the dance tonight."

Joan Miller's ears perked up. She looked at Perry and smiled.

"I'm not dressed for it," Haley said, shrugging and looking back at the field, where Hillsdale's finest were emerging, rejuvenated, from the locker room.

"I could drive you home to change," her dad offered.

"But I don't have a dress," Haley said.

"There's always the green dress from your piano recital last year," her mom chimed in.

"Mom," Haley said. What she thought was *My piano recital? How embarrassing.*

"You look great in that dress," her mom said reassuringly.

"You could just go in what you're wearing now," Perry said.

"Yeah," Haley said, pulling back the plaid blanket that covered her lap. "Sweatpants are really the latest craze in evening wear."

"I bet no one would even notice," said Reese.

"Coco would probably post pictures on the Internet."

"So it's settled, then," Reese said.

"What is?" Haley asked.

"Your dad's driving you home to put on your green piano recital dress." Reese reached down and grabbed Haley by the hand, pulling her to her feet. And before she knew it, she was climbing into the station wagon and heading home to change.

Later that night, as Reese and Haley danced to a slow song, he leaned close and whispered, "You know, Haley, I'm really glad . . ." He paused, torturing Haley, and added, ". . . that we've become such good friends."

The word *friend* wasn't exactly what she'd hoped to hear. *Of course,* she thought. *That's all this is. He was supposed to come to the dance with Sasha, and now I'm the last-minute replacement, the buddy who won't let him down.* Apparently, Reese wasn't all that "taken" with Haley after all.

"You're a special girl," he added.

Ugh, Haley thought. *Special? That's the kiss of death.*

At that moment, she didn't care that she was, in fact, dancing in Reese Highland's arms. All she cared about was getting rid of the buddy image Reese seemed to have of her. She silently vowed to spend the rest of the semester changing his mind about who, exactly, Haley Miller was. And by the end of the next song, she had already begun to formulate a plan.

THE END

Honesty may be the
best policy, but it
isn't the only one.

"I'm glad you told me," Irene said after Haley had confessed to stealing her drawing and submitting it to *The Mission*. "Especially since I already knew." Irene pulled her sketchbook out of her bag and turned to the place where the page was missing. "Did you really think I wouldn't notice?"

"How did you figure it out?"

"When Devon told me about the contest in *The Mission,* I knew it was you. I mean, who else would be that desperate for two tickets to San Francisco?"

"It's not like that," Haley began. "I mean, I guess I sort of assumed you would take me if you won."

Irene frowned. "If this is supposed to make me feel better, it's not working."

"But," Haley continued, "I also wanted your work to get noticed. You're so good, Irene. Seriously, if I had an ounce of your talent, I'd be wallpapering the school with my drawings."

"Even your drawings, would be better than that gross yellow paint."

"So does this mean you're not mad at me?" Haley asked.

Irene hardened her expression. "No. First of all, I'm not taking you to San Francisco. And second, don't even think about looking at my sketchbook again."

"Got it." Haley bit her lip. She was disappointed not to be going to California with Irene, but more than anything, she just felt relieved.

"You realize I'll be lucky if he still wants to talk to me after this," Irene said.

"Who?"

"Who do you think, stupid?"

"Right. Johnny."

Irene untied and retied the laces on her black combat boots. "He's bound to see it now. And then what's he going to think?"

Haley hung her head. "I'm sorry."

"I know," Irene replied.

At that moment, Shaun and Devon pulled up. Devon had just turned seventeen, and his parents had given him their old convertible as a birthday present. It was a little beat up, but it ran "like nobody's business," and he had promised to take Haley, Shaun and Irene for a drive up the parkway.

"Ladies, let's commence," Shaun said from behind his dark shades.

Devon smiled at Haley. "We still on for Saturday night?" he asked.

She nodded. "Like the wheels," she said.

Irene climbed into the backseat. "Careful, Devon. Haley co-opts things she likes."

"I'm about to co-opt me some chicken wings," Shaun said, squeezing his stomach. "Damn! The beast is stirring. Get this hunk o' junk to Pick-a-Chick, hoss. I need me something suicidal, but quick."

Haley climbed into the backseat next to Irene. It was a clear blue afternoon, and somehow, in that instant, with the wind blowing through her hair, she knew that everything between them would be okay.

"So are you taking Shaun to California?" she asked Irene as Devon pulled out of the parking lot.

"Come on, Haley. Do you really think I'd go to San Francisco without you? I was just making you sweat."

So somehow Haley had managed to hang on to her new best friend after all.

In spite of all her mistakes, life was working out

for her, and she couldn't wait to see where it would take her next. Like on that date with Devon, and after that, California with Irene and Gretchen. What more could Haley Miller want?

THE END

**A bad reputation is like
a shadow. It will follow
you everywhere
under the sun.**

Thanks to a series of pop quizzes in biology, Haley was about to receive the first D of her educational career. Between hitting the mall and "studying" at Coco's house after school, she'd fallen behind in several of her classes midquarter and had never been able to catch up.

Now report cards were about to come out, and Haley's parents weren't buying her excuses for the subpar grades. They had grounded her for two weeks to study for exams. The problem was, they'd chosen to impose her sentence at a critical point on the Hillsdale social calendar: homecoming week. And Haley just couldn't let that happen.

So instead of going to the library on Saturday night, Haley threw her new low-cut black velvet dress into her book bag and went directly to the dance.

The theme for this year's homecoming was, appropriately, "The Secret Garden." Hillsdale was, after all, in New Jersey, the Garden State. Accordingly, the gym had been transformed into a lush paradise, filled with potted plants and tall trees, all lit with white lights. In the center of the room, a large swing had been suspended from the ceiling so that couples could sit to have their pictures taken.

The magic was, in large part, thanks to Cecily Watson and her father's nursery. When an alternate theme for the dance had fallen through at the last minute Cecily's dad had loaned the school truckloads of ficus trees and towering palms at no charge.

Over on the refreshments table, a large fountain trickled ginger ale and pink sherbet punch. Of course, those weren't the only refreshments being served.

"Well, well, well," Spencer Eton said, approaching Haley. "If it isn't Hillsdale's most underappreciated sophomore. You should have been up there with me tonight," he said as he kissed her on the cheek.

"What's past is prologue," Haley said, brushing her hair off her shoulder.

"Like the dress," Spencer said, feeling the fabric.

For what I paid for it, he should like it, Haley thought.

Spencer lightly traced a finger over her bare shoulder and down her arm. "You want to go somewhere and have a drink?" he asked.

Haley looked up at his mussed hair, his deep green eyes, the little cleft in his chin and his perfect Italian suit. "Sure," she said indifferently. "Why not?"

They found a table in the darkest corner of the gym, and Spencer brought out a flask of whiskey. After taking a sip, he passed it to Haley. Determined to forget about her grades and her parents, she leaned back and gulped down a mouthful, paused, and then took another swig.

"You're a bad girl. I like that," Spencer said, brushing her hair away from her face. He nodded toward Coco, Whitney and Sasha, who were presiding over the dance floor. "They've got nothing on you."

Haley took another sip. She watched the other girls walk off the dance floor arm in arm and head for a table nearby. As her eyes followed the Coquettes, she began to feel the slightest bit . . . dizzy.

"Guess I shouldn't have skipped dinner," she said.

"No worries. I'll get snacks," Spencer said, caressing her back. He got up and walked toward the refreshments table but made a short pit stop at Coco's table first.

As he did, Reese Highland approached Haley's table. "Hey, Red, you feeling all right?"

Haley slurred, "Hi, Mr. Perfect."

Reese took a step back, realizing she was loaded, or at least getting that way.

"Don't you like my dress?" Haley asked, leaning forward to present her cleavage. Reese didn't respond. "Whatsa matter?" she asked.

"I just didn't think you were that girl, Haley."

"And what girl is that?"

"The last girl this school needs." Reese walked away, and before Haley could register her disappointment, Spencer appeared with a plate of finger sandwiches.

"Here we go," he said, setting it down in front of her.

Haley tried to eat, but as she watched Reese escort Coco to the dance floor, she suddenly lost her appetite.

"Let's take a walk," Spencer said, pulling Haley to her feet. She wobbled onto her high heels and followed him down a long hall.

"Where are we going?" she asked as Spencer opened the door of an empty classroom.

"Shhhhhh," he said, pressing his lips against hers.

Haley pulled away. "Don't you think this is a little fast?" she asked. "We didn't even come here together."

"But that doesn't mean we can't leave together," Spencer said, lifting the hem of her dress.

As she thought of Coco and Reese dancing in the gym, Haley minded Spencer's advances less and less. She just wanted to be somewhere else, far away from Reese and the image of him holding Coco.

"Much better," Spencer said, unfastening Haley's bra. Before she knew it, he was kissing his way down her neck.

"Wait," Haley mumbled. *Why am I hooking up with Spencer Eton in*—she suddenly recognized the room—*my Spanish classroom? Ew. Is this Dave Metzger's desk we're sitting on?* She jerked away.

"Okay, stop!" Haley said, and pulled her dress down.

"Come on," Spencer said, grabbing her again, this time more forcefully. "You know you want me."

"I said stop," Haley said. She heard a loud tear as she shoved him off her and ran from the room. It wasn't until she reached the parking lot that she realized her dress was ripped. Shivering and on the verge of tears, she stood on the curb, trying to figure out how she was going to get home.

At that moment, Haley spotted the Miller family's station wagon circling the parking lot. Clearly, her mother and father had just discovered that she wasn't actually studying at the library. But Haley didn't care. All she wanted was to be as far from Hillsdale High as she possibly could be. Even if it meant facing what was sure to be a legendary punishment from her mom and dad. Haley was starting to warm to the idea of limiting her social life to hanging out with Mitchell, Marcus and Freckles for a while.

THE END

LIZ RUCKDESCHEL was raised in Hillsdale, New Jersey, where *What If . . .* is set. She graduated from Brown University with a degree in religious studies and worked in set design in the film industry before turning her attention toward writing. Liz currently lives in Los Angeles.

SARA JAMES has been an editor at *Men's Vogue,* has covered the media for *Women's Wear Daily,* has been a special projects producer for *The Charlie Rose Show,* and has written about fashion for *InStyle* magazine. Sara graduated from the University of North Carolina at Chapel Hill with a degree in English literature. She grew up in Cape Hatteras, North Carolina, where her parents have owned a surf shop since 1973.

Haley still
needs your help!

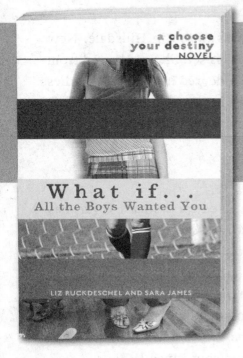

a choose
your destiny
NOVEL

What if...
All the Boys Wanted You

LIZ RUCKDESCHEL AND SARA JAMES

What's a girl to do with all these choices?

What kind of trouble will Haley find herself in now? Fill in the blanks below to guess what will happen to Haley in *What If . . . All the Boys Wanted You.* Coming September 2006!

Haley just can't stay out of _____. She's back at school with a new _____, but the same old problems, including _____, continue to plague her. Now that they've kicked Sasha to the curb, Coco and Whitney want Haley to be the next _____, but can she change her _____ so they will accept her? Meanwhile, Sasha seems to be in serious trouble, and Haley needs to decide if she will go to _____ with Irene.

What's next for Haley? Remember, her future is in your hands, so choose wisely.

www.randomhouse.com/teens

Delacorte Press   RHCB

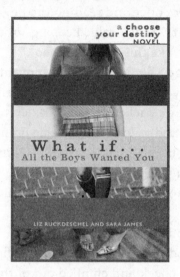
Haley somehow managed to make it through the night without looking at her haircut once. So, on Monday morning, about thirty minutes before she had to leave for school, when she could put it off no longer, she sat down to assess the damage.

What she saw when she opened her eyes was . . . actually, not that bad.

Haley hadn't morphed into a babyish tomboy, as she had feared. On the contrary, the layered,

shoulder-length bob made her look . . . sophisti-
cated, sexy, *older*.

Well, what do you know, she thought, smoothing
out the ends. *Mom was right*. Of course, Haley
would never tell her that.

Downstairs, Joan was sitting at the kitchen table
drinking her coffee and reading the newspaper.

"I hate it," Haley said, keeping up the act. "No
one has hair like this in high school."

"Don't be silly. It's very fashionable. You look
like one of your father's students," Joan said, holding out Haley's packed lunch as Haley took a bite of
wheat toast and gulped down some orange juice.

"Which means I could pass for eighteen," Haley
said, grabbing the brown bag.

Joan's face went white. "Like I said, it'll grow
back."

Haley rode to school in the new car with Perry.
"Have a good day, honey," he said as she gave him a
peck on the cheek and climbed out of the car.

"Oil slave!" a girl with long braids and a tie-dyed
T-shirt yelled, glaring at the SUV.

"But it's a hybrid," Perry said, looking at Haley
helplessly.

"Don't worry, Dad," Haley said. "You know it's a
hybrid, I know it's a hybrid and the planet knows
it's a hybrid, and that's all that matters." He forced a
smile as he drove away.

As usual, Coco, Whitney, Spencer and their

crew were holding court in the courtyard, with Annie and Dave Metzger hovering nearby. Sebastian was futilely trying to soak up some rays on the lawn, while Irene, Shaun and some kids from the Floods were congregating in the parking lot, near Sasha, Johnny and the guys from his band. Luke, Haley noticed, was actually in school for once. And for some reason Devon was also there. *Weird,* Haley thought.

The one person she didn't see was Reese.

Haley took a deep breath and headed toward . . .

● ● ●

The holiday season has begun at Hillsdale High, and if you think Haley Miller's first few months at her new school were exciting, just wait until you find out what's in store for her next. There will be sweet sixteen parties, holiday shopping trips, a California excursion and a game of strip poker, as Haley discovers the further benefits of being the new girl in school.

Spoiler alert: Haley Miller will soon have a boyfriend. But who will it be? Now that Haley has gotten to know most of the boys at Hillsdale, which one will she go after? And what if . . . they all come after her?

You can either send Haley to worship at the altar of the popular kids in THE COURTYARD, or have her veer toward the danger zone in THE PARKING LOT.

When all the boys want you, life should be perfect.

But is it? That all depends on how you work, love and play with Haley Miller, the girl with the most potential at Hillsdale High.